DARK MADE DAWN

JP Smythe is an award-winning author. The Australia Trilogy is his first series for Young Adult readers. He lives in London, where he teaches Creative Writing.

Dark Made Dawn

Book Three of the Australia Trilogy

J.P. Smythe

HODDER &
STOUGHTON

First published in Great Britain in 2016
by
Hodder & Stoughton
An Hachette UK company

1

Copyright © JP Smythe 2016

A CIP catalogue record for this title is available from the British Library

Trade Paperback ISBN 978 1 444 79639 1
Ebook ISBN 978 1 444 79640 7

Typeset in Sabon MT by Hewer Text UK Ltd, Edinburgh
Printed and bound by Clays Ltd, St Ives plc

Hodder & Stoughton policy is to use papers that are natural, renewable
and recyclable products and made from wood grown in sustainable
forests. The logging and manufacturing processes are expected to
conform to the environmental regulations of the country of origin.

Hodder & Stoughton Ltd
Carmelite House
50 Victoria Embankment
London EC4Y 0DZ

www.hodder.co.uk

PART

ONE

PROLOGUE

Outside the city walls, there are animals. They survived whatever happened before, and they're surviving now. Nobody in the cities really knows about them, or cares. They stay out of the way of people. The animals are terrified. They hide, cower in the scrub. The nomads who live out here don't hunt them, though. The people who live here want to preserve them. They want to leave them alone; nature is getting on fine without them. But some things can't do that. Nature seems to be able to replenish itself. But some things? When they're gone, they're gone forever.

I've seen pictures of what these animals used to look like; I've seen a stuffed one in the museum, with its brown speckled fur and soft down. Deer, they're called. They weren't for farming. Everything used to be either farmed or wild, and the wild things were the ones that humans left alone. The farmed ones, humans ate or put to work. Horses could be used as transport, or to pull machinery that tilled the soil. People rode them, for pleasure. Cows and sheep and goats would be used for milk, or for their meat. But deer sort of existed outside that. In the wild. Humanity never really tried to tame them. People watched them from afar, and marvelled. How beautiful they were, and how still, how tranquil.

But the deer outside the city walls are something different. They are white. Their fur is completely and utterly white, no spot of colour visible. The insides of their ears are pink, their eyes are red. Everything else is a white so pure it could almost be no colour at all. Clustered in their herds, on the horizon, they are easy to miss when the sun crowns the day and it's hard to see because of the glare and the ground is scorched to near-white as well. When they stand on the rocks or near the sand of the beach, the place where they cluster to eat seaweed that has washed up on the beach during the night and cooked in the sun, that's when they're nearly invisible.

I see some, now. A small cluster of them, heads bowed, jaws working in this pleasingly gentle, rolling motion. I creep towards them and I hold my hand out. They look at me as if I'm the strange one. To them, I'm something to be stared at, quizzical heads tilted to one side.

Who is she?

'I'm Chan,' I say. 'Don't be scared.' I have food in my hand – kale, which we grow easily here, because it thrives in the shade of the well, growing thick and coarse and bitter – and the deer come to me, their heads tilted. I tilt mine, to echo them. Maybe that will make them feel more comfortable. Do as they do, and they might accept me. 'Don't be scared,' I repeat, as if the words mean anything to them. And they come, slowly, one by one. They don't know if they can trust me. There's one at the front, smaller than the rest, but more eager. She – I don't know for sure, but I suspect she's a female – has her mouth open, her tongue loose. She licks the air first, missing my hand. Tentative, she wants to know if I'll meet her halfway. I do, arm outstretched, palm open. And then her tongue is on my skin, hot and wet, and I can smell her breath, and the kale is gone from my hand. She scampers backwards, chewing as she goes.

I wonder if the vegetable tastes the same to them as it does to me. If they can taste how bitter it is, and how it needs boiling down to actually make it palatable. Maybe they simply don't care. Maybe, to them, kale is like chocolate, a delicious treat. That's how different we are as species. The others wait while she comes forward again, closer to me, asking for more. I have spinach in my satchel, some cabbage. I took whatever we had that nobody wanted because it was close to rotting. I give it to her. She takes everything. Some of it she tosses over her shoulder, and at first I think she's discarding the food, but then the others run to it. Too scared to come close to me, but too hungry to pass up what I have to offer.

Then they all trust me. They all stand in place, around me, and they wait as I empty the bag, as I feed them or set the food on the ground in front of them. I step back to stop them nipping at my fingers. That's how hungry they are, how eager.

'Can I stroke you?' I ask the first who came to see me, but of course she can't answer, so I assume she won't mind. I run my hand over her head. Her white fur runs softly through my fingers. Like one of Alala's furs.

It feels the same, in some ways, as Mae's hair. Young.

I have this feeling inside me: that I still haven't done as I promised. She's still not safe. She's lost, and here I am, feeding deer, finding myself. It's been a year since we came here, and I can't stop wondering when she'll ever –

'Chan.' Rex half shouts, half whispers at me, from behind. I turn and see her: crossbow resting on her arm, her finger on the trigger. She raises the weapon. She's been hunting for birds, training herself, and that's been fine. But I won't let her hunt the deer.

'Stand away,' she says.

'Don't be an idiot,' I tell her. 'They haven't done anything.'

'Their meat is delicious,' she says. We found one a few weeks ago. It was already dead, had just died, but not by our hands. It was skin and bones, mostly, but Fiona showed us how to cure the meat, to strip it from the carcass, hang it, dry it, smoke it, to get these thin slices of amazing flavour, stronger than anything we'd ever eaten. We made it last as long as we could, but we ran out. I can almost see Rex salivating at the thought of eating more.

I am, too.

'Not these,' I say. 'We don't kill these.' The deer who first approached me comes close again, even with Rex's weapon pointed at her. She moves her head under my hand, not for food but for the touch, to feel my fingers on her. I rub her ears. She shuts her eyes.

'They trust us,' I say. 'And they've not done anything to deserve being killed.'

'We are hungry.' Rex says it as if that's it, the only truth that matters.

'Not hungry enough,' I tell her.

In the end she lets the deer go and hunts for vultures instead. When she's done we walk back to the nomad camp. The fires are being lit for the evening feast. There are so many more of us than when Rex and I first arrived here. We've spent the past few months doing runs to the poorer parts of Washington, finding the people who were forced to run when Alala's reign over the docks came to an end. We've brought them here, made the numbers in the camp swell. That means more food, more fires, more tents and shelters.

Rex drags three vultures behind her, their feet tied with rope to her belt, their heads dragging in the sand. Vulture meat is delicious if you cook it for long enough.

She asks me why it's okay to kill the birds but not the deer. What possible difference is there, aside from the fact that the deer let us pat them?

'The birds would eat us if we died,' I say. That's what Fiona told me. That's her rule. If it would eat you, were it able to, then it's fair. 'The deer, they don't eat people. They don't eat other animals.'

'That just makes them weak,' Rex says.

I watch our shadows on the ground seeming to join up as one, before they're swallowed by the dark shade of the city wall.

1

There are things which, the longer I have been down here on this planet, living with these people, living this new life, I have started to forget.

I am forgetting the smell, the stench, coming up from the pit, down in the depths of Australia. It is a smell that I was sure would be with me forever. A pungent, bilious stink, that filled your nose and your throat and your head. If you were unlucky enough to catch a cold or some other virus, once you got beyond the pain in your head, there would be another unexpected benefit: the stench was gone. To have no sense of smell for a few days, no matter how sick you were, was almost a relief.

I am forgetting what it is to fight, to really fight for my life. To think, every day, that there is a chance I am going to die. For the first six months here, not fighting wasn't an option. I fought for food, for safety. I fought with Alala, with her junkies, with the police. I escaped and I ran, and then I met Hoyle, The Runner, and I got to stop fighting. After I – we – Rex and myself – struck a deal with him, everything became a little bit easier.

In the mirrored fronts of the buildings here, in the reflections of car windows and polished glass, I can see that I am getting a little bit lazier, maybe even complacent. I wait around. I am endlessly waiting. That is what working for the police involves. I exercise, but that's no replacement for *fighting*. Maybe that's okay, I tell myself. Because maybe that next fight, the one I haven't yet had? Maybe that will be the one to take me out.

And I am starting to forget faces. They slip away in fragments. I have forgotten how my mother smiled. That memory was the first one that I realised I had lost. What has stuck with me instead is her face in the final few days of her life: teeth gritted, jaw clenched, eyes scrunched shut so tight that lines I'd never seen on her brow appeared, trenches running through her skin. I've forgotten Jonah's look of concern for me, never needed but always there. I used to find it reassuring. The first time I saw it again in Pine City, even when I didn't remember that he was Jonah, that he was somebody from my life, I felt that same comfort. But that memory is gone. And Mae's face. That's mostly gone too. I can't quite make her out any more. She was once so fully formed, so easy for me to conjure up when I closed my eyes, and now all of her features – her eyes, her mouth, the shape of her face – everything is foggy.

It's as if those memories slip away when I grab for them, and I'm left with an echo of what they were. What I picture isn't the same. It's not real.

But I tell myself that I'll know her when I see her again.

And I will see her.

Everything I've forgotten feels a bit like a dream, like a nightmare that I once had. But when I think about it too hard, it vanishes as if it's scared of me, and doesn't want to be caught. It doesn't want me, specifically, to catch it. And sometimes, when I wake up here, lying under my tent on the border of the city, surrounded by the sound of people feeling safer than they have ever felt before, and I'm warm and safe myself, I think that maybe I don't want to catch a hold of it either. Maybe, I think, Gibson was onto something with his experiments. Maybe it would be better if I forgot everything.

We get a message from Hoyle (I can't get used to calling him The Runner, even if everybody else on his team uses that name like it's the most natural thing in the world). He sends us messages through the drone-birds, which are homed in on our trackers. They hover above us, waiting for permission to deliver their mail, and when we signal they drop down next to us. They're odd things. Apparently, way back when, they were designed to look like something called a helicopter, a flying machine thing, like a car with blades above it. The resemblance made it easy for people to understand them. But the more drone-birds there were, the more people got scared of them. They looked unnatural, and people didn't like having them in the air all the time. After the governments began to rebuild their infrastructures, the companies who made the drones redesigned them. They modelled the new shape on real, live birds. They gave the drones wings; eyes where the cameras were; feet where their scanners were; a glossy sheen to their outsides, like oily tar-black feathers. Their span grew as wide as my arms, spread; their bodies the size of my torso. Their weight is probably about the same as mine. Maybe more.

After the real birds died out in the cities, the drones became a natural replacement. People who had previously been afraid of the mechanical drones didn't mind them when they looked like birds. They *expected* to see them in the sky. People wanted to be reminded of the life that they had once had, that they longed for again. They wanted versions of creatures that used to be a part of everyday life, and now existed only outside the cities, in scraggly, distorted versions of what they used to be.

Today, Hoyle's bird lands, sits and waits until we tell it to deliver its message. It makes no movement. It's not like a real bird at all, when you're up close. Real birds twitch. They're restless. They hop and flutter. They remind me of Rex, with their constant nervous movements.

'What have you got for us?' I ask the bird. The eyes flicker, blue light coming from them, projecting a holo of Hoyle.

He's calling us in. 'I've got something for you,' he says. 'Bring Rex. We'll need her.' Rex's ears perk up.

'What is it?' she asks, but I don't have a clue.

'He has never specifically asked for me before,' she says. She worries about it all through breakfast, and then as we get ready, dressing and arming ourselves for the city. No crossbows inside the walls. Out here, we dress for comfort: for the heat and the sun, and then the cold at night. In there, we try to fit in.

In the city, survival is all about blending in.

11

I watch Rex from the corner of my eye as we dress. She folds the arm of her jacket down, over the space where her hand once was, and she pins it rather than lets it hang freely. She likes it better that way. She has boots. I have sneakers. Mine are flimsy. They're falling apart; they aren't built for the abuse I give them. Hers are sturdier, but I don't understand how she can wear them all the time. They're uncomfortable, thick and too tight. And her feet stink when she takes them off. She'll go for a swim in the ocean to cool down every night – she's specifically trying to cool and soothe her feet – but then, every morning, she puts them right back on. I said that we could get her new shoes, but she refused. She likes them; who am I to argue?

Ready for anything, we move into the shadow of the wall and walk towards the gate. Anybody else in our nomad city would use the underwater tunnel if they needed to get inside the walls. We did, the first few times; and then Hoyle asked why we never used the gate. He'd given us passes to get in when we first started to work for him, but we didn't understand how they worked, not exactly. We didn't know we were free to come and go as we pleased.

We'd never had that anywhere before.

When we arrive at the gate, the guards raise their strikers and riot shields. They're afraid of us. It's nice to know we still look at least a little dangerous. We let them scan us, and we wait while they double check that the information they've got is correct, because they can't quite believe it: that we nomads from outside the wall are allowed to come and go as we please. Our passes don't have any information about us, not even our names. We discovered that when, one day, Rex put her hands onto the duty guard's uniform and dragged him over his monitor. Teeth bared, she snarled, 'Tell us what you know about us.' He showed us the screen. No information at all, just *Permitted Access*. And, above that: *Redacted*. No other information at all, not even pictures.

It's as if we don't exist.

There's always a car waiting for us, just inside the city's entrance. It's always the same car. It finds us, wherever we are, whenever we need it. It's a black marked car, police symbols on the side, no driver, with Gaia greeting us with our names when we step inside. And it always takes us where it's been told to take us. Ordinarily a car would ask where we want to go. We don't have any say in the matter.

While we drive, Rex pushes herself close to the window and stares out at the city. I think about myself when I first got here; how amazing I found this place – impossibly tall glass structures, all in the shade of that imposing wall. An impossibly busy city. People like I'd never seen before. New clothes, new hairstyles, new faces; skin dyes and augments and bodymods and tech enhancements. The cars, the birds. It was so jarring, so difficult to take everything in, to understand the rules of this place that had been here long before I existed. The history, the buildings, the people, the way of life.

For me, everything before had been constraint. It had been closed up, boxed in. Darkness. And then, here, there was light.

Sounds like something from Jonah's testaments.

Rex used to ask me what things were. She wanted orientating, context. She asked the same questions that I'd once asked Ziegler; so I gave her the same answers.

And after a while, the questions stopped. Now she stares in silence out of the windows, just as I do. Now, we both watch, soaking it all up.

Waiting.

Hoyle's accommodation is just the way I remember it being the first time I met him. It never changes. It's as if it looked exactly like this when he was given it, and now he lives here, and he's never made a single change. He barely has any possessions, even. I've got enough things in my own shelter, outside the walls, that it feels like my own. A painting that Fiona did of Rex and me one day, when we were fishing. A tatty copy of the book that Ziegler wrote about me. Some writing I have done myself, recording my memories. I hope that if I write down everything that I remember, I might stop forgetting it.

But Hoyle's room doesn't have any of that. It's white and clean and clear of anything that could tell you anything about him.

Until today. Today, there's a pitch-black sheet on the room's solitary table with something lumpen and bulky underneath it. When we walk in he's holding the corner of the cloth with one of his gloved hands, eager to pull it away. He's excited to show it to us, whatever it is. We don't often see him excited when he calls us in. Nervous, yes. Worried, definitely. Never usually excited.

'I have been waiting for this,' he says to Rex. She stands at the back of the room, near the door. That's where she feels most comfortable. 'I've got a present for you, Rex. Sorry it's taken so long.' She doesn't say anything. She's nervous, quiet, shifting her body to a position of drawn-back hesitation. She's not nearly as eager as he is. 'I've been working with the city's tech people,' he says. 'You're getting the absolute best. This is even more advanced than mine, I think. Stronger, faster reaction times. Took a lot of pulling strings to get hold of it; but then, you've done a lot to help us out.' He pulls the sheet away, and there's an arm. From just above the elbow down to the hand. It's so shiny, the fake skin that covers it glossy and smooth, as if it's been covered in oil or sweat. The colour is the only thing that gives it away as false: it's as white as the deer.

Rex's face is frozen. I can't read her.

'You like it?' Hoyle asks.

'It's an arm,' she says. Hoyle nods, smiles this half-laugh of humouring her. He finds the things she does, the way that she reacts – or sometimes doesn't react – amusing. He says that everybody else is what other people think about them. Rex isn't. She's herself, and she couldn't give a damn if you don't like her. Hoyle likes that. He says it's refreshing. He hoists the arm up – I get no sense of how heavy it is, because his own limbs are far stronger than the ones he would have been born with – and he walks to her, holds it up to her.

'You put your arm in here,' he says, holding the false skin that covers the arm apart; and Rex rolls up her sleeve and slides her own arm into the hole. She's tentative, as if she's reaching in to pull something from a fire. There's a snapping sound, and she winces for a second.

'Okay, so there'll be a tiny bit of pain,' he says. 'It's got to hook in to your nerves. It's going to feel like getting an injection. You okay with that?'

'Yes,' she says. She tries to act as if pain doesn't faze her. But I know different. She braces, and Hoyle squeezes the arm just above the wrist, and there's a slight hiss from the mechanism inside the arm. Rex shudders as it pulls tighter to her body, hooking up to her.

Then it's done, and the new limb drops limply to her side.

'It doesn't work,' she says. I can sense her frustration.

'Just wait,' he says, 'it's calibrating. Patience in all things,' and he looks at me, and he smiles. Then we watch as the new limb's fingers tremble and twitch; as the false skin changes colour, shifting to match Rex's own skin tone; as the arm itself tightens and adjusts around her skin, pulling itself even closer.

And then, she lifts her new arm, holds it to the light, moves the fingers, one by one. There's a twitch on her lips: not quite a smile, but definitely not the stoic freeze that was there moments ago.

'Comfortable?' Hoyle asks.

'Yes,' she says. She sounds assured about it.

'You got the first one of these in the world.' He grins. 'Newest tech on the market. I'm not even getting these firmware upgrades until next month.' When he smiles, the scars on his face seem to fade away to nothing. People here seem too concerned with what they look like. Hoyle doesn't care about the scars. He wears them like badges of pride, just as I do, just as everybody on Australia did. And when he talks about them, I can tell that their permanence means something to him. 'Look, don't think of it as a replacement for what you've lost: think of it like you've found something that's even better. This arm isn't a replacement, it's an advantage.'

'How strong is it?' she asks. There's a glint in her eye.

'*Strong*. The old hydraulic ones were stronger, but they sacrificed control. This one, you have total control over.' He steps back. 'Give yourself some time to practise with it, and once you're good it'll crush pretty much anything. Lifting things will still be a function of the strength in the rest of your body, but your grip will be unbeatable. Yeah, it's pretty powerful.'

'I could crush a bird,' she says. Her voice is casual, matter of fact.

'Absolutely.'

'And your skull.' She looks at him seriously, eyes calculating. As if she's trying to work out the logistics of such a deed.

'She's joking,' I say, quickly, because I think that sometimes I have to stress these things. People don't realise when she's joking and when she isn't. Sometimes, even I'm not sure. In those cases, I assume she is. Easier that way.

'I know,' Hoyle says, and rubs my arm reassuringly. 'It's okay,' he adds. 'Rex and I are good. I know when she's screwing around with me. Right?' She smiles. It's still an unnatural movement for her. Like it's taking all of her willpower to move the muscles in her face into the proper position.

'I'm very funny,' Rex says.

'And those jokes about crushing my skull will never get old.'

'You're welcome,' Rex says. We've been working on politeness.

'Just pleased I could do something to help,' Hoyle says. And he means it, I can tell. The way he says it, the slight nod when he smiles, that's how you know. 'There's something I need from you, though.'

'Of course.' Rex understands bartering. She gets a new arm, Hoyle gets us to do something for him. 'You need somebody captured.'

Hoyle smiles again. It's a different smile from before. There's a sadness there, a realisation that we're not just visiting him for fun. That this arm is to help Rex do what Rex does. Rex will do the things for Hoyle that he and his people don't want to – or can't do. Things that even I won't do. But Rex? She doesn't think about it quite as hard as I do. She doesn't worry about it, and they don't worry about her.

'We don't need them captured,' Hoyle says.

He doesn't say it outright, but it's clear to us all; he wants somebody killed.

After Alala died, we gave all of her files to Hoyle and his team. She had been holding information on old-school physical burner drives – ignoring Gaia's cloud, which is what most criminals do, we've been told. She had stuff on hundreds of people in the city, stuff that the police didn't have a clue about. Terrorism, murder, drug smuggling. Outside the city, people can do pretty much anything they want. If they can stay away from the law, then they can get away with it. But the bad things that happen outside the city, Hoyle has explained, seep through the walls eventually. He's not talking about nomads like us: he's talking about the tribes, the gangs who live in abandoned places, who make drugs, who traffic in people. It's all the things the inhabitants of the cities never actually see, never get exposed to. Hoyle explained it once. You can't impose a system that will make everybody happy. It's impossible. And sometimes, the unhappy people end up doing whatever they can to make the others suffer. Bitterness or regret or rage, they're fuel to do bad things. On Australia, it was violence; it was death. But here, it's drugs, and it's terrorism. It's the way people have always been, Hoyle said. Since forever.

His team spent weeks poring over Alala's files, weeks that we were forced to spend living in an apartment in the same building, just a few doors down from him. The police – the people who run the city, really – own the building. It's not just where Hoyle and people like him live; it's also where they keep witnesses, people who have information or that need protection. Usually, Hoyle told us, it's better protected than when I broke in there.

Hoyle lives here because he's the leader of his police unit. Ten years older than I am, and he's got all these people, a whole team, working for him, trusting him; like Rex did with the Lows, but without the same sort of control, without the violence. He doesn't need violence. The Lows didn't trust Rex, but Hoyle's people trust him.

The day they finished decrypting Alala's information, he asked us if we wanted to help the police out with something else. And in return, they'd help us 'acclimate' to the city a little better. I had to look the word up: they would help us to fit in.

I already knew that fitting in here was the only way to survive.

Rex said that we'd do it. She didn't even give me a chance to think about it.

I'm not sure I'd have said any different; especially not when Hoyle showed me the photograph of Mae that he'd found in Alala's files.

'Your target is Cair Mooney. She's British.' Rex nods as if she knows what that means. 'Only arrived in Washington a few months ago, but she's being tracked in New York and Seattle for quite a while now. She didn't come in through the gates, she made her own way in. She's got some false ID set up, messes with the scanners. It's been hard to pinpoint her, but we know she's here. She's not a good person.'

That's one of the rules in this new world: your past will always find you. Doesn't matter if you've done bad things and then tried to make up for them. Rex and I are rare evidence to the contrary.

'She came to the US three years ago, and we don't actually even know how she made it out of the holding pens.' They keep the people who come to the cities, looking for new homes – travelling either from other countries, or from just outside the cities – in prisons outside the walls. Policed and locked down tight. But people break out, sneak through the walls somehow: they find cracks in the wall, places they can tunnel through, swim through, fight or bribe their way in. There have been groups that pushed their way through, on occasion. You get enough people together and they can force their way anywhere. The authorities are pretty naïve about how much people will fight to do something they really want to do.

Hoyle brings a picture of Mooney up in a holo. No smiling now; he's all professionalism when he's giving us a mission. She doesn't look like a criminal, though I don't know what they're meant to look like. Mooney is pretty. Dark hair, really bright eyes, like they're almost lit from behind. It's probably an augment, but maybe not. I've been here long enough to know that some people are just born lucky.

'Do you know where she is?' I ask.

'We don't have a clue. That's part of the problem. We know she's in the city, but that's it. None of the usual informants are talking, so . . .'

'So you want us to find her.'

'Yeah. Officially, we want you to subdue her, bring her in. But, you know, if you can't, sometimes it's safer when people are just gone. It's better that way.'

'But you'd prefer if she's alive?' I ask. I need to check these things. I get nervous about getting something wrong, balls of tension in my stomach.

'The important thing is that she's taken out of the picture,' he says.

He doesn't look at me as he says it. Eyes firmly on Rex, and she stares back.

'What did she do?' I have to know. I always have to know. It helps, I think. Rex doesn't care. She'll do what she's going to do regardless.

'Watch,' he says. He taps something on his wrist, like he's writing on the skin itself. It's not a watch. Everything is built in to him, all the attachments, all the augments. He joked once that he's like one of those knives you get in antique shops – Swiss army man, he called himself. I didn't understand it, but I've learned now that it's easier – and faster – to laugh as if I do. Otherwise people just explain the joke, and explanations are never as funny. They're always disappointed when they have to tell you why they said the thing they said.

A holo plays on his command. A city, as seen from above: we're watching footage recorded by birds as they swoop and swirl. It's disorientating, following them as they fly. This isn't Washington. The streets aren't as well laid out. It's sloppier, somehow, less structured. On the ground, the people are as small as the fishes that swim around my feet as I cool them in the shallow waters of the shoreline.

The birds hover around a building. We can see police down below, trucks full of them. Uniformed officers rush out of the trucks, their shields up to protect themselves. They move to surround the building entirely.

'That's a services facility,' Hoyle says. 'It's a rehabilitation centre.' Rehabilitation is what the people here call what they did to Rex and me in Pine City. As if we were broken and needed to be fixed.

It's a prison.

'This particular facility is in Seattle,' Hoyle says.

There's an explosion. The windows go first, glass shattering in all directions as flames spew into the air. I see

people run out of the building. They're confused, disorien-
tated. They flee down the streets. The fire continues.

'Mooney and her people blew up the staff facilities. Took
out guards, police. Set the prisoners—' He stops talking
and looks at me for a second, to see how I'm going to react.

'We know that's what they are,' I say.

So he nods, and carries on. 'They set them free. But the
important thing to remember is that innocent people lost
their lives in this explosion. People who were just doing
their jobs, trying to make the world a better place. Doctors,
workers from the Services. It's murder, pure and simple.
And Mooney has to be punished for it.'

'Why did she do it?'

'She said that she was saving them. She doesn't think the
way our government treats criminals is right – says that
we're not giving them a chance to fix things, to own what
they've done, to pay their dues and rejoin society. It's ironic.
When we catch her, she'll say that she wants that too. Even
though we know she can't be changed. She won't see the
error in her ways.' He clears his throat. There's a mechanical sound to it when he swallows. It's strange, the moments
where I remember that he's not entirely organic, that there's
something different between him and me.

'Alala's files pointed us to Mooney and the people that
she's been working with. They bought the explosives from
some gang we've already taken care of. When we catch her,
we can find out who else she's working with. We start with
her, she'll break. We can make her break. The whole thing'll
unravel after that. We got this –' another video, of Mooney
outside one of the malls in the north-east of the city – 'a

few days ago. Only caught her on the high range birds, and then we lost her. Hasn't popped up on the radar since. But she's in Washington, we know that much. Hasn't left yet.'

'Why is she here?'

'We believe she's looking for Alala.'

'Alala will be hard to find, I think,' Rex says. I think that's a Rex joke. The equivalent of it. Alala's been dead a while, and we all know it.

'That she will,' Hoyle says, almost laughing. 'But Mooney doesn't know that, not yet. We've managed to bury enough of what happened the day Alala died, and we've been dropping hints she's alive. We've spread word among some of the junkies that she's squirreled away somewhere, waiting to make her grand re-entrance into society. Doesn't help anybody to think she's dead, because her contacts will move on. We want them looking for her. Just like Mooney here. She's not as smart as she thinks she is. So you're going to put out that you know Alala, that you know where she is and how to contact her. Then? You'll wait for Mooney to find you.' He shrugs. He pulls something – a bag of dried fruit – from his pocket and pops a piece into his mouth. As he chews, there are flashes of the metal deep inside his mouth, where his jaw was rebuilt. 'Start around the docks,' he says. 'That's as good a place as any.'

Rex reaches out with her new arm. She's made it into a fist. 'We will go now,' she says, never one to waste time when it could be spent doing something.

'I've put some credit onto your chips, for food, any supplies you might need,' Hoyle says. 'Dress warm. Gets cold in the docks.'

'I know,' I say.

'Of course you do,' he replies.

Rex walks into the hall. I hear her talking to the officer stationed there. They're getting to know us well by now. This building is filled with older police who've been injured in some way and want to stay useful, but out of the firing line. They're glorified watchdogs, but we like them, and they seem to like us. The one Rex is talking to, Crofts, is about as entertained by Rex as Hoyle is. He always shares his pastry with her, just to get her reaction. Gives her different kinds, to see her responses, which ones she prefers. I listen as he gives her something called a cinnamon bun – 'I got the recipe from my cousin, she's Swedish, or she was!' he says – and as she murmurs her pleasure.

'You're alright?' Hoyle asks me. I don't reply. Instead, I grab his shirt and I pull him close to me and I kiss him. I feel the heat of his lips on mine, the pressure of his mouth. My hand goes to the back of his head and I can feel the cold there, where the bone gives way to metal underneath his skin. That part of him is never warm. I find it quite reassuring, how constant the temperature is.

'I'm fine,' I say as I push him away; but only far enough that I can still feel his breath on me, the faint scent of the dried peach that he was eating. 'Have you got any news about Mae?'

'You think I wouldn't start with that if I did?'

'I know you would.'

'You have to stop asking. I'll start to worry it's all you're interested in me for.'

'Shut up.' Another kiss. Harder, this time. I pull him closer. I can hear the sound of his jaw as it opens against my mouth, feel the cold of his head beneath my palm. I slip my hand through the hole in the top of his t-shirt, and feel his skin there, my fingers tracing the line where his skin becomes false flesh, where the bone becomes metal.

'I am getting tired of waiting,' Rex shouts from the hallway. Hoyle smirks his way out of the kiss.

'Another time,' he says. And then, as I'm going to the door, he grabs my hand. 'I'm working on the Mae thing,' he says, 'pulling as many favours as I can.'

'Thank you,' I say.

He smiles. I can tell he's satisfied that he's doing enough. I'm not sure that he is, though.

Rex and I take the stairs down to street level. There are tourists outside the buildings. Slightly off the beaten track, they're probably lost. A family. Two parents, and a child who must be adopted; she doesn't look the least bit like either of them. Hoyle's told us that it's tough to adopt. It means you've got power or money. There are so few children permitted in the cities – because there's no space – so as soon as one is found abandoned, or taken from parents that the government feels can't look after them, they're snatched up by people who've been on a waiting list for months, or even years.

They look at us. The father's got an augment in his eye. I can see it spinning as he scans us. I wonder if he's more than he appears. Skin leathered by the sun. I have learned that it's so hot in some parts of the country that it's even harder to cool the cities down than it is here. In Texas, they couldn't do it at all, so they abandoned the idea of coolant entirely. I like to imagine a fully functional city in this hot land that no one lives in. The father's clothes give him away – bright shirt, tasteless patterns, slightly too much flesh showing for how cold Washington manages to keep. He's rich. His wife's dressed nicely as well. Her sparkling necklace looks old. Old things tend to cost. And the kid's got augments of her own. Some sort of game thing. I can tell because her eyes are twitching, left to right. She's seeing things on the streets, fighting them off in her peripheral vision. She's barely even here.

'I wonder,' the man says, approaching us. He walks with something of a limp. It could be an old injury, or it's affected, because it doesn't look quite right. People use limps to make themselves look harmless. That's something I haven't forgotten from Australia.

I'm constantly on my guard. Even now.

'I wonder if you can help us. We're looking for –' He turns to his wife. I notice the big ring on her finger. I can see it sparkle, even in the shade of the buildings. 'What was it?'

'Ford's theatre.'

'Ford's theatre, that's right. It's somewhere near here?'

'I don't know,' I say. I stay back from them. Rex stares. I wouldn't like to be on the end of her gaze, unblinking and fixed. Her shoulders shift backwards, getting herself ready. Putting tension into them, in case she needs to react. I see her flexing her new hand. Open, closed. Ready.

'Can I show you my map?' He steps forward.

Open.

'We're not from around here,' I say. Understatement. Closed.

'Oh, sure. Okay.' I wonder why they don't use Gaia. Just ask her. Every device here is on her network, so they must be logged in. I see the wife's got augments in her ears, something – a thin strip – running along the base of her skull. They're all augmented, the whole family.

Then we freeze, all of us, and we stare at each other.

Hold still, I think at Rex. She glances at me, on my wavelength. I can't tell if the tourists are dangerous or stupid. Or both. We wait, tensed, as they size us up – either to push for information, or because there's something else going on – and then the man shrugs.

'We'll be moving on, then,' he says. And they walk off. The wife pushes the kid by the head, guides her back onto the main road. The man keeps looking back at us. I watch them ask other people for directions the way they asked us. They don't just look like they don't belong here; they act like they don't belong here. I can see it now. I watch them till they're out of sight. And then we turn away.

It's only when Rex and I are back at the car that I think about that *we*. That Rex and I are both becoming more used to this city; more comfortable by the minute. It's not just me. It's *us*.

The docks haven't changed. I rarely come back because it's hard to see this place and feel the memories it dredges up. Not that they're bad memories, not entirely, it's just that they're different. They're a different version of me, from when I was at my most terrified. Back then I was scared, living in a hovel, subsisting on whatever I could find or whatever Ziegler gave me. I had nothing. Now I can bury those memories, mostly. Those feelings. I've got something that feels like control over my life these days. I have a place in this city. A job. A role. A purpose.

And so does Rex.

It doesn't matter that our job is doing what they don't want others to do, or what the others won't. It's still *ours*.

It's cold out, today, the wind biting. I forget how cold it can be in the city, given how hot it is outside the walls; the air feels like somebody blowing hard on my face, a sharp chill. The ground is slippery with iced-over patches of water. Black ice that you can't even see, and then suddenly your feet are giving way and you're desperately trying to rebalance yourself. Rex doesn't have that issue. Her boots are better on ice than my sneakers. They're better when she kicks somebody, too. She grabs the back of my jacket when I slip, to keep me upright.

'Where do we begin?' she asks. She must be as cold as I am, but she doesn't show it; she doesn't pull her jacket tighter or wrap her arms around herself. She clenches her jaw to stop it from quivering. That's the extent of it: the rigidity in her face.

'Start with the junkies.' Mooney will have come to see them, knowing full well what Alala provided them with.

'They will know Alala died.'

'The ones who were here died with her. The others would have heard whispers, but maybe Hoyle's whispers have gotten to them as well.' I think about Zoe, the girl that Alala had working for her before she met me. I wonder

29

where Zoe came from. Was she born in the docks? What situation had she got into, that meant she gave herself up, got addicted, found herself at Alala's mercy? A cycle she was never going to break out of.

It doesn't take long to find the addicts. Those who have cleaned themselves up ended up outside the city; we introduced them to the nomads, welcomed them into our community. The ones that are still here are stuck fast, too far gone to want to change. They're queued up outside a shanty even more derelict than Alala's was. Everything about it is temporary. The addicts are wrapped up in clothes that barely keep them warm. Through the holes in their shoes, their flesh looks sore, tinted blue from the cold. Some of them appear in worse shape than others. You can see the puncture marks on their arms and legs where the needles go in, where the skin's begun to rot itself away.

At the end of the queue there's a boy. Hair long, unwashed. He's younger than I am, with something like a moustache on his face, almost comical it's so thin. He's already ruined by his sickness, being here.

'Are you muted?' I ask him. He stares at me, eyes weeping from the cold. He shakes his head that he's not, but he still doesn't actually say anything. 'Good,' I tell him. 'I need to ask you some questions.' I can feel my own teeth chattering in between the words. I'm so cold it's hard to even think properly. I swear it's gotten colder than when I lived here. Or maybe I just feel it more, now that I'm no longer used to it.

'What about?' His accent's not from around here. Another stranger to this place: like the tourists, like me. His voice is clipped and hard. He sounds much older than he looks.

'Have you seen this woman?' I bring up the holo image of Mooney.

'Pay me,' he says. It's not forceful, the way he says it, but desperate.

'If you've seen her, then I'm sure we can come to some—'

He shuts down. I know he won't talk unless I give him some incentive. I reach into my pocket. I have a few cash notes, for occasions like this. I pick a low value one and hold it out. He snatches it from my hand without looking.

'Not enough,' he says.

'It absolutely was,' I say. I move to put the rest into my pocket.

His hand darts to grab the notes. The fingers of his other hand stab into my throat, closing in on my windpipe.

I wasn't expecting the attack and I stagger back, cough, sputter, choke. My eyes blear as he tears off, as I see him running amongst the shanties.

Rex takes off after him. She's faster than he is, of course. She's ridiculously fit. Over the past six months, she's devoted herself to becoming as strong and as agile as possible, lifting rocks as weights, running for miles every single morning, even in the midday sun. She works out until her skin stretches taut over her muscles, until you can see the veins in her limbs, the sweat on her chest pooling on her puckered, scarred skin, running down like trickles of water on the bed of a drying-up river.

All of which is to say, it's not a surprise when she catches him, and quickly. Using her new arm, she grabs his hand from behind and wrenches him nearly clear off his feet, heaving him backwards and upwards and then down, slamming him into the dirt. I hear the snap of his wrist from where I stand, and his howl of pain is so loud I think it must be audible for miles around. She leans down and speaks to him as I approach.

By the time I get to them, my throat still aching, she's done her damage. A lump is already rising on the side of his head. One ear is swollen as if it's a fungus. She pulls the money from his hand and passes it back to me.

'He saw her,' she says. 'Mooney was here, asking for Alala.'

'And?'

'They told her she was in a hospital somewhere. They think maybe in another city altogether.'

'So where did Mooney go?'

'He doesn't know.'

I kick him between his legs. I'm not as scary as Rex is, but it's never not effective to target where it hurts them the most. It's worth a shot, anyway, to see if he's holding any information back. He curls up, cries out again. 'What was she trying to get hold of?' I ask him. 'Why does she want Alala?'

'I don't know!' And I believe him this time.

'Where did she go after she left you lot?'

'Somebody said . . .' He spits something up: bile, yellow and thick. He hasn't eaten in a while, or it would come up as well. I feel sorry for him but squash the feelings down. 'Somebody said she should ask the journalist. Seeger, something like that. He would know where Alala was.'

'Ziegler,' I say. It comes out like a sigh of disappointment: that I'm going to have to see him again; and of tiredness, because the city really is so small. Of course Ziegler's involved in this. On the floor, the boy rolls himself up into a ball, clutching at his legs, trying to make himself as small as possible.

We walk away from him. The other junkies watch us as we go, backing away from us, trying not to make eye contact in case Rex goes for them as well.

The only one who doesn't take her eyes off us is their dealer: a big mute woman who's stepped out of the shack to watch us. She looks strong. A different sort of strong to Rex. She's not muscular, she's *huge*. Big arms, and it's obvious there's a brute power behind them. She stares to let us know that she's not scared of us. She hasn't been here long, doesn't have a hold over the place yet – not like Alala. I think about how Alala must have started like her: she found a place with a need, and she filled it. It doesn't matter what she was before, just what she ended up doing.

There is more to this woman, as there was to Alala. But this is the point where her story starts, the first that anybody will tell about her. No one cares about anything but the right here, the right now. Nobody is interested in what came before.

2

The Girl who Fell to Earth.

Ziegler told me that he wanted to write a book about me, and then he did. Some words I struggled with as I read it, but I've still got the dictionary he gave me when I first met him. That felt satisfying: to be looking up the complicated words he attributed to me, using the book he learned them from. The book about me was dismissed as fiction by the people he most wanted to impress. It held my story, but there was no other evidence: no footage of the crash, no other survivors to back me up. Serious journalists ignored it. And other readers? They couldn't believe that their ancestors could be so cruel as to condemn people to such a slow death; to send them to the stars and abandon them. People acknowledged that the ships were up there but believed them to be empty. People believed that the prisoners from Australia and South Africa were brought back to Earth before they could die. People believed that the experiment failed. People believed that Ziegler's book was a story. A lie.

It didn't stop the book from selling though. There were piles of the book in bookstores, and those piles all sold.

Everybody on the networks was talking about it. People thought the story was entertaining enough, I suppose. And it was; it just wasn't my story. There were times when it felt like a different story altogether, when I almost forgot who it was meant to be about, and I could get involved in the love story, the revenge story, in the tragedy of it all. But then occasionally, it was almost verbatim my words, recorded by Ziegler and transcribed: and there I was, fighting for my life; falling, over and over again; breaking my body; losing Mae; not understanding Washington, or Earth itself. Lost to all of the rules. Getting what I'd wanted my whole life – somewhere permanent – and not feeling like I fitted in, as if it wasn't made for me at all, or I for it.

Ziegler invented a lot about what I went through. I read about a girl who sounds like me, who looks like me when he describes her – he writes about her looking into a mirror, when we didn't have real mirrors on Australia. And then he puts her through hell. It is the same hell that I went through, but tweaked and altered. He gets my mother wrong. Maybe I didn't tell him enough about her. And he gets Agatha wrong as well; crueller in the book than she really was. Maybe Ziegler didn't understand why we were so close: why I loved her and she loved me. And Jonah . . . Ziegler changed him entirely: made him a romantic figure. The Jonah of the book saves my life a lot. Over and over, Ziegler says how much I needed him. That's not how it was. It was more fair than that, more equal. We saved each other, when we had to.

Sometimes now I think about Jonah. I wonder if that's what drew me to him: that he, in his own way, could understand the loss I was going through; perhaps his own loss

– the Pale Women, who were his mothers as much as Agatha was mine after my mother died – meant he needed me as much as I needed him.

I wonder where he is now. Hoyle said that his records are sealed, but if he survived, he would have been put into another facility. Maybe he's even back under Doctor Gibson's care again.

He could be released by now, living in a different city altogether. He could have a life, a job, another relationship, just as I have.

I could have pushed harder, demanded to know the truth, but Hoyle would have asked why, and then maybe he wouldn't help me find Mae. So I didn't. When I've found Mae, I tell myself, I'll find Jonah. He's next on my list.

In Ziegler's book, Jonah is strong. He sweeps me off my feet. When I read that I laughed. Because that's not the way it happened. But so little in the book is the way it actually happened.

'This is where Ziegler lives,' I say. Rex and I are standing at the side of the road, looking up at The Royal. It's been a while since I was last here. I can remember the smell of the bacon, the taste of the drinks he made for me; the softness of the bed that I slept in, the strange mustiness of the room that he never used, that he kept like a shrine to his long-gone daughter. And I remember the shelves groaning with books that I borrowed, read and discussed with him. He was my friend, for a while.

Only, I haven't spoken to him since he abandoned me on the side of the road, desperate and running for my life. He didn't message me to tell me about the book he wrote about me; he didn't ask me to read it. He didn't even thank me in the back of it, and Hoyle's told me that's customary. You steal somebody's story, you thank them. It's the least you can do.

But he was weak. I know that now. He was using me. My past was all that mattered. He wanted to know about the story that was already told; not about what was going to happen next.

Rex and I walk into the lobby of The Royal. Our security clearance will let us get in anywhere. Gaia's been taught to accept us. The camera scans us and we let it. Rex hates this part. She doesn't understand the system: the computers, Gaia, all that stuff. I barely do, but I can pretend better than she can. She worries that the scanning process is insidious. I just know that the more you get used to something, the more you stop wondering if it's right or not.

We head into the elevator. Rex hates these as well. I've tried to explain them to her: that there are chains hauling the box upwards and downwards; but she doesn't care. She doesn't like the sense of being closed in, the voice of Gaia telling us what floors we're passing when it feels like no movement is occurring.

She'd always choose to take the stairs.

'Are we going to go in?' she asks for the third time, as we stand outside Ziegler's front door. I ignore her. I'm trying to get my head in the right place before I see him again.

'Just give me a second,' I repeat. She's doesn't understand why I'm nervous. As far as she's concerned, we're here to do a job. Nothing else comes into play.

'You are irritating,' she says.

I ignore her. Deep breath.

I press the buzzer. He's been informed we're here; Gaia will have already let him know. There's no answer. So I press it again.

Rex shakes her head, already done with waiting, and slams her new fist into the door above the handle. The door cracks, the wood splintering. It's not reinforced with metal, like some doors in the city. Rex looks wide-eyed and delighted at the power in her arm. She is impressed with herself.

'I am so strong,' she says, under her breath. She slams the door again and it swings open, and there he is, cowering, surrounded by piles of his book, a badly drawn version of my face printed on their cover.

He throws a copy at me, as if that will keep me away. It bounces off Rex's arm.

'Keep her back,' he hisses. 'What are you doing here?'

I don't reply, and Rex keeps on walking. He throws more books and she swats them away, unblinking. Then she grabs him by the neck and hoists him into the air.

'Gently,' I say, and she glares at me.

'I am always gentle,' she says.

'I'm not here to hurt you,' I tell Ziegler. 'I just want some information.'

He makes choking sounds as he struggles. 'I don't know anything,' he says.

'You don't know what I was going to ask you,' I reply.

I watch Rex's fingers squeeze for a second and then relax. He gets the message.

'Please, put me down. Please, I'll listen. I'll talk. Whatever you want.'

She opens her hand and he falls to the ground in a heap.

I crouch next to him and bring the holo up. 'Cair Mooney. You recognise her?'

'No,' he says, but he's lying. He's so obvious to me now.

I walk to his window. I open it, as wide as it can go. He's taken the protective bars off it so he can get fresh air. It's an old window, back from when they first built this place. The glass is new, sure – it darkens, protects the books – but the frame is the same. The window is big enough to climb out of, I reckon. I nod at Rex and she hikes him into the air again, moves him forward towards the open window. Then he's through, outside, head first, face down; held up only by Rex's strength. He screams, so she pushes his whole torso out, and his arms flap, beating the air around him as if he's trying to fly. I can see how effortless this is for her, how strong she is. She holds him tight and he reaches behind himself, scratches at her arm, pulls at the false skin.

'You know Mooney,' I say.

'I think she came to a signing!' he yells. He sounds absolutely terrified, his voice gulping in the air around him as he spits out the words. 'She asked me about Alala, about you; asked if the book was real. That's all—'

I stop listening and signal to Rex to scare him a little more. I don't really need to tell her. We both know how the process goes – we've done it enough.

Rex lets him go, just for a second. His body slips further out the window. She grabs his ankle just as he falls all the way, and he swings in an arc, smacks into the building. His screams are so desperate now they remind me of when somebody went off the edge of a floor on Australia. The long fall to the bottom of the ship.

The knowing what was down there, when you finally landed.

'She came back here! To my apartment! She was . . . she was a fan, she said, and she wanted to see where I worked.'

I swirl my finger in the air to indicate that he's done. Rex drags him back in, hitting his head on the window frame on the way, and she smirks at the sound his skull makes against the wood. No accident. He lands in a heap on the floor, red-faced and snivelling.

'You had sex with her.' I stand over him. I don't know if I'm disappointed in him or not. Maybe it's something I expected.

'No! She—'

'You wanted to, then. That's why you brought her back here.' He doesn't reply. 'We need to find her. Got any ideas?' I ask.

He starts to say that he doesn't, that he's not got her contact details; and then he looks at Rex again, and he changes his mind, goes with the truth instead.

The plan is simple. It's not what Hoyle asked for. He said we should wait for her to find us, but I want to be done with this job and out of the city. I don't like these things hanging over us. You start something, you finish it. And Rex can't abide waiting. So we've made our own plan. Ziegler's contacted her, asked for a meeting. He will wait for Mooney outside the museum, the same place where he and I first met – Mooney's suggestion, an accidental circumstance that I appreciate – and I'll be on a bench across the street. Rex will be inside the museum, out of sight but close enough to watch. We'll chase her down, catch her, give her to Hoyle and be done with this job. Back to the outside world.

We walk to where Ziegler's parked his car. 'Nice to see you again,' it says to me when I climb in. I'm surprised that he didn't wipe its memory.

Rex pulls at the skin on her new arm.

'Stop it,' I tell her.

'It's wrong,' she says. She holds the limb out in front of me. 'Look at it.'

'It looks fine,' I say. The skin is loose, admittedly, but it needs to be. It's obviously not quite as elastic as real skin, and it needs to move with whatever she puts her new arm through. It needs to be resilient as well. I explain that and she shakes her head. She pulls it again, tugging almost, and the skin loses its colour as she does so. 'You'll damage it,' I say.

'Good,' she says. She holds up in the other arm in comparison. Even without the colour difference, it looks somehow more real: scarred, burned, with scratches all down it, evidence of where she's been and the things that she's done: who she is.

She runs her fingernails down the skin of her new arm, trying to leave a mark. She does it so hard it really looks as though she wants nothing more than to draw blood.

From my park bench I watch Ziegler fidget. Mooney is late, which isn't a surprise. He didn't give her much notice to meet up, and he didn't tell her what information he had for her, why he wanted to see her in person, just that he'd heard something about Alala. She probably thinks he wants a second date. Another chance. I watch him pace in a small circle. I don't let him out of my sight and he knows it. Rex has already told him what will happen if he tries to get away from us.

I watch him, and through the permanently open doors of the museum, Rex watches me. We're both ready.

I yawn. It's infectious, I spot Rex catching it from me. She doesn't like yawning; she sees it as a sign of weakness. I told her that it's not tiredness, not really: in the wild, when there were predators everywhere, yawning was a sign of power. A lazy, controlling way of showing your teeth. Now, when she can't stifle a yawn, she grits her teeth together at the end, showing them off, making sure everybody can see.

I smile and look back at Ziegler. He's perked up. His head tilts, as though he recognises somebody he knows. I look for her. There's a crowd of children and adults, probably a school group, coming down the pavement towards the museum.

Ziegler catches my eye, then tilts his head again towards the group.

She's there, pushing her way through, smiling the whole time, even as she seems concerned that they're in her personal space, ready to pull away from the crowd if there's any danger someone will brush up against her. She's pretty. Long, long hair. It's rare to see hair that long, and it looks like it's all hers. Without the sheen of an augment, it's just tangled and messy enough you know it's real.

She smiles at Ziegler as she approaches him. Raising her hand, she greets him, leaning in, her hand reaching for his chest. So immediately close and personal, it's more than I would like from somebody I knew as little as Ziegler knows her.

I stand up. I need to get closer.

Rex fidgets. I wave her down. Stay there, I mouth. I sidle towards Ziegler and Mooney, like I'm waiting for somebody myself. As I get closer, I can hear Mooney's voice: soft, curled words, like she's singing. This should be easy. It should be as simple as getting up behind her and grabbing her arm. Rex will pile in, and we'll tackle her, stick an Unabler on her hands, bundle her into the car, take her back to Hoyle.

I can hear what she's saying now.

'When you didn't call, I assumed you didn't have anything,' she says. Her pretty voice makes me want to listen. I'm close enough that I could get to her in five steps. Ziegler's eyes have glazed over. He isn't looking at me. 'But you've betrayed me, haven't you? You've lied to get me here.' Her voice makes me want to sit, to listen. I feel dizzy.

It's augmented. Too late, I realise, and—

A blade drops from her sleeve, and then in a fluid movement the tip of the knife is held firm at Ziegler's neck, pressed into the skin with enough pressure that I can see the indentation, the skin puckering under the sharpness of the blade.

'You need to stay back,' she says. She isn't looking at me, but I know I'm who she's talking to. I raise my hand slightly, telling Rex to hold off. Not yet. 'I'm going to walk away from here,' Mooney says. 'You won't follow me. I'm assuming from this betrayal that Alala isn't here? Doesn't matter.' She looks over at me, right into my face. 'Maybe I just need you instead? I've heard all about you. You're the one he wrote about in his book, aren't you?' Her voice is so at odds with everything else about her. It's not persuasive, exactly; it's more that it's confusing. It's throwing me off balance.

'No,' I say, and I glance into Ziegler's eyes at this, 'I'm really not.'

'Did he bend the truth? He seems like he bends the truth a lot. I could tell that after just a few minutes with him. Awful man. Why don't you kill him?' She pulls the knife away from his throat and he sags against the wall. 'I'll bet you've been wanting to.' I shake my head. 'The things he said about you. If they're true, then you're a killer. If they're not? Well, then, this man right here's a liar. Deserves all he'll get.' I glance around us. Nobody's watching us. Nobody cares.

From the corner of my eye I see birds in the sky. They'll pick us up. More likely, they've been trailing us. So why aren't they acting? Hoyle said they needed evidence against Mooney. Surely threatening Ziegler's life is enough?

Then I notice that Rex isn't in position any more.

Where is she?

'Or I can just kill him for you, if you'd like?'

I try and find her, glancing around, but I don't want to focus on one place too long. I don't want to give Rex up, if Mooney doesn't already know about her.

'Chan? That's your name, isn't it? Are you watching?'

'Yes,' I say, retuning my gaze to her.

'Good,' she says, and in a single movement she pulls the blade across Ziegler's throat. Her movement is sure and hard. I think, that's going to scar, because I've seen cuts like that before and so, so many times; but this time, the blood arcs out brighter and somehow wetter than I remember blood being.

When I remember blood on Australia now, I remember it being a deep, thick red. Viscous. Like syrup on pancakes; like tar on a road. I remember how it would sludge and clump together, globs of hair and fabric and mulch leaching together.

Not this blood.

This is the blood that ran down my hands as my knife jutted from my mother.

This is the blood that bubbled out of Agatha as I cradled her.

This is the blood I have tried to forget.

The rest happens in a blur. Mooney is gone and Ziegler's collapsed, his hands to his throat, and I'm shouting for somebody to fetch help, looking up at the birds and praying that they're watching. And I can't see Rex. Not at all. She's not come out of the museum; she's not chased after Mooney. Then I see the van: old, decrepit. And people, wrestling with Rex: dragging her. I can't do anything. She can hold her own. She'll have to, until backup arrives. I hold Ziegler, press my hands to his neck, try to and keep him whole. I don't want him to die. I don't have time to wonder why. Then Hoyle's here with me, picking me up, even though I'm covered in Ziegler's blood; and Ziegler is totally still, head lolling back as I let go, as the medics take over. Hoyle asks me what happened and I tell him, but my words sound like they're coming from somebody else; like my mouth isn't even my own any more.

I'm sitting in the back of the car, being driven back to the building where Hoyle lives, when a beep comes from Hoyle's arm. He brings a holo up, a map springing from his wrist. 'Rex's tracker is active,' he says, 'so we should be able to find her.'

'Her tracker?' I ask. I don't know why I'm surprised that they'd be keeping tabs on us. Everybody here's tracked. It's a part of living in this world: everything you do, everywhere you go, is watched by somebody somewhere. Hoyle told me it's easier to prevent crime that way.

But he brushes my question off, doesn't offer me an explanation. But I can guess. The tracker is in our chips, I think. The things that give us credits and security access, that let us through the wall. If Rex has one, I do too.

'She's being taken north. Towards . . . They're going to leave the city, looks like.' He zooms in on the map. There's the dot that represents Rex, moving fast. It has *Informant 1219* underneath it, not her name: not Rex. 'They're going fast.' He changes his tone, barks orders into his wrist. 'Get some birds out there, bring her back.'

'What if she leaves the city?' I ask.

'They won't. They'll shut the gates. We'll scramble cars to cut them off. And the birds'll catch up with them anyway.' But he doesn't sound sure. He reaches for my hand and squeezes it. And that makes me feel better.

I don't know why I care so much about Rex. I've thought about it long and hard. Once she wanted to kill me, and I her. She murdered Agatha. In so many ways, she's responsible for everything bad that's happened to me. But still: we're here now, and we're together. She's the only person here who has gone through what I have, who grew up where I grew up. Who knows how I feel about the place we live. She knows my story.

No. There are two people who know, I remind myself; as Hoyle's fingers snake through mine, as his thumb rubs the inside of my palm.

Jonah's still alive.

We're going faster than I've gone in a car before. Everything's handed over to Gaia, and she's in total control. She turns on the sirens; she makes sure the other cars on the roads move out of the way; she flips the traffic signals to green; controls the walkways, the drones that are used to hold people back and let us through. Everything is synchronised, perfect. It's astonishing to see. And, more than that: she tries to block off the escape by the people who have taken Rex. She shuts the roads off, lifts bridges, changes their route. Their car must be hacked, to be off the grid; and they must have manual controls in there, because they're going through parks and off roads. We never lose them on the map.

'He's not dead,' Hoyle says. 'Ziegler. They got him to hospital. He's unconscious, but alive.'

'Okay,' I say. I'm astonished to realise that I'm relieved.

Another holo comes up in the car. This time it's a video feed by the drones. They've found the van Rex is in. The birds flying through the air, then diving and darting through the traffic, so fast, and so focused. It feels like they're coming in far too close to the van that Rex is in.

'They're not getting away from us,' Hoyle says. My hands are sweating. I'm actually scared. I don't need another person to have to rescue, to have to worry about. If Rex gets taken somewhere, I'll have to get her back. Her, and Mae, and Jonah, they're all I have, and if they're all gone, if I don't know where any of them are . . . That's just too much.

Hoyle expands the holo, putting together a composite image feed from all the birds chasing after Rex. At the top of the holo, I can see the van she's in. It's bigger than most cars in the city, and armoured. It's so old, it looks like an antique.

I recognise the area around it. This is where we found the lander ship that never flew up to join the others, the one that sits derelict on the edge of the city. The New World.

Gaia orients the birds to surround the van, then makes them dive down to attack it.

'What are they doing?' I yell, certain it'll careen off the road and kill Rex.

'The driver'll get out of the way. They always get out of the way,' Hoyle says. 'Trust me.'

The birds make it to the van. They scrape along the top of it, then two of them go down onto the windshield. They cover it almost entirely, their wings blocking out the view. There's probably a way for the driver to see the road still – a camera on the bumper with a video feed inside the van or something – but the van swerves, just as Hoyle said it would, careening to the left of the road, and then back to the right, furiously. In the distance, Gaia moves more cars to the side-walk, out of the van's way, clearing the roads, keeping all the bystanders safe.

The van shakes the bird loose, and the image on the holo shows us a bird's eye view through the windshield, for just a moment. The driver's face, scrunched up in terror, not because of what's on the road but because of what's in the van. Whatever happened during that moment where they lost control, Rex got loose.

And she looks absolutely furious.

The driver doesn't see the tyre puncture strips that Gaia's raised in the ground near the city's northernmost gate-way. The tyres are old-fashioned, real rubber tyres that burst as they ride, torn up by the tarmac's new teeth. The van hits the curb, goes onto it then spins off, smashing through a fence. As the back wheels hit the curb, a bit of dirty dark metal comes loose from the guts of the vehicle and the van flips up and over itself. I shout something; I don't know what. The birds swoop around the van, form-ing a circular pattern in the air, giving us the best possible view. The van comes to a rest upside down. Smoke pours out of it.

The back door of the van bursts off and Rex climbs out. She drags the driver out with her, throwing him onto the pavement like he weighs nothing. Then she pulls a passen-ger out, this one unconscious. And then, finally, she goes back in and yanks out Mooney, the terrorist's long hair wrapped around Rex's new fist.

'Can I get a message to her?' I ask.

'We can transmit through the birds,' Hoyle says. 'She'll be out of internal comms range, but they can—'

'Transmit this,' I say. 'Rex, don't let her speak. She's got a vocal persuasion augment. It's dangerous, so don't let her—'

Rex looks up at the birds and she nods, still clinging to Mooney's hair.

'Backup will be there in a few minutes,' Hoyle says. 'Rex, don't do anything but keep her subdued. We'll bring her in.'

I know what he's saying. He's saying that this will have to be an arrest. There's still no real evidence of what she's done, and the birds were watching it all. We made too much fuss, too much commotion. Everything now will need to be by the book. I know it's not what he wanted, that he hoped we'd get Mooney quietly, without more people knowing than would need to.

'What if you don't bring her in?' I ask. Mooney bites at Rex's arm as Rex lifts her higher, drags her to her feet. Her teeth sink into the skin of Rex's new arm, and Rex swats her away. She opens her lips to speak, but Rex puts her hand over Mooney's mouth. Clamps it tight. The birds get closer, priming their weapons. 'What if you call the birds off. Call the backup off,' I say.

'They're on their way to help Rex.'

'She really doesn't need it.'

He thinks, for a second, then nods. He takes my hand again. A different squeeze. This one grateful or proud, or something. I listen as he calls his colleagues off; as he says that backup isn't needed, stops Gaia's intervention, and the birds pull up and away from the van, from Rex and the bodies. He issues a command: to wipe the footage from the birds. Maybe I didn't realise before how powerful he is, that he has the authority to do something so drastic, so final.

The last thing I see before the birds turn away is Rex reaching into Mooney's mouth, her new hand taking hold of her captive's tongue, ensuring that she won't be able to say anything ever again.

Mooney is still conscious when we arrive, scrabbling around on the ground, moaning. Blood is dripping from her lips, but she keeps her mouth shut tightly. The streets are still closed off, but there are no police to be seen, and no birds at all in the sky above us. Rex is sitting on the ground near the crashed van, picking at the skin on her new arm.

'We'll log it that she died in the crash,' Hoyle says, as we get out of the car. 'Mooney, not Rex. Rex was never here to begin with.'

Neither of us were, not really. According to the files, to our ID chips, we don't even exist. Not by name. I remember the dot that represented Rex on the holo map: *Informant*.

I can't tell if the other two people Rex pulled from the van are alive. Hoyle's men attend to them but Hoyle rolls Mooney onto her front, Unables her then hauls her to her feet. I go to Rex.

'You're okay?' I ask.

'This arm is frustrating,' she says. 'She cut me. She bit it, when I was fighting with her. There's no mark.'

I was asking if she was safe, unharmed. She doesn't care. 'That's a good thing,' I tell her. 'It'll stay like it is.'

'I hate it. Give me your knife.'

'What for?'

'Give me your knife,' she repeats, snapping the words. I pull it from its sheath and hand it to her.

'She tried to kill Ziegler,' I say, as Rex lines it up against the flesh on the augment, right at the top.

'He was an idiot,' she says.

'He doesn't deserve to die.' But Rex ignores me. She strokes her new arm with the tip of the blade. She isn't pushing hard enough to break the skin. Instead, it's like she's teasing it. 'What are you doing?'

'I can't feel the skin,' she tells me. She's quiet, her voice monotonous and deep. Disappointment drips from her words.

'Again: that's probably a good thing. If somebody stabs you—'

'If I get hurt, I want to feel it.' She puts the knife up near the top of the limb, where her real arm sockets into the prosthetic. 'I want to know.' Then she pushes hard, teeth gritted. I watch as the metal goes into the skin, puncturing it. The flesh almost seems to deflate as she does it, and then she clamps her jaw tighter – not because it hurts, but from something more like concentration – and slices around the prosthetic, cutting a circle around where the flesh is attached to the metal underneath.

'Here,' she says, when she's done, and she hands me back the knife. There's a liquid on it, some sort of nasty dark oil. She pulls at the fake skin with her other hand, tugging it down the limb. She takes the fingers and yanks at them, as if she's wearing dainty gloves; loosening the skin digit by digit, until she can strip the arm of its skin, shaking off the wetness from the structure that lies beneath it. 'Better,' she says, bringing it up to examine closer, a frame of skeletal metal, in blacks and bronzes, dripping with that same oil. When she flexes her fingers, as she does now, the whole arm seems to move: lines of metal bone and coiled chain-link muscles tighten or twist. As she tests it, it acts exactly like the covered one did. I don't know if it's horrifying to see it like this, or really quite beautiful. Either way, she looks pleased. She drops the empty flesh glove to the ground.

'That flesh cost more than I make in a year,' Hoyle says, watching from behind us.

'The arm is better now,' Rex tells him.

'I don't see how,' he says.

Rex leans over and takes the knife from me again. She holds it over the metal – the longest piece of it, a red-gold tubing that runs the length of the limb – then scratches at it furiously, slashing the knife down so hard it almost sparks, metal against metal. Then she hands the knife back, smiling, satisfied. She holds up her arm.

A deep ridged scar now runs down the red-gold tube. It's evidence: of what she's done, and who she is; proof that she can still be damaged.

I'm sitting in the car, waiting to leave, when Hoyle leans in through the door.

'I need to talk with Rex, okay? Check she's holding up. Check we're clear on the story of what happened. You know how it is. Rules.' He reaches to my head, touches the

53

hair at the base of my skull. The top of my neck. His fingers are gentle and I wonder if that's how gentle he naturally would have been, or if his own augments let him be softer, somehow. More in control. 'So, look. You want to go back to headquarters? I'll come back soon, after I finish up here. Maybe wait in my room for me?'

'Okay, fine,' I say, but I don't mean that. It's not fine. I don't want to be sent off. How long can it take, really? And Mooney is not registered, she's not official, so whatever he needs to do can't be for the official records, can it?

He leans in further, his shadow falling over me, and he kisses me. His lips are cold. We're close to the wall, and the air feels a few degrees chillier than it was at the museum. It's not as cold as the docks, but cold enough.

'I'll see you later,' he says. He pulls back and pats the top of the car with his hand, giving it permission to leave. I turn. Through the window at the back of the vehicle I see Rex stand and watch me go. She holds her augmented arm across her chest; and on her shirt there's the imprint of it, where the oil has left its mark.

We're driving through the city when we pass a bookstore. I've been to this one before, when Ziegler's *The Girl Who Fell to Earth* was first released. I wanted to read it but refused to pay for it. It was my story; I shouldn't have to pay. Hoyle said he could just find me a copy on the network somewhere – there's always a way to get stuff you don't want to pay for, he said – but I wanted to see the actual thing. So I went in and there was a stack of them at the front, and a holo of Ziegler, standing next to them advertising that he would be there, in person, to sign them. To tell more tales about the amazing girl who fell to Earth.

It took me a while to find it on the shelves, because I was looking for the real stories, the true life ones. But instead it was at the back, nestled amongst books I'd read before; fantasy stories that Ziegler had recommended to me. An old story about a time machine; a teenage girl who saves the world; gods who came to Earth as musicians. I saw the cover, gaudy and luminous: the girl on the cover who looked nothing like me, posing as if she was ready to take on the world. I took the book to a seat in a corner away from everybody else, and I sat down and read it in one go, maybe not as diligently as I should have done, flipping the pages hard and fast to see what he'd done to me. Rex was training somewhere, running in the open air and heat until she made herself sick; and Hoyle was on a mission, so I had nothing else to do. I had all the time I needed. I wanted to lose myself in the book, just as I'd managed to lose myself in the books that Ziegler had lent me before.

Then, at the end of the day, as I raced through the last chapter, Ziegler arrived. He was wearing a new suit, or at least one I'd never seen before. He'd lost weight since I'd seen him last, lost the paunch of his belly. His hair was cut smartly, and slicked to his head; his beard trimmed. It was the first time I'd seen him in months, and he was only barely recognisable. He looked more like the pictures of him I got when I searched the network: younger, healthier. Before he went through whatever it was he went through.

There was a queue of people who wanted to meet him. And he wanted to meet them: putting his hand out to shake theirs, flirting with the women. *Enchanted. Who can I sign it to? What a beautiful name.* And so I queued. I listened as some of them spoke about me, in this weird tone, like I had never existed, as if Ziegler had invented me, a strange creation whose story was too unbelievable to not be a work of fiction. They wanted to meet Ziegler, because he understood them, they said. He knew what it was to be an outsider; what it was to feel as though they didn't belong. *What an amazing character she is. Her isolation is so total. I feel like her too. I feel like that sometimes. I feel like there's a pit at the bottom of my life that I'm in danger of falling into.*

He saw me when I was three away from the front of the queue. I was holding the book still, having just read the last page. He ended my story with my death, a death that never happened and never would, as unsatisfying a way to finish things as I could imagine – and I was trembling because I was so close to him. Everything I wanted to say – about how he betrayed me, and in so many ways – clogged in my throat.

'No,' he said. He looked right at me and he said that single word, and then he whispered to somebody standing with him, one of the staff from the shop, and they came to me, took the book from my hands, dragged me out of the queue. They told me that I had to leave, that I wasn't welcome there.

I thought about making a fuss, saying who I was, arguing that this was my story, that I was the person he had written about. I could tell them that he had ruined me, murdered me. He'd made me weak and desperate, and then he had killed me. But I thought better of it. They would scan me, and I wouldn't exist. There was no evidence of anything I was saying. There was just me, looking like I was crazy, standing there screaming at Ziegler, delusional and deranged.

I left the shop. I watched him through the glass for a while, until security told me to leave. I didn't wait for the signing to finish.

Now, I tell Gaia to stop the car, to wait for me. I'll only be a few minutes.

In the back of the shop, I find two copies of Ziegler's book, both of them signed, from when he was here before.

I take one of them to the register. I listen to Gaia's voice tell me the price, let her scan my credit. I hold the book close to me, as if it's worth far, far more than it actually is.

It's dark outside by the time Hoyle gets back to his apartment. I'm on the floor, curled up underneath his duvet, jammed in safe between the bed and the wall. I don't remember going to sleep. I was watching some thing on holo, an old movie from back before the world collapsed. A man and a woman, sitting and talking: nothing but talking, like the characters were in love, but couldn't say. It must have flicked off when I fell asleep.

Hoyle tries hard to be quiet but that doesn't work on me. I wake at the slightest sound. I always have.

'Don't wake up,' he whispers. 'I'm going to take a shower.' He bends down and kisses me, then helps me onto the bed, rearranging the duvet, tucking me in. But I'm more awake than he thinks. He leaves the bathroom door open, and I watch as he strips his clothes off and throws them into the trash; as he washes his bloodied hands in the shower. I listen as he cleans the parts of his body that detach – he cleans and oils and dries the legs, then rests them next to the bed – and then as he lowers his damp body onto the mattress, feeling it clammy beside me; and I stay awake as he falls asleep and dreams bad dreams, as he murmurs and turns and scratches at the sheets as if he's trying to get away from something; as if he's so scared he can barely cope with sleep.

His limbs are magnetised. When he wants them to attach, the magnets – only attracted to each other through some technology that I don't understand and don't need to – are turned on, and the limbs find their partner. This is how he puts himself together in the mornings. But he says it hurts: the pull of the magnets, the thud of the connections. So some days he asks for my help. He sits on the edge of the bed and I hold the pieces for him, slide them into place then press them tight until they click and latch and he can move them again.

'You're too good to me,' he says.

'What happened yesterday?' I ask.

'When?' He's still while I adjust the placement of his left leg.

'After I came back here? You were gone for hours.' I want to ask about the blood, but Hoyle can be uncommunicative and I have found I need to slide into conversations with him instead of asking directly. He won't talk about things I don't have security clearance for. But I can tell he doesn't like shutting me down. He wants to talk, he just can't. 'Is Rex okay?'

'She's fine. We just debriefed, really.'

'What about Mooney?'

'What about her?' He turns to look at me. I'm pushing and he doesn't like it. He's only attached one leg so far. He stands up and activates the magnet for the other, which snakes along the ground, hoists itself up into the air and slides into place. 'Chan, you know how this works. We laid out the terms when you started working for me. You do the missions and I'll help you find Mae. It's amazing, you're amazing, but you can't ask—'

'I wanted to know about Rex, why you needed to keep her back.'

'You asked about the target from yesterday, and you know—'

'Fine,' I say. I stand up. I pull my trousers on and I grab my jacket from the hook behind the door. I strap on my belt – knife in a sheath hanging from it – as I open his bedroom door, as I walk out into the hallway.

'Don't be like that,' he shouts, still half-naked.

I don't reply. Rex will tell me, I know. I wish Hoyle would talk to me – I wish he wouldn't lock me out – but I don't actually need him to get the answers I want.

I find her outside the city, back at the nomad settlement. This place doesn't have a name. We wondered why, at first, and then one day Fiona told us, out of the blue, since she thought that we might have been wondering.

'It's easier if we don't name it,' she told us. 'Naming something gives it power; makes others think it's worth caring about. It makes a thing tangible. Leaving it vague ensures it's safer for everybody.' So they don't call the settlement anything: it's just the place where they live. But they do have a name for it. They say, We're going home, and you know exactly where they mean.

The exact place that they're talking about sometimes changes: sometimes, when there's a terrible storm, the tents and the yurts they've built get blown away; they get burned by the sun, and the sand soaks through so much that nobody can sleep there. And then they move, picking up their homes, dragging them up the beach, finding somewhere new to set up. Everything is temporary; everything is meant to be movable when they need it to be. It was Fiona who first described her people as nomads to me, a word that I needed to look up at the time; it means that they move, that they have no permanent residence. Maybe one day they wouldn't even live in this part of the world, she said. Maybe they would find somewhere better. But their concept of *what* home is never changes, even if the location does.

I'm not sure I've found somewhere to call home since the days when I lived with my mother, in our berth.

Rex and I sleep slightly away from the rest of the nomads. Fiona made tents for us out of fabrics she had woven and metal rods taken from the wall, where it's started to crumble beneath the waterline. We set our tents up where we felt comfortable, slightly away from the crowd. We've been invited closer, to share in their community, but it's easier if we don't. Not like the people we've helped to find this place.

The displaced, the desperate and wandering: we've brought them here, when they've needed somewhere. Helping them like that reminds me of when I tried to save the people on Australia, by offering them a better place to live. But the settlement is even better. New people turned up in dribs and drabs, small groups at a time. The nomads helped them find or make tents, like Fiona did with us.

Rex is in her tent now, asleep. She's tired after yesterday. I can see her feet through the open flap in the front of it, trying to get some breeze inside, if any can be found. The sun's oppressively hot already, even this early in the morning, making me sweat as I trudge across the sand. I call her name as I approach – better that than surprise her. I've had scratches that bled for hours when I've made that mistake before.

Once she's awake, after I've fetched her a cold drink – chilled coffee, which Fiona keeps in jars in the cold water, nestled under the shadow of the wall – she sits outside our tent and digs her new arm through the sand, picking up handfuls of the stuff and letting it run through her skeletal mechanical fingers.

'What happened yesterday?' I ask her. 'After I left you with Hoyle. What happened?' She doesn't say anything. She holds a small shell between the metal thumb and fore-finger, squeezes it then crushes it to dust. Then she finds another and repeats the action. 'Hoyle told me that—'

'I don't trust Hoyle,' she says, interrupting me. She's been fine with him before.

'Why?' Again, she doesn't answer, just scoops up more sand into the palm of her augmented hand, letting it run between the fingers. 'What happened?'

'He told me to say it was between us, that I shouldn't tell you.'

I take her hand, partly to stop her playing with the sand, partly to let her know it's okay. I wonder what she can feel through the robotics: it's linked to her nerves, but can she tell that I'm squeezing her fingers to console her? That I want the warmth of my hand there to let her know she's not alone? 'What did he make you do?' I ask, but I know. From looking into her eyes, I already know.

3

I grab Hoyle by the neck before he can say a word. He opened the door at my knock and I saw his team inside, but that didn't stop me from lunging at him. His team know me and I know them, but that doesn't mean they'll let me attack him. I do it anyway, for show as much as anything; to let Hoyle know how serious I am. My hand clamps around his throat and I heave him backwards, slamming him onto the floor.

The others pull their weapons and stand at guard. Rex, my own team, waits in the doorway behind me. Her response is a noise that sounds almost like a growl. They turn their heads to look at her. They want to keep their eyes on the person that they're most afraid of.

'Nice to see you too,' Hoyle sputters, mocking me. He knows why I'm here. His voice is choked up by my grip.

'How dare you,' I say. I let go of him, leave him gasping on the floor. He coughs, rolls to one side. Pushes himself to his feet.

'It has nothing to do with you,' he says.

So I hit him, hard and fast, my hand tucked loose into a fist, smashing into the side of his cheek. I'm not as strong as him, I know, with nothing augmented in my arms, in any part of my musculature; but I don't think I've ever hit anybody as hard in my life. His head snaps back like it's going to come off. After a long moment he raises his hand to his jaw. There's blood on his lips.

He looks at his team. 'Get out. Start mission prep,' he says. He's mumbling; his lips are swelling, maybe there's a loose tooth or two. I can tell. I know what it sounds like, speaking through a jaw that's been hit hard. 'You too,' he says, addressing Rex.

'Don't go with them. Wait in the corridor,' I tell her. Hoyle goes to contradict me, but then nods. He knows better than to tell me what I can and can't do, now.

He pulls a tooth out from his jaw – only one, and it's one of the false ones. He puts it under the tap, washing it clean of blood – blood, and something else, that same thick oil that coated Rex's arm – then places it gently on the shelf above the sink. He rinses his mouth out, head bent under the faucet. I wonder how much of this Rex can hear. Maybe all of it – it's not like we're keeping our voices lowered – but I'm fine with that. I don't want to hide it from her.

'It wasn't an easy decision,' he says. I don't know how to respond to that. 'Rex is different. She's not like you or I.'

'She's—'

'Just let me talk. She's able to do things. She doesn't let them get to her. She doesn't let what she is bother her – not like I would, or you would.' I know what he's talking about. He doesn't need to say it. 'I've been there. I've done things that I'm not proud of.' He touches his neck, at the point where metal joins skin. He always rubs it when he talks about the deal he made with Alala, the betrayals he committed that ended with him being so terribly wounded, so physically altered. He touches it when he's trying to make amends, and he touches it now. 'There are certain things you or I can't come back from, can't undo. But with Rex, it's like there's a filter. And the things that we can have her do? They're not even close to the worst she's already done.'

'So that makes it alright to use her as a weapon?'

He sighs. He doesn't want to answer my question. He just wants to carry on explaining himself to me, like I'm an idiot, like I'm still new to this place. 'The rules are different here. They are. You come from a place that's . . . I mean . . . Jesus, Chan. Where you grew up? The things you went through? That would destroy an ordinary person. You're lucky, because you had your mother, you had . . . what's her name . . .'

'Agatha.' He doesn't remember. I've told him so many times about her, and he doesn't remember. Something inside me sinks; all this time, I've been talking to myself. He hasn't been with me.

'Agatha, right. They taught you what you should and shouldn't do. That's true, isn't it? They gave you rules. But Rex didn't have those. The only rules she had were kill or be killed. So she killed. *Quod erat demonstrandum.*' He's used that before, says it's a language from centuries ago. I don't know what it means. I don't even know if he's entirely sure. 'She's a killer. She'll always be a killer. We're letting her do what she's good at.'

I feel sick knowing that he thinks this about her, that he can't move past it. I struggled, but I got there in the end. And what must he think about me?

'Look at what happened when you were in Pine City. They tried to break her and they couldn't. They gave her a new name, a new identity. But they couldn't give her a new purpose.'

'You have no right to assume that,' I say.

'She's more human now, right? That's what you keep telling yourself. But they couldn't stop her being a killer and neither can you. So why not let her use that? Why not let us use that?'

'There's no death for criminals here,' I say, 'no executions', and that makes him laugh.

'No, there isn't. Doesn't mean it doesn't happen. You're not naïve. You know what people are like. Some people are so deeply set that nothing you do can alter who they are. Then you have to take matters into your own hands.'

'You betrayed your friends before, when Alala told you to,' I say. 'Does that mean you'll do the same to me now?' I can't help but think that he already has. What he's done with Rex feels like betrayal.

'I haven't betrayed you and I haven't betrayed Rex. She's a weapon, and I'm using her as such.' His face is deadly serious as he says it. 'Look, there have always been people who have done the dirty work. People who don't mind. But there's a scale of involvement. Ordinary people: they're at one end, the high end. They don't want to be involved. They don't want to do anything bad. They don't even want to think about it. My team, we're somewhere along the other end of the scale. You wanted to know why we don't work out of a police station, have uniforms? It's because the rest of the police are ashamed of us. We'll do what they won't. Or what they can't. But we've got our limits. Rex . . . she *is* the other end of the scale. Her limits are different to ours. She's not like us.'

'Of course she is,' I tell him.

'You're blind,' he says. 'You think I'll do something bad to you? That I'll betray you? She'll do worse, Chan. She'll *kill* you. She killed Agatha, remember? Because you act like you've forgotten about that.'

'I haven't,' I say, 'I remember it every time I look at her.' But something twists in my heart. I never told him how Agatha died. I didn't want him to judge Rex, to wonder why I trust her now, or to worry that I couldn't be trusted with her. So I never told him the whole truth. The only person I told was— 'You read Ziegler's book,' I say. Hoyle doesn't reply. He doesn't even look at me. 'I told you that it was made up, that it was nothing to do with me or my life. And I asked you not to read it. But you read it anyway.'

'You have told me pretty much nothing about yourself. And then this happened,' he says, meaning us, meaning our relationship, 'and I needed to know more. I needed to know what sort of person you were. I needed to be sure you weren't like Rex.'

'Maybe you didn't need to know that. Maybe it's got nothing to do with who I am now, who she is now.'

'Of course it does. She killed this woman who was basic-ally your mother, or your grandmother, something like that . . . important to you; everything to you. And yet here you are, acting like you're – I don't know – sisters or best friends or something. Like she's not a murderer—'

'Shut up!' I scream, and I slam my hand into the door, right next to his head. The wood cracks; a splinter punctures my skin. 'You don't have the first idea about me, and her. You don't know what we've been through, who we were, or who we are. You can't.'

'No,' he says, 'I can't. And right now, I'm pretty glad of that.' He steps closer to me. 'Because maybe you're just as broken as she is.'

I don't hit him again.

I don't want to prove him right.

I push him to one side, pull the door open, and I walk into the bedroom, slamming the door shut on Hoyle. I open the door to the hallway and look at Rex.

'Get ready; we're going,' I say to her, and she stands up. She's been crouched on the floor. Her head is bowed. A deep red is spreading across her cheeks: shame, I think, embarrassment. We never talk about who she was. Not any more. When we first got here, when I first helped her escape from Pine City, she worried about it. I told her not to.

I told her that people can change.

I believed that. I still do.

I grab my things, and then snatch a couple of items from Hoyle's own bag: a few Unarmers, a couple of EMPs. He won't notice; and even if he does, he won't come for them.

Then we leave the room, and walk down the corridor. As we go down the stairs, we pass Hoyle's team coming up; and I know that they know what's been going on, because they won't look at Rex. They nod at me, expressions frozen, mouths tight.

'Where are we going?' Rex asks.

There's only one place I can think of.

It used to be that Ziegler's apartment was a haven of sorts; somewhere that I could rest, be fed and clothed, sleep if needed. He told me that he could be trusted, and he wasn't lying. Not entirely. He meant, I will never betray you or turn you over to the police, or try and kill you. And I trusted him. And then he betrayed me. He left me when I needed him most. He abandoned me. I got over the hurt, but I know I can never go back.

There's a kind of serenity to be found outside the city walls, but as they keep telling us, it's transitory. The community could be gone when we get there. If they decide to move on, they won't wait for us. They won't let us know where they are. We could return to an empty beach, to scraps of cloth and the embers of a fire, to having to fish for our own meals.

But I want something more than that. I want safety, familiarity. Those things I don't have.

I remember the lander ship for the New World. It's the same as the one I lived on in the last days of Australia: the smaller ship that I brought down here. That was our sanctuary for a time. But I don't know whether the New World's lander will be the same. We can't get into it anyway; it's locked down. Outside the yard where it's been lying for decades, there is almost a jungle of sorts: trees that provide shelter, overgrown grass to lie back on, soft enough to cushion, firm enough to feel familiar. That's close enough to what we need. That's where we go.

Our IDs get us into the compound, but I have no idea how long they'll keep working. I reckon that Hoyle thinks we'll be back – that I'll be back eventually – with my tail between my legs, asking for another chance. Because he knows he's our way of living here, of making ourselves a part of the infrastructure of this city and this world.

But he's wrong. We don't need him.

I don't need him.

After a while, we sleep. I think we both find some comfort in being near the ship, in remembering what happened before whilst understanding that it was a different time and a very different place. We're not the same people any more.

Memories of my mother have started to fade. It used to be that most of the things that happened to me here in the city, most things I saw, would trigger some memory deep in my mind; a door opening just a crack, to remind me of her. They come less and less often now.

I'm stuck on a memory that I can't quite reach: my mother and me, the first time she took me to the arboretum. There was a hard year when the water stopped working properly. Some of the people from the forges, those who claimed to understand how it worked, decided to take the system apart and then put it back together, hoping to discover what was wrong and set it right. For months the arboretum struggled, and everybody who could was called to try and work on it, to find ways to water and tend to the crops, to nurture them; to try and save what we had to eat, and somehow save ourselves. Only now do I realise what would have happened if everything had actually died: the protein recyclers could only do so much for our nutritional needs, and we would have devolved further. More of us would have died. There were always stories about people on the ship who ate other people, who scavenged the pit for their food. That would have been everybody, I suspect, given enough time.

So my mother showed me what I could do, taking me with her when she went to help in the arboretum. She wanted to keep me safe, out of trouble and within eyesight. She set me to work tending to the runner beans. They were the easiest to look after, I think. They'll grow in very little light, very little water. All they need is the soil to be cool, which meant turning it. Making sure it was churned up around the roots, using third-use water – the stuff that had already been used twice to water other plants, then run off back into the now-still river that went through the heart of the arboretum – to cool and wet the soil, then patting it all down. She knelt next to me when I had done the whole row and told me what it meant.

'Those beans, they'll be a stew for everybody who wants it. That's as much as there is, one for everybody on the ship. And after we pick them, more beans will come from the plants, and then more. That's how it works. They get taken by us, turned into food, and the plants try and give us more as soon as they can.' Then she took one and snapped it in two. She ate half of it and gave me the rest. We ate a bean every day I worked there. Then, eventually the water started working again.

That's as much as I remember. I don't know what happened next: if I kept working on the beans; if my mother stayed working there a few months longer; if the arboretum returned to exactly as it was in the time before, or if it took years to recover. I don't remember.

It's not what happens in the story that troubles me; it's the telling of it. It's the gaps, the holes. Because they are only going to get worse.

When I wake up, it takes a second for me to adjust; a second in which I'm sure I am lying back on Australia, cradling Mae. The warmth of her small frame, pressed into the nook that my own body made for her; her thumb in her mouth, her hair swept back, tickling my chin. The soft sound of her breath, the rise of her body as she drew in air, as she seemed to hold it, making me panic, making me think that she had simply stopped.

Then I wake up properly, and of course she isn't here. But I'm not alone. Rex is with me, lying next to me. She's moved closer while I slept, and she's here, now, perfectly still, asleep. She must have needed the warmth. She's taken her arm off. I notice a bruise at the part where her arm meets the tech, just above the elbow, and then I see that it's scratched and cut, and the marks are not just from where the augment's been resting and rubbing. She's been picking at it. I notice that some of the scratches are from finger-nails, but some are from something else. Something sharper, finer. A blade of some sort.

She moves, and I think she knows I'm awake. But she doesn't open her eyes. Instead, her face scrunches up like she's chewing her lip, or the flesh inside her mouth, the insides of her cheeks. She's grinding her teeth, murmuring. Something is wrong.

She tells me that she never remembers her dreams, her nightmares.

I don't know if I believe her.

I reach down to touch her, to stroke her arm, and her hair. I worry that she'll panic and lash out, but she lets me brush her shoulder with my fingertips. She lets me soothe her as I would have soothed Mae. I run my fingers through her hair, soft as I can manage, and that stops the murmurs for a second.

She shivers, but not from the chill. And then she opens her eyes, and I could swear that she's been crying.

'We should go,' she says, without sitting up. She lets me keep stroking her hair, even now she knows that I'm doing it.

'Or we sleep for a while longer,' I say. She doesn't respond. She lies there and lets me continue, and after a while she's fallen asleep again; and she's making that same noise that Mae made, that soft snore, that quiet rumble of breath in and out. It's exactly the same. I shut my eyes and I imagine it, back as it was. Just for a second.

'We have to get the little girl,' Rex says. I've been back to sleep, and now here she is, standing over me, fixing her arm in place. 'You need to wake up.'

'I'm awake,' I say. I wasn't, and she grunts to let me know that she knows it's a lie. I can't pull the wool over her eyes.

I was dreaming about somebody. A boy. No, a man. I don't know who it was, exactly. Parts of Jonah and parts of

Hoyle. 'We don't know where she is,' I say. 'Without Hoyle's help—'

'We don't need his help,' she says.

'I've tried everything,' I tell her.

'Not everything.' She shakes her head.

'I don't know what—'

She throws the copy of Ziegler's book down to the ground next to me. She's been through my things. It was in my bag, and she's found it. She's not much of a reader, but she's learning. I've been teaching her, in our spare time.

'I don't see how that helps,' I say.

'Everybody knows this story,' she replies. 'They have read the book.'

'So? It's not true.'

'Some of it is. The girl. She's true. Maybe somebody who has read the book knows where she is.' Her voice rarely sounds this excited. A break to her usual raspy monotony. 'You could ask them. Ask the people who have read it.'

'No,' I tell her.

'Yes,' she replies. She nods furiously. 'You tell everybody who you are. You tell them, and then they will help you find Mae.' She's right. That is definitely something I haven't yet tried. 'What have you got to lose?' she asks. It's something she's heard me say, heard Hoyle say.

'Nothing,' I tell her. 'Right now, nothing.'

We walk through the city, back towards the centre and the museums. We have a plan but it's sketchy. I'm going to find a reporter; I'm going to tell him or her everything and ask for help. And I'm going to insist that they put what I say on television, so everyone can see it.

Ziegler was on television a few times. The day the book came out, reporters and their drones swarmed, following him everywhere. It seemed like he was famous in that moment. But since then I've seen reporters – or, at least, their drones – at other times, hanging around crime scenes or on the edges of the docks. I didn't see them when Ziegler was attacked by Mooney, but they would have been there eventually. Chances are, a few of them will still be hanging around, hoping for something else exciting to happen there.

'What are you going to say?' Rex asks. We're nearly out of breath we're walking so fast. I'm in good shape, but not as good as I used to be. Not like on the ship, when I was constantly running, jumping. Now I feel like one of those people on the holos: out of shape, with sad advertising pleading with them to get diet or fitness augments.

'I'm going to find a reporter and tell them who I am,' I say. 'I can ask if anybody knows where to find Mae.'

'What about me?'

'What about you?'

'Will I be with you?'

'On the show? If you want to be.' Then I realise she doesn't mean that. She means in general, if I'm doing things – interviews, whatever – will she be able to come. 'But I won't leave you alone. You can stay with me, you know. We're in this together.'

'Okay,' she says.

I can see she's uncertain and it's strange, to see her so out of her depth. This woman I was so afraid of, so terrified of, and yet here she's reduced to something else entirely. Here, what she knows, what she's good at . . . the only way to use her is to abuse her. She's like a fist made in your hand with nothing to hit, to lash out at. She's expendable energy.

As we walk, she treads harder than I do. Her boots slam into the concrete with each step and she's not out of breath despite our pace. As the sun gets higher, as the day gets on – both of us in sync with our footsteps, not talking, not even looking at the city – now we're more used to it, now it's less astonishingly new to us – I swear she could run and not even properly break a sweat.

The reporters waiting by the police tape where Mooney attacked Ziegler look sleazy. They're not the ones first on the scene, camera birds at the ready to get the juicy details. These people are older; they look tired. They have their own birds, sure, but they look like hack jobs: lumbering with old batteries hanging from their bases, making them unbalanced. These journalists can't afford better equipment. I feel sorry for them. Their lot is mopping up after the better journalists have come and gone, hoping for something salacious at the last minute, something they can hop onto and sell to some of the bigger outlets. Bottom-feeders, Ziegler calls them. I can see why.

One of them, the only woman here, looks even more worn out than the others. She's leaning on a stick, putting all her weight onto it. Something's wrong with her hip that she can't afford to get fixed. Grey hair, not augmented. Her drone, hovering aimlessly a few feet above the ground, is a repurposed police bird, sold on when it was decommissioned. The paint's been scraped off, but you can still make out the tell-tale scratches of blue and silver.

'Her,' I say to Rex, and we make a beeline for the woman. She stares as we approach. 'I've got a right t' be here,' she snaps as we get close. 'Same as anybody else. I'm not doing anything wrong.' Immediately on the defensive.

I like her.

'I don't care,' I say. 'I want to talk to you about what happened here.'

'You've got information?'

'Yes.'

'I can't pay.' She glares at me, her gaze travelling up and down my body. Then she does the same to Rex. She looks at our clothes, our hair, our faces; she spies Rex's augment and I can see her wondering about it. She's trying to work us out, to suss what we want.

'I don't expect you to.'

'You need me to sign anything before you talk?'

'Why?' Rex asks. 'Are you famous?'

She smiles sarcastically, as if Rex is taking the mickey out of her. 'You've got a story, you own it,' she says. 'But you can trust me.'

I can't trust her. Of course I can't. But I don't care. This isn't about money. 'Ziegler, the man who was attacked.'

'I knew him. Good guy. Used to be. Was one of us, back in the day. Used to work the same streets, same stories.'

'What about his book?' I ask. 'Have you read it?'

She laughs, this sound that almost feels like it isn't coming from her. It's deeper than her voice, affected. 'Yeah, that . . . It's great for him. When people find an outlet for their, shall we say, wilder moments . . . He was always full of that sort of thing. Conspiracy stuff. No money in conspiracy, though. Not unless, you know, you do what he did, turn it into a nice piece of fiction.'

'What if I told you it wasn't fiction?'

'Then I'd say you're a few days late. Only person who can verify his story is himself, and he chose not to – chased the cash, went with it being a world of his own making. They're doing a movie now, you know.' She leans in closer, as if we're conspirators together. 'From what I've heard, he's not going to survive to reap the rewards, if you know what I mean.'

'What if I could verify the story. If I had real proof,' I say. She stares at us again. She's read the book, I know.

'What are you saying?' she asks. She sends the drone higher into the sky, to take a shot of us as we're talking, get this all on tape.

It hurts to say the words, but I know what I have to tell her. I know what people want to hear. 'Okay,' I tell her – I shouldn't be doing this, it's a mistake, it's a mistake – but: 'I'm the girl who fell to Earth.'

4

The studio where they'll be filming the interview is enormous. Hundreds of years ago, this was the building where the city sorted all of its mail. It's beautiful from the outside – one of the few structures that wasn't altered or tampered with when they rebuilt the city. Although patches had to be rebuilt, here and there, where the masonry had crumbled away, they're hard to spot. One of the assistants gives us a tour of the site before the interview. They tell us that the building was gutted on the inside and turned into a nasty hotel sometime before the collapse; but the architects kept the character of the place, protecting its grand appearance. The assistant says this with some pride, pointing out the original features.

The studio is in the old sorting office (the dining hall of the revamped hotel). The room is enormous with white walls featuring digital screens – holo projectors – nothing but brand new technology. Rex and I are ushered through to a smaller room. The assistant tells us that this is 'hair and makeup'. She doesn't stop smiling.

'They'll fix you up in here. Can I get you anything? Coffee? Vita?'

'Nothing,' I say. Rex remains silent. The assistant doesn't seem fazed.

The interview will be going out live, they say, a holo feed that everybody will see. The reporter, Elia, passed us to the network for a finder's fee. She was happy to. She didn't want the story herself. Ziegler was nearly killed, and she doesn't know why; it could have been because of me. Who's to say she wouldn't end up the same? It's for the best, I think, that she passed us on: the interview feels much more important now. Inescapable. I recognise the two presenters we'll be talking to from the shows that I used to watch sitting on Ziegler's couch, or lazing on Hoyle's bed at the end of the day. They're not serious reporters, they're light entertainment, more used to interviewing singers or holo stars.

We sit in tall chairs while people move around us, touching our hair, trying to tease it into styles that leave us looking nothing like ourselves. Rex gets it worst: hers is pulled into something like the kids in the richest parts of the city might wear, dye and structural augments applied to make it a shocking pink, to hold it in place. In the mirror in front of us I see her expression turn so sour and disgusted it makes me laugh. She bares her teeth when I do, and I realise that maybe she actually likes it.

They ask if they can shave mine.

'Like in the book . . . It says you shaved your head, for the creepy crawlies.'

'No,' I say.

'We can augment it back to –' the hairdresser lets what I've got run through his hands as if it's filthy, as if he barely wants to touch it, 'well, we can augment it back to this afterwards. But for your appearance, everybody feels that—'

'Leave it,' I say. He nods, then slicks it back, tight against my head, so that from the front it looks like it's barely there.

I don't argue. I think, as he's finishing it, neatening it at the back, how much I like it. It reminds me of who I was, but it's new. I touch it, gently, tentatively, and it's rock solid, fastened with spray. Immovable, I think; and I like it even more for that.

When our hair is done they turn to our faces. They put dark marks around our eyes and what look like smears of dirt on our cheeks.

'No augments,' I say, when they try to put something on my lip. When I look at Rex, I see they have changed the colour of one of her eyes, so they no longer match. It kind of suits her.

Then they leave us waiting. Somebody will be along to tell us when the hosts are ready. Have a drink, they say. Make sure you've used the toilet.

'Are you going to be honest?' Rex asks me once we're alone. We are looking at ourselves – and each other – in the mirror. Rex is still slightly freaked out by them. She stares at herself; moves her body slightly, watching the smoothness of her own movements.

'About what?'

'About me,' she says.

'What is there to lie about?' I ask.

'I tried to kill you. In the book, you talk about that.'

'I didn't say it. Ziegler wrote it. Different.'

'Still, I tried to kill you,' she says.

'And I tried to kill you,' I say. 'So I reckon we're probably about even.'

I want to give her a hug. I want to tell her that it's okay, that everything is, and will be, okay. But I'm not sure I believe it; and I'm not sure she will either.

People in sharp-angled clothing – bright, fancy, expensive-looking – lead us through to the studio. The lights are impossibly bright. It's hard not to squint. I can't see what I look like, but Rex's face is in a permanent scowl. I wonder if that's just what she always looks like and I've stopped noticing. Drones hover around us; the walls have cameras mounted on them, to capture the full holo. Then the hosts come out, and they shake our hands. They're immaculate: beautiful human beings, so beautiful they appear hyperreal. Their clothes are even brighter and more fabulous than everybody else's. Rex and I are dressed head-to-toe in black, newer, cleaner versions of the same clothes we always wear. Against the white walls and bright lights, I feel even less like I belong here. I've never felt so out of place in my life.

Someone counts down, the drones get into position, and then we're live. The presenters speak to the audience watching on the other end of the network, introducing themselves and the news that they've got something really special today. They turn to us.

'Chan,' the female presenter – Nancy something – says. She's all hair, blonde and augmented so that it's constantly shifting in gentle waves. *The Girl Who Fell to Earth*, the book that the world was told was a work of fiction . . . And yet here you are, informing us that it was, in fact, the truth. Have—'

'Not the truth,' I interrupt. I speak slowly, considering my words. I want to make this right. 'Some of the stories that I told Ziegler have been changed.'

'So you didn't kill your own mother?' She pauses, for effect. It's an accusation, and it stings because it's true, at least in part. 'The ship wasn't full of brutes, of horrors and murderers?'

'I suppose,' I say.

'And, of course, one of those murderers is right here with us. Rex. We're lucky enough to welcome you here, as well.'

'Rex,' the male presenter says, turning to her. 'You were the leader of the Lows, a gang which, it has to be said, didn't exactly seem to include people we'd want to know. In the book, we all read about how you earned your name as a sort of title, following a battle to the death with your gang's previous leader. So what's your real name, if we might ask?'

I watch as Rex's whole body tightens up. She shouldn't be here. I shouldn't have done this to her.

'Rex is her name,' I say, cutting in. 'Doesn't matter if it hasn't always been.'

'And after the two of you fought over and over, nearly killing each other, now you've forgiven each other. Are we to believe that?'

'Yes,' Rex says, small and quiet. 'Chan is my friend.'

'There was a lot to forgive, if you don't mind me saying. I'm not sure that many people could find the fortitude, the strength, to forgive some of the things you did to her. You murdered the woman who raised her, after all.' He looks at me. There's something in his eyes, the same thing I saw in Alala's eyes when she was about to take advantage of a situation. He doesn't believe me. They don't. We're here to be mocked: a sideshow.

'Now, the American government, the collected governments of the world, have denied the existence of the prison spaceship Australia, as I'm sure you're aware. And there's simply no empirical evidence to back up your accounts. The country itself is long gone, of course. No one remembers seeing your 'pod' land here. What, a year ago? The government, the police, the military, they have all denied everything. What are people meant to believe? What do you say to the detractors, the non-believers?'

'We're the proof,' I say.

'You could be lying. You could be trying to take advantage of a credulous public, desperate for excitement and adventure, hoping for grand conspiracies. It's easy enough to come forward now with the author of the novel injured in a terrible attack just a few days ago. And we happen to know you were there when Mr Ziegler was attacked. Who's to say you weren't responsible?'

He gestures to a screen and I see footage in the corner of the holo where Ziegler's throat is slit; me standing near, hopeless and helpless. 'There's no real way to corroborate what you're saying.' He goes silent. Glances at the female presenter. 'So *do* you have any actual evidence?'

'Mae,' I say. 'I want to talk about Mae.'

'The little girl? You'll remember,' Nancy says, speaking to the cameras, 'that in the story, this little girl named Mae was rescued by Chan, and then lost when the ship landed here in Washington.' She says it with the voice of somebody who's explaining an elaborate lie – patronising me – us.

'She's missing,' I say. 'She's here, in the city, or maybe in another city, but she's *here*. She's alive. I want to know if anybody's seen her, if anybody can tell me where she is. I made a promise to keep her safe, and—'

'Chan, let me ask you this. If the stories we're meant to believe are true, then you're a *murderer*. You're *both* murderers. You've racked up a hell of a body count between you. So why aren't we locking you up? Why aren't we reconditioning you? If your story is true, why aren't you both in prison?'

The lights flash out. The studio turns pitch black.

The door at the far end bursts open and police swarm into the room, strikers at the ready. A squad of them. Over the shouts and the yells, I can hear a voice screaming at us to stay where we are, to stand perfectly still; this is a raid.

The voice is Hoyle's. I'd know it anywhere.

'What were you thinking?' he asks me. We're alone in an interrogation room. The walls are grey, a smooth, polished metal. The floor is metal, the ceiling is metal. The table between us is metal. I'm not locked down, but I keep my hands on either side of the slot where the Unabler usually rests, where prisoners are usually secured as they're interrogated.

'Where's Rex?' I ask him.

'She's fine.'

'I didn't ask how she was. I asked where she was.'

'She's here. Don't worry about her, worry about yourself. Nobody's talking to her, nobody's making her do anything she doesn't want to do.' He's exasperated. He doesn't have a clue how I'm feeling, how much I want to hurt him right now. 'You shouldn't have done this – the interview. It won't help you.'

'It might,' I say.

'You think somebody from the government's just going to step forward, say, Oh, I saw that kid! You don't have a picture of her. You've got nothing but a name, which they've more than likely changed. The only people who can help you are here; and now we won't. Not unless you help us first.' There's a coldness to the way that he says it. He rests his arms on the table and they're perfectly still. That's what I find weirdest about the augments: how they don't twitch or tremble. They impart a curious calm to everything he does: a fluidity to his movements, a security to his resting.

'You told me that you were helping me, that you would help me find her.'

'And I was. I am.'

'You told me not to give up hope.'

'Without me, you have no hope. Without me, your search is over. She's gone. Maybe she's gone anyway. Maybe there's—'

'She's alive. She's here somewhere.'

'She could be. But she could have a new name, a new family. She might not even remember who you are any more.' I wish his arms would shake; I wish his jaw would quiver, just to show me that he was feeling something. His eyes are augmented; I wonder if that's why he doesn't look sad. 'Maybe she doesn't want to be found, Chan. You have to move on.' He pauses, for a moment. He doesn't want to say what he's going to say, I know. 'Maybe she's dead.'

He's believed this for a while, I can tell. Ever since we met, he's believed I was chasing something I wouldn't find: a ghost.

He lied. Everybody does.

I feel more hurt at these words, and the way he's behaving, than I can remember being. It's a different sort of pain to the kind I've experienced before. It's not the pain of being stabbed; not a dislocated shoulder; not losing my mother.

It feels as though the ground has been pulled away.

It feels like I'm falling, right through the hole that's opened beneath me, and into the dark below.

If I try to picture Mae's face, I get flashes of her features, the memory of her hair tickling my chin. But nothing comes together. She's a blur; she's there, but she's not there. I picture a nose that's hers, but maybe not; maybe it's a composite of the shadows that I saw her in; a mouth, missing milk teeth, her lips chapped and dry. I can't remember the colour of her eyes, just the shape and the darkness of them: reflecting back myself, and the fire.

I try and remember these details, because I want to tell myself that I would recognise her, if I were to find her. I want to be able to say, I know you.

And if I've forgotten, what chance is there that she will remember me? How will she even know who I am?

*   *   *

'Drink this,' Hoyle says. He hands me a cup of water. Cold on my lips, and refreshing. It's so good, I realise that I've neglected myself these last few days. I haven't eaten enough, or drunk enough. Stupid of me.

'I want to see Rex,' I say. He nods, walks to the door. Turns.

'I didn't want to hurt you,' he says.

'But you did,' I say.

Then he's gone and I'm alone. I wonder if anybody has been watching us in here, if they'll let us go now.

The door opens and Rex walks in. She looks angry. She doesn't like feeling captive. She doesn't want to be trapped, tied down. I see Hoyle behind her, waiting outside; he doesn't look at me. I wish it hadn't ended this way. There was something there once. I thought he was a good person. It seemed like he was. I need a good person, somebody to ground me, to guide me and tell me when I'm steering myself wrong. I had my mother once, and then Agatha. For a while, it felt like Hoyle could be that person, just like Jonah was before him.

He closes the door. There's no lock on it, but there doesn't need to be. We're in a police station; there's no way to get out of here. Not without a serious fight, at least.

'Are you alright?' I ask. Rex sits opposite me.

'I do not like these people.'

'No,' I say. I reach over and squeeze her hand. She flinches slightly at my touch.

'Are you alright?' she asks. I can tell it's not a question that comes naturally to her. Worrying about others isn't really in her vocabulary.

'I'm fine,' I say. I smile. 'Thank you for asking.'

'You like it when I let you know I care about you,' she says. That makes me laugh.

'I do,' I reply. 'It's good.'

'They're watching us,' she says.

'Yes,' I tell her, 'probably.' I hand her the cup with what's left of my water in it. 'You should drink this. Keep your strength up.'

'I'm also hungry,' she says. She finishes the water, pours it straight down her throat.

'They'll have to let us go,' I say.

And then we don't talk. Maybe an hour passes while we sit in our chairs in silence, and wait. Sometimes the chairs creak as we shift in our seats; or we stand and pace, stretching against the walls as we wait to see what happens next. But otherwise the room is silent.

Rex's stomach growls, suddenly. A deep gurgle, and it surprises us.

I laugh. She's embarrassed for a moment, then she smirks, ever so slightly.

Then we're silent again.

After what feels like hours, Hoyle opens the door, comes in and stands in front of us.

'We've got an offer for you,' he says. I don't reply. Rex doesn't even look up. She leaves Hoyle to me. I think about what could happen if she didn't, if she took matters into her own hands. She's different now. I know that. But Hoyle thinks she's still who she once was. He thinks she's an animal, capable of grabbing him now, pushing him against the wall, tearing out his throat. Us escaping in a spray of blood, a cloud of chaos, out into the open-plan part of the station where she'll tear through the police, holding back less than I will, cutting them down, fighting them off, fending them off until we're out, in the city, Rex's hands doused in their blood, and mine clean.

Hoyle waves his hand. 'You with me?'

'Yes,' I say.

'So. You know that you're not meant to be in this city. You had a record—'

'Which you cleared.'

'Which we cleared, yes. But your allowance will be revoked. If you're not working for us, we can't help you any more. You won't have any security access, not even an ID, and no ID would mean you're illegal. Illegal, in the city, would make you a criminal. You know what that means. Best case? Exile. Worst? Reconditioning.' That makes me shudder; a knife blade tickling my spine. 'We both know you don't want that. So let's assume you escape. There's no coming back to Washington after that. No going to any city. We'll find you and catch you.' We. Not they. 'You get caught? Pine City again. Maybe worse. Philly, or Jersey.'

'What's Jersey?' Rex asks.

'You don't want to know,' he says. 'But that can change. We still have work that needs doing, and you can do it for us.'

'Like before – the same sort of work,' I say. It's not a question.

'Yes,' he says. 'There are situations we cannot handle. We're not . . .' He walks to the table and leans in, close to us. He softens his voice. 'We don't have people here who are like you.' He looks directly at Rex. 'But if you do one more job for us, then we'll change all the shit that could happen to you. We will put you on the system with real identities. Permanent identities. You'll get jobs, and as long as you're working, as long as you're contributing to the infrastructure, you'll be able to stay here. You can have normal lives. Live in the city, in a real house, with real friends. You'll get the lives you've never had before – never had a chance to enjoy. You'll finally have somewhere to live. A permanent place to call home. Forever. And we will – I will – leave you alone.'

'Both of us?' I ask.

He nods. 'This is it. One last job.' I don't say anything. I don't know what to say. If I'm not in the city, finding Mae will be harder. Living outside the walls as a nomad is comfortable, but it's not a home. It's moveable. There's always the fear it won't be there when I next return to it. The city is here, and it's not going anywhere.

But the price we have to pay to stay is high.

'We need time to think,' I say.

He nods. 'You can't stay here, though. We'll escort you to the gate. You can go back to your tents.' He says *tents* with derision. I know he thinks I've spent too much time there with Rex, when I could have been in an apartment inside the city walls with him. When I should have been integrating myself. 'You want to come back inside ever again, you have to accept the terms I've set out. You don't want to accept, that's fine; you just don't come back into the city, and we won't have to—' He stops himself. 'We won't have to find you, and do something none of us wants to do.'

He stands upright again, stretches his back. There's a crack: a sharp, quick click, of bone on metal. 'I'll prepare a vehicle to take you to the gate. You've got until tomorrow to give us your answer. This is time sensitive.'

Then he leaves us. He doesn't look at me again.

We're only alone for a few moments before Rex leans in close to me.

'I'll do what they want,' she says. And then she sits back and looks down at her hands resting in her lap; the augmented hand squeezing and rubbing at the skin on her real one, wearing at the skin. She's grazed herself. A trace of blood on the skeletal metal thumb of her augmented arm.

I notice that the eye pigment she was given for the interview is still bright. The colour of one eye is a startling green colour, so light it's almost white.

'I don't want you to do it,' I say.

'It's my choice,' she says.

She's right, I tell myself. She's right.

The transport vehicle has a cage in the back, for those the police arrest. This is where they make Rex and me sit while they drive us outside the city walls. Hoyle sits opposite us, head in his hands for most of the journey. Sometimes he leans back against the wall, not looking at us. He doesn't say anything until we hear the guards at the gate usher us through. It's only as we're leaving the city that Hoyle leans in and indicates for me to do the same. He drops his voice to a whisper.

'Come to me if you decide to take us up on our offer. Just promise me that.' I nod and he glances at Rex. 'She'll bounce back,' he tells me. 'You need to be selfish,' he says, and I remember how many times I've been told that before in my life; how many times I promised that I would be.

'I'm trying,' I say.

'This is the only way you get to Mae. The only—' The van stops and Hoyle sits back again. 'Your stop,' he says to us.

Someone swings open the doors to the cage and we step out into the sunlight, the burning heat, escorted by two police in full armour, weapons at the ready.

And I wonder, even if we do what they want and get our IDs and become totally free, if they'd ever fully trust us; if they would ever assume we weren't going to fall back on violence, on what they think must be an innate part of our natures.

Back at the camp, Fiona hands us bowls of stew, even though it's not dinnertime, and sits with us, handing out chunks of bread, freshly baked in the sun. The bread is flat, pock-marked with air holes and almost too sweet to eat with the savoury meal. We use it to mop up the fish stew in our bowls, and smile at Fiona, who nods, pleased we're enjoying it. We sit back and watch some of the people from our camp splash about in the water, catching dinner for the next couple of days. My eyes drift across familiar sights: a boat bobbing on the waves; people dragging a net full of fish back to shore; a man beating a squid to death, just as we saw the day we arrived here. It's quiet, peaceful.

'You're one damned stubborn girl,' Fiona says. I nod, mouth full of food. 'Not many people would have gone as far as you've gone to find someone. They'd give up, take the easy route.'

'There is no easy route,' Rex says, through her own mouthfuls. We haven't told people here about Rex's past; about what the police would have her – us – do. We don't want the nomads scared of us like the police are; or, worse, try to use her as a weapon like the police do. As far as they're concerned, she's quiet. They've never seen her fight.

'There's always an easy route. Sometimes it's as simple as lying down, letting things wash over you.' She smiles. 'I ever tell you about when I left Australia? *My* Australia?'

'No,' I say. She's described Australia the country to me before: a place not unlike this, when she left it; a hot desert punctuated by cities, with water lapping at jagged cliffs; greenery sparse and animal life sparser.

'The end was hard,' she says. She lies back, stares up at the roof of the tent we're sitting inside. We can't really see her face and I get the impression that's what she prefers. 'The last few months, it felt like the the rest of the world was abandoning us. We were stuck out in the middle of nowhere, the middle of nothing. An island that nobody wanted to help, because everybody was preoccupied with their own nonsense.' She laughs at that word. 'That makes it sound like the world wasn't coming to an end. But that's what we thought, what everybody thought: that the world was just going to get too hot and we were going to die.

There wasn't a plan to save us, not out there. Not that far away from the rest of the world. We were forgotten about.

'We lost TV signals a few months before the end – TV was like the holo, before it was the holo – so all we had was the radio. And all the voices broadcasting were talking about how we should have seen the end of the world coming. That's all anybody said, over and over. That humanity had had blinkers on our eyes, like we were horses.'

'Horses?' Rex asks.

'Like donkeys.' Rex shakes her head. 'Like . . . deer, but bigger. They were animals used for pulling things, for riding. People would put blinkers on them to restrict their field of view so they wouldn't get scared of things that rushed up on them.'

Fiona puts her hands on the sides of her face, by her eyes, so she can only see straight ahead. 'That was us. The heat, the collapse, it rushed up on us. It surprised us, even though we should have known it was coming. And in Australia, it hit us harder than so many other places. Some countries were okay. Here, you can live in the heat. It's hell, too hot to stay out in the sun and not blister and peel, but it's *bearable*. There, it was a nightmare. The air became so warm that you didn't even want to breathe it. It hurt to suck it in, like you were being cooked from the inside. People died so fast in those days. You had to stop letting it get to you. Ships came, from the rest of world, to carry those who could afford it away. Asia totally shut its borders, so the people fled to Northern Europe, to Russia, if they could. The seas were rising and there was nothing we could do. I don't know if you know how much land we lost to the sea?'

'I've been to the museum. I've seen what it was like,' I say.

'Then you can appreciate what we went through. The things we witnessed – whole cities, gone – where we lived, worked; and the people who lived there gone with them. The land was just vanishing into the sea. So the rich saved themselves. They paid their way off the country, and they went to another life where it was cooler, safer. For those of us who couldn't pay . . .' She shrugs. 'I was a little girl. I watched my mother die. My father die. My brothers and my sister, they all got sick, because the bugs ran rife and they carried diseases that we couldn't even hope to fight off, illnesses that raised your temperature: a death sentence given by your own body. But I survived. I got stronger, because they died. I fought off the illnesses they passed on. And I haggled and bartered. I lived in caves, in the shells of abandoned houses in the hills, in holes dug out under the shade of dead trees. I fought to survive. I gather you did the same, in your time.

'And then, eventually, we began to give up. We didn't have any power after a while. We tried to make do with solar panels for a while, but the heat had made parts melt, made the tech unusable. It was like we were losing everything we had developed – hundreds of thousands of years of civilisation, snuffed out in an instant. We were forced to abandon everything. People turned to strange ways to survive.

Just when I was about to abandon all hope, I saw a boat. One solitary boat. Pillaging, it turned out. From China. They'd stopped caring about their borders at that point. They were as desperate as the rest of us. I didn't speak their language, and they didn't speak mine. Still, I swam out to it. I didn't give them any choice but to save me. I persuaded them to take me somewhere else, away from Australia. And they did.'

'They brought you here?' Rex asks.

'No, no. Not even close. To the other side of the world. That's when I decided that being a nomad? It was as close a thing to a calling as I'd ever found. It makes sense. Sometimes it gets too hard and you settle somewhere, for a while . . . I have travelled my whole life, running from everything I lost, looking for something to replace it. Never found it. And now I'm here, and . . .'

She's still smiling, but there's something desperately sad in her eyes. It takes me a second to remember the exact look; I've seen it before. My mother. The day she told me what was happening to her, what would happen in the end.

'You're dying,' I say to Fiona.

'We're all dying,' she replies. 'Some of us are simply closer to death than others.' She takes our bowls from us and pours purified seawater into them before upending them and wiping them down with a cloth. 'Eventually everyone is forced to stop travelling, forced to settle somewhere. I'm guessing that now isn't that time for you two. Not yet. But my time is coming, sure.'

'Maybe you're wrong,' I say. 'You told me that you move on when you want to. When you need to, or when you feel like it.'

'We've been here, at this site, for just over ten months now,' she says, gesturing. 'Longest I've stayed anywhere in as long as I can remember. I've got one more move in me, I reckon. Either I journey until we find it, or it'll find me.' She takes my hand, and then reaches for Rex's augmented hand. Rex flinches at the touch but Fiona doesn't care. 'You listen to me. Whatever you have to do, you should do it. Finish what you started. Don't regret anything.'

'What do you regret?' I ask.

'Everything I haven't done. And everything I'll never get the chance to do. That's the sad thing, girls. I've tried to do whatever I wanted, and now the end is coming? All I can think is how much I wish I had more time.'

'She does not act as if she is is dying,' Rex says when Fiona's left us. We're getting changed to go for a swim. It's a way to cool down, to make some time to think. The sea is still tonight, which is unusual. The boat has been dragged in; the nets bustled up and settled under rocks to keep them from blowing away. Rex undoes her arm, pulls it free of her body. 'I have seen dying people. She is not nearly as weak and useless as they were.'

'Some people stay strong until they're suddenly weak,' I tell her. My mother looms large in my memory at that moment. Her voice is clear in my head. I can still hear it. It's the only memory that I have of her which never fades, never changes.

Be selfish, I hear her whisper. I shudder and turn away from Rex, hoping she doesn't see.

'I hope she dies peacefully,' Rex tells me, untroubled, and she leaves the tent, walks down the beach to the edge. She doesn't hesitate as she wades out into the water; and then, as she braces herself, raising her arms – one complete, one not – above her head and carving an arc into the sea, under the waves. I follow her, running to keep up, but she's gone, so strong a swimmer that I can't possibly catch her. Nothing slows her down; not even what she's missing. If you didn't know you couldn't tell; it doesn't affect her one little bit.

When we return we sit in the light of the setting sun to dry ourselves and then we offer our help to the fishers to get more squid for the evening meal. Squid and salt fish: a meal we're so used to now, a meal we eat so many times a week I lose count but which we are not yet sick of. We stand at the edge of the shore, our feet in the soft waves, and we throw spears whenever we see a tentacle, then we drag the creatures out, hurl them up the beach to be gutted, cleaned, cooked, served.

We're tired and so we don't speak about what happened, about Hoyle's offer. Rex will let me make the decision and she'll stand by me. I know that.

It's what she does.

The next morning I move quietly so as not to wake Rex. Even though she's in her own tent, she's like me – the slightest sound wakes her. I creep through the camp as soon as dawn breaks. Some of the nomads are awake. They keep strange hours, preferring to sleep through the hot days and make the most of the nights. They hunt or brew drinks or build things. They produce crafts, which are then smuggled into the city and sold to people who'll pay artisans far too much money for knocked-together driftwood and cliff-rock carvings. Nobody notices me as I creep out of bed and slip away. The sand's quiet to walk on and the front of Rex's tent doesn't even twitch as I go past.

Fiona catches me on the outskirts of the camp.

'You're not leaving us forever,' she says.

'No,' I tell her.

'Good. It's not your time yet.' She takes my hand and presses it to her chest so that I can feel her heart. The steady thump of her life.

Then she lets go and almost pushes me away, with her fingertips, gently but surely. I don't know why she does it.

'I'll see you soon,' she says.

I carry on walking through the dawn. The sun is just coming up. The sky is a beautiful hazy dark that isn't quite holding together, like there's a battle between the morning and the nothingness that was there before.

I come to the wall and I follow it around to the gate. It's shut. I wait at the scanner, hoping. I breathe in.

I've done this before: felt like this, stood before a scanner hoping it works, holding my breath until it does. Then it was at the archives, when I first began my search for Mae. Then, I was on somebody else's identification. I had no right.

I'm lost, thinking about that day – the guard I accidentally killed to get his pass; how Alala manipulated me – when I hear the gate doors grind open. I've wondered, when everything else in the city is so shiny and clean and now, why they've let the wall become filthy and run-down. I've wondered why this was the gate that they put in, why here. Why did they build it this way, so it's not something inviting, but something that feels archaic, as if it's made out of chunks of the ships that should have joined Australia in orbit around this dying planet.

I step through and into the city.

The guards stationed here look up as I pass, then down at their screens. They are probably checking my pass, my access. I nod at them and they nod back. They appear slightly more relaxed than usual. People rarely come through the gates this early. It's the end of the night shift. At this time of day, when the sun is low on the horizon, it's even darker in the city than it is outside. Inside the walls, the shadows linger until the sun rises higher. I walk through the darkness to a terminal and call Hoyle. His number, his private line, is linked to my ID.

I remember the day he fixed this, three weeks into our training with him. He told me that I would be able to use it to get hold of him wherever I was, wherever he was. I think it was something he wanted to do to make me feel safe. We were in an apartment that they provided for us, waiting for our processing to be completed, doing nothing all day but sit and exercise and watch holos and train. Rex and me, side by side, beating the dust out of punch bags that Hoyle hung from the ceiling for us. The night before, when Rex was asleep, he told me about himself, about the time before his accident. He said it was only fair because he knew all about where I came from, and I knew nothing about him. And then he kissed me, and I kissed him back. It was nothing like kissing Jonah, where everything was tentative. With Hoyle, it was urgent. Kissing Hoyle was understanding that, with him, whatever was happening it was for the moment, it wasn't going to be forever. But it would be something, in that moment.

This is the first time I've used his personal number. Next to the log, by his name, it says I've only ever called the station when I've tried to get hold of him before, never his private line. I press the digits for the first time. He won't be at work yet, and I want to be the one who wakes him. I'm the one who's going to be saying goodbye, who's giving up the life, the being here, the chance to find Mae. Everything I've worked so hard for.

As I hear the beep of the connection being made, I know he'll know; that he'll understand why I'm calling before I even say a word.

I wait. The beeping continues.

Then the beeping stops. Gaia tells me to leave a message. I tell it to try again, but there's nothing. Tell it again, and—

The system boots me out. The screen resets, asking me to identify myself.

I press my hand to it and it scans me.

'Please step away from the terminal,' Gaia says. 'You have used an unauthorised city identification. Remain where you are. The police have been notified.'

'About what?' I ask. Frantic. Something's gone wrong. My access has been taken away, and now . . .

I check my log in. Nothing. Not even an Informant number.

I'm nobody again.

Hoyle lied. He must have lied. He told me to come here. It was a trap.

It must have been.

I run back to the gate. The guards look up at me. One of them I half recognise. He's older than most of the others. He has a kind face, and he's out of shape. I've always guessed they gave him this position so he's somewhere he's no hassle. He doesn't have to do anything, other than stand around all day.

'You're leaving so soon?' he asks.

'Yes,' I say. I don't want him to scan me. I don't want to fight them. I don't want to have to do what I would have to do to get away from them.

'Did you find your friend?'

'Hoyle?' He knows about Hoyle?

'Don't know her name.' *Her.* 'The one with the arm.' No. 'Came in here about an hour before you did.' No. 'Said she was going to do something, some job.'

I stop dead in my tracks.

'It was definitely her?' I ask.

'I can check,' he says. He shouts to the other guard, the one waiting by the terminal. 'You bring up the stats for earlier? Her friend, who came through here? She's still in the city?'

'Yeah,' the other one shouts. But then he sees something on his screen. I watch his face change. He raises his hand to his ear, speaks quietly. I think he's telling the kindly guard that my access rights have been redacted. They look at me with big eyes.

They're going to have to take me in and they really don't want to try doing that.

'Is something wrong?' I ask, but I know the answer already. I can't leave. Not yet. Not now. Rex is in the city somewhere. She's taken the deal. So why has Hoyle shut me out? Why has he taken away my—

'Chan? That's your name, right?' the guard in front of me asks.

His hand drops to his side. He does it slowly, in a way that he thinks I won't notice. He's been out here too long, away from action.

I don't want to have to fight him.

'Yes,' I say. I start to edge backwards. Away from him.

'Wait there a second,' he says.

Two options: I run or I fight. If I run, they'll call the birds. Swarm me. If I fight, I can stop them raising the alarm, which I know they'll do if they can't subdue me. And they can't subdue me. They just don't know it yet.

But fighting these men – out of shape, lazy, tired – feels almost unfair.

At least, that's what I'm thinking in the split-second before the guard in front of me raises his striker – a whip – and it fizzes and it slashes toward my face. Instinctively my arm comes up, and the whip coils around my wrist, tightens, pulls me close.

It's almost unfair, but not quite.

The second one doesn't have a chance to react. I hurl the first guard over my shoulder, using his momentum against him. He ploughs into the second one and they both go down. They hit the floor with a thud and a collective moan, and then I'm on top of them. I whack my forearm into their bellies, one after the other, winding them. I don't want to hurt them, but I can't risk them raising the alarm. I need to get out of here. They've got Unablers and I snap them onto their wrists, lock them to each other, back to back. It won't hold them for long, I know – somebody will come through here and find them soon enough – but it'll give me the time I need.

No sign of any birds yet, so I walk away. If I run that might alert people that something's wrong. I know the routes through the city where there are the fewest cameras, fewer places to be spotted, so I stick to those. I need to find somewhere quiet, somewhere that Hoyle and his team – or whoever's looking for me – won't find me. I need to prepare. I need to find Rex, to get her out of here; and they won't give her up without a fight.

I pass an old terminal. I want to try Hoyle again, so I keep my face hidden, holding the arm with my ID chip away from the terminal so it doesn't try to read me. I log in with the old ID that Ziegler once gave me: a name that wasn't mine, from when I first came to the city. I struggle to remember the password. It was the names that were important to me, but I can't remember the order. My mother, first. Surely. Then Agatha. Then Mae. And I'm not sure if that's right.

My password works. I breathe a sigh of relief and then message Hoyle, going through the official channels. He'll be able to pinpoint this terminal's location and send birds here within minutes. If – as I suspect – he wants me gone from the city, or captured, he'll waste no time. But it might not be him who locked me out. It might be his superiors, who never liked that Rex and I were given pardons; who never liked that Hoyle was training us, using us. Hoyle might not have a clue what trouble we're in. I've got three minutes, I reckon, until I have to leave. If he hasn't replied by then, I'll know it was probably him that betrayed us. But I can escape with enough time to hide.

And I suddenly remember: the tracker. It's in my arm. If they want to find me, they can through my ID chip.

No time to think. I draw my knife, poise my blade over the spot, grit my teeth and pierce my skin. Blood wells up. I press down and try not to howl, but I don't know if I succeed. Just when I'm sure I can't press the knife in any deeper I feel the tip of the blade grind against something, so I pull it out. A neat cut and a lot of blood.

Back in with the knife, trying to flick the chip out.

Somebody comes up behind me. I hear their footsteps. 'Not now,' I say. I tense my fingers around the knife handle and I yank. No good. I'm going to need to use my fingers. It's too embedded.

The person behind me coughs, clears his throat – exaggerated, because he wants me to know he's there. I glance back. He's not a threat. A man, a few years older than me. Thin. Even his head is thin, long and thin.

'Are you finished with the terminal?' His voice sounds like he looks. Same thing.

'No,' I reply. I glance around. No sign of the birds. No sign of backup. No sirens in the distance. Come on, Hoyle.

Come on.

'I've got important business,' the man says, and then he looks down at my arm, blood dripping to my wrist, over my palm, spattering on the floor.

'Can't be that important,' I tell him. 'If it was, you'd be rushing to find another one.'

'I'm sorry, I'm sorry,' he says, his face going ash white at the sight of my wound. He gags, like he's going to throw up.

Some people really aren't good at the sight of blood.

'You've got mail,' Gaia says, as the man turns and rushes away in the opposite direction. I open the message as I push my index finger into the cut. I find the chip, hook under it, flip it out. It feels warm and slimy, but getting free of it is a crazy relief.

The message is from Hoyle. Three words.

Leave the city.

I don't know if that's his instruction or a warning that something's happened and he doesn't want me here. But I know, in that moment, I'm going to find him, and Rex. I'm going to rescue her and then we're going to get Mae, and then finally everything will be alright. It's time for me to stop waiting.

My time is here.

If Hoyle has Rex, his apartment will be empty. I need to know where he's taken her. It won't be the police head-quarters, because the job he offered us is so dirty, so awful, they won't want to admit to it. So I have to start with his apartment. There may be clues. Getting to it is the easy part. I know the city so well now that I don't need to stop and reorient myself and I don't need a map from terminals, or to ask Gaia for directions. I just move. There are no birds chasing me. Just the usual ones on patrol. I stay where they can't see me, close to buildings, under shelters. I wait until they pass and then I move on. I let the city move around me: the people, the cars, the birds. I just have to be a part of the normal flow of the city and the birds will let me alone.

That is the way this world works. You have to know your place in it and let it be. You're just a part of a larger whole; a cog in a wheel.

I stand outside the building where the apartments are. Breathe. My pass is dead, so I can't use it to get in. I got up there once before without a pass. I think I can do it again. I wonder which security guard will be on duty, sleeping in the chair in the hallway.

I wonder if they'll try to stop me.

Up the steps, open the front door. The Gaia terminal blinks at me.

I don't stop to talk to it. I act as though I should be here. Maybe they wiped my logins, but didn't bother to—

Please wait, the Gaia terminal says. *You are not authorised to be here.*

I broke this door once before, to get to the stairwell. I kick through the door now, thinking I can do it again. It hurts and the door doesn't budge. They've reinforced it.

'Open the door,' I shout at the terminal.

The police have been informed, Gaia says.

I hear the elevator descending, and fast. Okay, Chan. Okay. There's likely only the one guard. Whoever was up there on patrol. I hope that it's Barney.

The doors of the elevator open, and Barney steps out, striker ready, but he's practically yawning. He sees me and he drops his guard.

'Chan?' he asks. 'You're the threat?'

'I don't know,' I say. 'I need to get upstairs.' He hasn't been told. He doesn't know that I'm not meant to be here.

He looks at my arm, sees the blood. 'Why didn't your ID register?' he asks. He doesn't wait for an answer. 'Let me call this through,' he says, and he turns away from me. He'll find out. He'll have to stop me.

'I'm sorry,' I say. I thump him in the gut, in the right spot to bring him down, and he keels forward. My arm tightens around his neck, to get him to sleep, just for a while. 'I don't want to do this,' I say, as he struggles, 'but I haven't got any choice.'

I know that's not true. There's always a choice. You just have to make the right one and stand by it. That's getting harder and harder.

As soon as he's slumped on the floor, I get into the elevator. It won't move – Gaia won't let it – but there's a hatch in the ceiling. I leap up, hit the hatch with my forearm, slamming it open. I grab the edge of the hatch and pull myself up and into the shaft. There's no ladder here, but I can climb the cables if I'm strong enough.

Which I am, just about. Hand over hand, I haul myself up. I use my feet to steady myself, pass the door for the first floor, the second; and I keep going until I'm at the right floor. The door is shut but it can be prised open. I just need to get to it.

So I swing. I start moving my body, back and forth, and when I'm close enough I reach out and grab the doorframe and plant my feet on the edge. Once I'm steady I pull my knife from its sheath. Reinforced metal, Hoyle said, when he gave it to me. It should be unbreakable.

I jam it into the space between the elevator doors, worried it'll bend or snap, but it doesn't. It holds and the doors wedge open enough for me to get my fingers in, then my hands. To force it open.

Then I'm on the floor. The chair that Barney was sitting on is empty now. There's no sign of other guards, not yet. They'll be here soon enough. Minutes at most. The birds'll be here even sooner, clamouring at the windows.

I run to Hoyle's apartment. His door isn't reinforced. I kick in the lock and I'm in. I don't know what exactly I'm looking for. There's a satchel on the bed and it wasn't here when I last left. I turn it upside down, let everything fall out. A holotab tumbles out. I pick it up and flick it on.

Password? Gaia asks.

'Marathon,' I say. He gave me his password. He trusted me. He can't have totally betrayed me, not if he trusted me with this.

The screen unlocks. I scan through his files, the messages he's been sent: requisitions, permission papers, a conversation about Rex and me. Even with everything that's happened, I feel a twinge of guilt at reading his private correspondence.

Do you trust her?

Rex? No.

What about Chan?

She's not a part of this.

So we take Rex out?

When we've done what we've got to do.

Where is he being kept?

Bethlehem.

Okay. Get the transport. Take her along.

I have no idea who Hoyle is communicating with. It's an unidentified number. But now I know that they've got her. And I know where. I'm about to throw the holotab onto the bed and leave when I see another file, waiting there, as if it's been dying for me to open it.

Missing person #112363: Mae X.

It can't be.

But I open the file, and it is.

Hoyle lied to me. He's known Mae's whereabouts since the day we met. Before. Her records go back to the day we landed here, when she entered the system. Upon arrival, the social services asked for her name, and she told them. Mae. Her file says that she spelt it out for them, repeating the letters I taught her. Everything else, they said, was subnormal: arithmetic, language skills, physical endurance. They brought her to a facility in upstate New York first, along with the other children they took. *Rescued*, is the word they use in the statement. The children were so happy to have food, beds. Mae, it says, needed only a doll to sleep with, to hold. She named the doll Chan. My hands shake as I hold the holotab. I can hear muted shouting down the corridor. I can hear something outside, too. Birds. I keep reading.

Mae was adopted by somebody; a woman, who, according to the file, is one of the doctors working for the services. No name. I know what those doctors are like. I met one – Gibson – in Pine City. The memory of him tampering with who I was – the thought of someone like him changing Mae, taking away her personality and her memories

– makes me seethe. My knuckles go white as I grip the holotab. I can hear the birds swarming outside. And the footsteps in the corridor let me know there are four police out there. There'll be more downstairs, waiting for me.

There are two ways out of this. The hard way – the way I was taken out of here when I first came and met Hoyle, kicking and screaming and right into the hands of Gibson and Pine City – and the way I've never tried before.

Okay.

I throw the holotab hard at the window. Really hard. Not expecting the glass to break, because most windows won't; but this building is old. I just need the holotap to make a crack, a splinter.

That'll make the next part hurt less, I reckon.

The holotab bounces off the window, but the glass ripples for a second, like a stone being thrown into water. Thin lines, not waves, not cracks, but something.

It's probably not enough.

It'll have to be enough.

'Come out with your hands up,' somebody shouts from the corridor. One of the police, I think, the sound of her voice changed by the helmet. 'Open the door.'

The handle rattles. They'll have a ram and the longer I wait the sooner they'll start using it on the door.

'I'm coming,' I shout back. Give them a moment of wondering if that's true. Of course it is. I will come, just not the way that they're expecting.

I grab a chair, hold it at shoulder height, brace myself. Legs pointed at the glass. I take a deep breath and then charge towards the window, slamming the legs into the glass, into the point where the ripples appeared. Outside, I can see the birds hovering, watching.

'What is that?' the police outside the door shouts. I don't answer. 'Prime the ram!' she shouts to her colleagues. I hear the shuffle of their feet as they get into position.

'Ram primed,' one yells back.

The ripples have turned into cracks. I hit the glass again until those ripples splinter. The chair bends and buckles, so I use my forearm, my elbow. Slamming into those cracks until they spread further and further. It hasn't completely given way, not yet. Fingers crossed it will.

I go to the far side of the room, pull my hood up over my eyes, pull the sleeves down over my hands. I need to try and protect myself. There's a bird right outside, staring at me.

I run. I run in a straight line and then I launch myself against the glass. I drive with my shoulder (always my shoulder, which you'd think would make me more used to it, make it hurt less). I feel something – bone or glass, I don't know what – crunch under the force, and then I'm through, the sound like a scream as the glass shatters all around me and the rush of the cold air comes up from the streets, and the whirring of the birds. I reach out, hoping they're slower to react than I am.

My hands meet the body of the bird, and it flaps its wings violently, trying to shake me off. But I grab hold, slotting my finger in beneath the flaps of metal, even as they tighten, as they cut into my skin. I can't focus on what's happening. I can't do anything really except hold on. I hear the other birds rally, trying to help the one I'm holding.

One of them zooms towards me; it thuds into me, into my left arm, whacking it away from the bird I'm holding. I lose my grip with that hand, and, as my bird struggles, we both sink towards the street, lower and lower, my weight dragging it down. The bird moves towards the buildings opposite Hoyle's apartment – a burst of power, to try and drive me off. It slams me into the brick at the side of a building, and that hurts, but I keep hold as we sink lower still.

The other birds come at me. I think about letting go. I'm only a floor away from the ground now, maybe. I could survive that. I've taken falls like that before. There are no police below me, just bystanders, gawping. I can run. I'll have a tiny headstart, as long as I can lose the birds.

But then it slams me against the building again, and this time I crash into a window. It's open, half open, and the bird smacks against the glass while I collide with the windowsill. I manage to grab the ledge, hook my arms inside.

I manage to hold on as the bird, dazed from the collision, stays back to readjust itself. I pull myself up, climb in through the gap. The room is full of people at desks: grey suits and cubicles and headsets and holocalls. Some of the workers stand up, and they stare at me. Glass windows on every side; and, in front of me, past the desks, I can see big double doors opened up on to some sort of balcony.

I run through the office.

At the desks the people stare. To the balcony. A woman in a suit shouts at me, asks what I'm doing, but I don't even glance at her.

I'm on the balcony. I'm up on the railing. There's a building opposite, another window, close enough to reach.

I launch myself, curl into a ball, and I smash through the glass; and then I'm rolling forward onto the floor of a shop, clothes hanging from racks all around me. I get to my feet and run, down the stairs in front of me, leaping the bannister halfway, over the heads of customers; and then I'm out the front door as I hear somebody who works there shouting at me, telling me to come back, to pay for what I broke.

I shout that I'm sorry, but the air carries my voice away as I run so fast that I can't even hear it. Around me, in the sky, I see no birds; I hear no sirens. I don't stop running, sticking to the streets I know are safe. Never stop running, I tell myself. Never stop.

When I make the wall I swim out, through the icy water, through the sluice drains and then I'm outside the wall, in the open sea. I follow the rope that's tied against the concrete in the sea, round to the shore. The sea is not calm; the waves are crashing against the wall, threatening to take me under, either pushing or dragging. My body is confused: hot above the water level, freezing cold underneath it. I'm exhausted and bleeding. But I can make it now. Not well, but well enough.

When I reach the shore two nomads rush into the waves to help me get to dry land. Fiona rushes down the beach holding a towel. She hands it to me.

'Are you alright?' she asks. It's been months since I used this way into – or out of – the city. I haven't used it since I got given security access.

'I'm fine,' I say. I dry myself. My clothes are ordinarily water resistant, but the shattering glass ripped them and

I'm soaked, so I start to take my clothes off as I walk up the beach. She follows me.

'You're alone?'

'They've got Rex,' I say. Or they will have. Once she's finished their dirty work for them, they'll take her and who knows what'll happen to her. 'Where's Bethlehem?'

'I don't know. Is that in the city?'

I shake my head. 'It's outside. Another city, I think.'

'We've got maps,' Fiona says. And she takes my hand, looks at the wound on my arm from my torn-out ID, and she squeezes my fingers tight. It stops me from moving and getting myself dry, but that moment feels secure and safe and good. We pause for a moment, then she nods, lets go of me, and rushes towards some of the other nomads, leaving me to bask in the heat coming from the sand and rocks we're standing on, even as the wall throws everything here into its shade.

5

His name is Randolph and he's been here a long time. Longer than any of the other nomads. He used to tell them where to go, front of the pack; now he's old and his leg means he can't walk far, so when they move they hoist him up on their backs and bear his weight for him. He doesn't tell me what happened to his leg and I don't ask. He smiles. Fiona tells me that I can trust him.

'Eventually, they won't want to carry me any more,' he says, and he seems calm about that, like he's already made his peace with it.

'Randolph used to live in Bethlehem,' Fiona says. 'I asked around and he answered.'

'Where is it?' I ask. 'I tried to look on the maps, but the towns around here . . . There are a lot of them.'

'Not a town, no,' he says. 'Fiona tells me you used to be in prison.'

'Yes,' I say. I don't tell him that it was twice. Twice I was locked up, forced to break out of somewhere I was trapped against my will.

'Well, so have I.' He reaches for one of the maps, brings

117

it up close to his eyes. He squints to be able to make out what's what. 'Here,' he says, jabbing a finger. 'Bethlehem is in New York state. Nowhere near the city, though. Somewhere around this part.' He moves his finger across the map. 'You can't miss it.'

'A prison.'

'It was. A supermax, they called it. Worst of the worst. It's not that any more, of course. That's when I got out. Couldn't afford to keep prisoners there, so they reconditioned them. Most of the time, it stuck. Me? Didn't take.'

'Why were you there?' I ask.

'I don't know,' he says. Sad eyes, as he speaks. 'That's the strangest thing. There are gaps in what I remember, gaps in what made me who I am. That's one. I did something, must have been terrible. They put me there and then they erased my memories. Threw me out and told me it was freedom. However you want to think of it.'

'You don't know what you did?'

'We've told him it doesn't matter,' Fiona says. 'Everybody deserves a second chance and Randolph's been a real asset. A good egg, as my mother used to say.'

'And I've told you you're wrong,' Randolph tells her. 'Of course it matters. Who you are when you start a journey is why you start it. Doesn't matter if you change; you can't entirely accept who you are unless you know where you began. I did something bad, I should know what. Without knowing I can't really ever be truly better. No one can help me.'

'You don't need the help,' Fiona says.

'I need to get to Bethlehem,' I say. 'My fri—' I stop myself. I was about to call Rex my friend. But she's not. She's closer. She's family. 'Rex is there. I need to get to her, and quickly.'

'There are no transports that go that way, not unless you're coming from the city,' Fiona says. 'Some go to New York, maybe. They could get you closer.'

'How long to walk?'

'Days. A long while.'

'I need to get there fast,' I say. 'Do you have any ideas?'

Randolph stares out to the sea. 'Maybe,' he says.

I watch the nomads rub the fishing boat down with something to keep the hull watertight, then drag it down the beach to the shore, right to the point where the waves tickle the dry land. Randolph watches it as it bobs in the shallows. He leans against his stick as if his weight is too much for his bones and he needs the support.

I walk up to him. 'You're sure you want to come?'

'I know the way.'

'You told me to follow the shore. I can't miss New York, you said.'

'And you can't. Be there in a few days. Head up to Bethlehem from there, up the Philly creek.' Days. I need to be as fast as possible. I don't know what they want Rex to do, but Hoyle's efficient. That's his thing. Get the job done and then it's dealt with. Then you can move on. And she won't last long after he decides she's finished. 'I want to come with you. I'll wait by the boat while you get your friend, then come back to me and we'll come right back here.'

'You don't have to,' I say.

'So you know how to sail one of these?' he asks. The nomads working on the boat are tying sheets of fabric to a pole in the middle of it – the mast, Randolph called it – and fastening them down. 'You know how to deal with tides, with the wind? How to steer us?'

'No,' I say.

'Well, then.' He looks smug for a moment, pleased at his own usefulness. 'You'll need my help, won't you.' He climbs into the boat. He's so slow, you can see the pain of movement on his face every time he changes position, as he lifts one leg to step into the boat, and then the other; as he sits on the wooden slat at the back; as he exhales, from the exhaustion of doing all those things. 'We should hurry,' he says.

I thank Fiona for her help. She hands me a scarf wrapped around a lumpy bundle, presses it into my hands. 'Food,' she says, 'and some purification tabs, for water.'

'You'll be here when we come back?'

'We'll see each other again,' she says, which isn't an answer, not really. But I follow Randolph, climb into the boat and sit opposite him; and some of the people on the shore grab the back of the boat and push hard, rushing us down the soft sand and into the water, and it crashes up around us, and then we're floating, drifting out into the sea.

'You didn't say goodbye to them,' I say, looking back at the shoreline.

'I didn't need to,' he tells me.

* * *

I learn quickly.

I learn that you need to watch the sail at all times, because the wind changes direction so quickly that you can be caught off guard, and then you're suddenly not hugging the coastline any more, you're heading out into the blue, off to somewhere you don't know at all, somewhere that's just as scary to me as what was outside Australia, nothingness all around you. I learn that Randolph is old, and he's weak, and that he's either unable or unwilling to do anything, and that as he barks orders at me – his mood increasingly stressed by the tide, the waves, the wind – I'm expected to juggle more than I thought possible, all the while with the salt water smashing itself across us, soaking me, stinging my eyes; and I learn that being on the sea makes me sick, sicker than I've ever been, leaving me hauling myself to the side of the boat for the first few times I vomit, until I stop, until I force my body to stop, because I can't, because I don't have anything to vomit up any more, because I need to keep control of this boat.

And then the waves die down and there's incredible calm; and we're moving slower, and he lets me recover. He purifies water for me to drink, and I sick up the first few sips, but then manage to keep the rest down. He tears off bits of bread for me – none of the meat, none of the cheese, because he says I won't be able to take it – and I eat it, slowly. I chew it until it's pulp in my mouth, even if everything in me wants to swallow it as fast as possible, that's how hungry I am. And we watch the green and gold shoreline, and I wonder where we are.

As night falls, he asks me if I want to hear about this place, about where we are right now.

'Yes,' I say. I need to stay awake, to get through the night. If we sleep, who knows where we'll end up. I want to suggest that we go inland, onto the shore, but we're making good time. The faster I can get to Rex the better.

'This,' he says, indicating the sea all around us, 'this used to be land. Used to be some towns out here. Not many, but a few. Over there, that used to be a town called King of Prussia. Darndest name, I know. Stupid name. All underwater now.' He squints his face again, stares out into the distance. 'I can't see it, not with my eyes the way they are,' he says, shaking his head. 'You try. You'll see the remains of it.' So I do. I stare off. My eyes aren't great either, so I squint as well; and then I notice the glints of things jutting out of the water, just above the surface. Things reflecting the moonlight. Metal, stone. In front of us, I see something closer: a cross, jutting out of the water. More things follow it, lit by the moon: the tops of rooves, the scalps of statues, the girders of tower blocks.

'I grew up here,' Randolph says. 'I don't remember it, not exactly. I remember a feeling of what it was like. In the time I was away, the waters rose and they abandoned the town. Before I went to Bethlehem, this is where I lived. Then they locked me up and twenty years later they kicked me out and the whole place was gone. There's a saying: you can't go home again. Well, you can't if they take it from you. If they steal it, bury it, sink it, abandon it.'

'Twenty years?'

'It was supposed to be life. They offered me the fix and I took it. That was a few years before they let me out. They say they've perfected it now, but I don't know. It didn't take with me.'

'Nor me,' I say.

He grins. 'They tried it on you? Well then. Nasty thing, eh? Where they take away who you are? That's insane. No one can do that. You are who you are. Simple as. Remove that and you're nothing. A shell. People who've had the fix, they seem like normal people, you can't tell. But you wonder if, inside, they're hollow. Or, I wonder . . .' He wipes the water from his face; the slight spray of salt water coating us both, drying out our lips, our skin, making our eyes sting. 'So they let me go and I had no place to go home, no people I could ask for help. I knew I wasn't who they told me I was, that I was somebody different. But I didn't know who exactly that person was.'

'So you didn't go to another city?'

'They gave me a name, you know. Randolph's the name they gave me, and I don't know if it was mine to begin with. That's what it said on my pass, but my records had no history. It's like I started my life when I was forty years old. The city I'd grown up in was gone, so they put me in New York, on one of the smaller islands. Gave me a job, working upkeep on coolant water. Got me working on the river.' He nods at the sail. 'S'how I know so much about this. Did it for a year, then I ran. Didn't even know why. I came back here, to good old King of Prussia. I tried to follow the streets, staring down in the water. Tried to find out where it was that I came from. But there wasn't anything worth finding. Everything was under the water, and it was lost.'

'So you became a nomad?'

'So I became a nomad.' He sighs. 'Where are you from, then?'

'Australia,' I say.

'Like Fiona. You don't speak the same as her. Accent's different. I don't know it, and I know a lot of them.'

'There was another Australia.'

He nods. 'There's another Bethlehem, you know. Or, there was. In some stories. Met some who went there, once. There's places with the same names all over. You know how many Birminghams there are? You know how many times I passed through a Springfield? Makes sense there'd be more than one Australia. What was it like?'

'Dangerous,' I tell him. 'It was very dangerous.'

'Is there anywhere that isn't?' He points off, into the distance. 'New York used to be the most dangerous place in the country, for a while. Then the government raised prices, forced people to live in the outskirts. The bits they didn't care about. You make people live somewhere you've neglected, treat them like they're not worth a damn, tell them they're worth nothing? Sooner or later, some of them are gonna prove you right. In my experience, at least. So the good folk, the honest folk, those wanting to survive by making a living, they fled, wound up in Philly, in Baltimore. That's when everything was destroying itself, anyway. Of course, the government saved New York first. They built dams and they dredged the islands. You ever been to New York?' I shake my head. 'Used to be amazing, hundreds of years ago. People and life, you know? Like it was somewhere that all types of people lived. There are holos, in the museums, of what it was like. And you can watch any of the films they used to make there, get a sense of the place. Totally different now. Now it's got no soul. It's polished to a shine, but there's nothing beneath it. You can just about make it out now, in the distance. Maybe see it in the morning, if there's no fog.' He shifts his gaze to me. Looks like he's about to say something, but doesn't. 'You should sleep. I suspect you'll have a long day tomorrow. No idea how far we'll get towards Bethlehem, but it's going to be a long day.'

'What about you?'

'I don't sleep much, haven't done for years. I'll catch some when you wake up. For now, I'll steer.'

'Wake me if you need anything,' I say, and he nods, grumbles something in reply. So I curl myself up on the damp wood. I shut my eyes, and I try to ignore the rocking of the boat, the rocking in my gut; and I think about where I came from, and how the rumbling of Australia was the only way we knew we were moving, because we didn't have windows, couldn't see a thing.

Of course, the truth is that on Australia we weren't actually going anywhere. We were just in orbit; waiting.

'Girl,' he says, 'wake up.' I rub my eyes. It takes me a moment to see what he wants to show me; at first, it's just a mess of far-off mist. Then I see them, in the very far-off distance: what must be massive towers, taller than anything in Washington, and so many of them, clustered in spikes, like fingers reaching upwards. Shining the light off the sun behind them, reflecting themselves, longer and more improbable in the water surrounding them. 'It's islands. Used to be only a few tiny islands, and the mainland. After the dredging, they had six. Six islands, bridges joining them.'

'There's no wall,' I say, wonderingly. From what I've been

told, every other city in this world is shaded, protected, cooled by a wall.

'They cool the city with water. That's what they had me working on. Pipes run underneath the buildings, under the streets, flowing with some coolant the scientists developed. The water between the islands is cooled down, and it keeps the islands cool. They run it through everything: the concrete, the buildings, the roads. It's quite the piece of engineering. Expensive, but the people who live there, they didn't want a wall.' He's disgusted. His voice is almost shouting. 'Didn't want the view spoiled.'

'Do you want to get some sleep now?' I ask him. We're still a ways away, having left the sea, now slowly going down a river.

'I'm fine for the moment,' he says. 'A few more hours, wind permitting, and we'll be as far as we can go.' He holds a finger up in the air, puts it to his mouth, licks it, holds it in the air again. 'Put the sail up to full. We'll take advantage of this breeze. There's a real wind coming.' And then he sits back and he shuts his eyes as I raise the fabric, and I hear the sounds of him breathing as if he's going to sleep. I let him be.

He wakes up when the water does, when the river gets angry. I was distracted, staring at the land as we pushed past it, the brown reminding me of Mae's eyes; the occasional real bird – as scraggly as the vultures that Rex likes to kill – pecking at something, pulling something from the ground. Then the wind kicks in, and we're rocked from side to side.

I struggle with the sail, with holding the boat steady. We're blown down the strait, almost like we're heaved down it, the front of the boat dipping low as the waves behind us force us forward.

'You let me fall asleep,' Randolph shouts over the wind and waves, as though it's my fault he couldn't stay awake.

'I didn't know this would happen!' I shout back.

'You don't know much, it seems,' he grumbles. He wrestles with the sail, and he grits his teeth and squints his eyes, and we hold on. Above us, the sky darkens, clouds blocking the heat of the sun. He looks up, and I watch his eyes as he looks for a place to stop, to take the boat to shore. At the same time we spy a bank up ahead, and he steers us into it; and the water forces us up, into the silt, the sound of the grainy ground beneath us churning as we come to a stop. He doesn't move from the boat. Instead, he stays sitting, brings his mug to the water flowing around our feet, drops a purification tablet into it.

'You should do the same,' he says. 'Long walk ahead of you.'

'From here?'

'You're going to want to keep following the river. Not far, now. Half a day. Then, from there, stick to the highway going north. It'll be torn up, broken, sure, but it's a straight line, all the way. You'll see Bethlehem off it. Signposted as well I reckon, unless the metal's been scavenged. Don't rely on meeting anybody on the way. This part's been cleared, purged.'

'Okay,' I say. 'You'll be here when I come back?'

'I'm not going anywhere,' he says.

The sky tears apart. Thunder roars in. The rain comes.
'You should go,' he says, so I nod my thanks, and I do.

It's easier to run along the roads in the rain. The rain keeps
me cool. There's a gnawing in my gut that I know to be
nerves; I don't know what I'll find at Bethlehem when I get
there. Nothing good will come of what they've asked Rex
to do. Nothing good at all.

And Hoyle. Hoyle will be with her, and I'll have to face
him. Tell him . . . I don't know. Tell him that he betrayed
me, that I don't even know if I was really surprised.

But I know what needs to happen after I find Rex. I repeat
it, over and over, speaking the words to make them sound
more real, more tangible. I get Rex back, and then we find
Mae. Hoyle knows where she is, so we make him tell us.
Then we get her, and we take her back to the nomads, and—

What then? What happens after that? I get Rex back,
then we find Mae. And after that, there's a fog, an uncertain future of being on the run, of hiding from the people
who want Mae back, who will want to arrest Rex and me
for what we've done. What we're going to do.

So we keep running. I always told myself that one day I
would stop running, one day I would be able to pause, to
sit, to be still. Maybe I was wrong. Maybe running forever
is all there is.

The boredom of the road gets to me. It's so long and so
dull. It is a straight line going on forever, passing the shells
of settlements and towns, of road signs torn down, of
abandoned buildings that once were motels or diners. I

drink the last of the purified water and eat the last of the bread, and as soon as they're gone I feel hungry and thirsty all over again, as if they never even passed my lips.

I try and think of stories to tell myself to pass the time, but they're all too old. All the ones that I remember about my mother, about Agatha, about Jonah, I've told them so many times. There needs to be something new, some new way forward. I miss them all – and Mae, who I miss most of all, even though I knew her least, even though she was in my life for the smallest amount of time.

There has to be something new. There has to be.

The road goes on. The rain smashes into the ground, onto my body, my face. I stare at my feet as I walk; and I think about how tired my shoes are looking, and how, when this is all over, somehow I will get new ones.

It takes longer than he said it would to get here – it's nearly night, now – but I don't need the signs to tell me when I've reached Bethlehem. The fences alert me first: wire mesh with spiked metal coils wound around it. Torn through in places, then patched up, but nearly all of it rusted and old. The concrete poles that hold the wire in place jut out like teeth, cracked and split; and the ground around them is sopping wet, water puddled and pooled in the scars that run into the hard soil. There's no sound here but that of the water thwacking into the earth. This is a soaked desert, and I know it should be scorched and cooked, but instead it's a grey-brown colour, nothing distinct.

Through the mesh, in the distance, I see a few buildings in grey and red. Not that tall. Wide. I can't tell how many.

The name 'Bethlehem' sounds quite nice, I think. Like a place I might want to live. I can make out lots of trees, or at least the dried-up stumps of trees, and shrubs hunched across the land. And I can see what was once a road, or a few roads, or many roads. Perhaps they were paths through ancient woods.

I have no immediate plan. There's nothing I can predict about this place. I'm going to go in, and I'm going to find Rex, and then we're going to leave.

I throw a handful of grass at the fence, to check it's not electric. The top is a twisted mesh of sharp-angled metal, spiked out. It looks dangerous, but it's designed to ward off trespassers rather than inflict true damage. It wouldn't hurt that much.

But as I'm walking along, looking for the easiest point over, I realise that there's no need to climb. I can go under. The puddles of rain water along the bottom of the fence show dips in the ground where I might be able to squeeze through. I take a layer of the fence in my hands, haul it upwards. The mesh digs into my palms as I bend it up, but it stays. And then the second layer, and the third. I fold them just high enough to get my body through the hole I've created. The rain seems to be falling even more heavily, and I'm wet all the way to my skin. It doesn't matter.

I drop onto my chest and crawl through. Something scratches my back, through my clothes. It really hurts, but I don't cry out. I don't make any noise at all.

Bethlehem is a few buildings all nudging up next to each other, attached by walkways with guard posts dotting the landscape. I can see no signs or maps, and no guards on duty. There are no birds flying around, keeping watch. The place would look abandoned were it not for the lights I can see coming from one of the buildings. There are a handful of rooms lit up. Doesn't mean that there aren't people in more of the prison, just that they're not using the lights. Maybe the power's out. There could be hundreds of police here.

Or, it could be just Hoyle and Rex.

I run towards the buildings, unconcerned about being spotted. It's deathly quiet. It's also dark enough that anyone out here would be using torches or blu-beams, and there's none of that. It's dark and my clothes are dark, and I'm quiet. I'm invisible. Even if somebody's patrolling, and I don't see anyone, they won't notice me until it's too late.

The lit building is the middle one of three that I can see, each four storeys high. The door is red. There appears to be one single entrance point. As I get closer, I see the locks on it: four of them, all different types. High security. No way I can get through here.

I look for another way. A window that's cracked; a patch of crumbling wall, where the root of some plant has forced its way between bricks.

A garbage chute.

The garbage chute is along one of the walls, high up. It's a hollow tube fixed to the side of the building. The bottom end is only a few feet off the ground, over a pile of garbage. The top part must come from inside, higher up. It's probably a few hatches on different floors of the building, for easy disposal of whatever. I eye the trash heaped below it. Maybe it's high enough to climb. Maybe.

The pile of garbage is unstable and I slip as I climb up, my feet sinking into the stink. Rotten food, packets of produce, filthy towels that have red-brown stains on them that I'm sure are blood. And clothes. Whole outfits, shoes, jumpsuits. The sky rumbles; lightning flashes, and I see that the clothes are orange, all of them various shades, brown in places where they've been soaked in dirt.

The chute is higher up than I can reach, even from the top of the pile.

I jump. My fingertips scrape the edge of the chute.

I wish that I was taller.

In the sky, more thunder, then flashes of white and the lightning again. The storm will pass soon, I know, but for now it's good cover. I back up, scuff away the garbage at my feet to clear a path I can run on. The wall might work as a springboard, to push myself off.

I try – dash, leap, push backwards, miss the chute, tumble gracelessly, face down into the mud and trash, which spatters filth all over me.

Come on, Chan.

So I try again.

This time, my fingers get inside the lip of the chute. This time, I haul myself up, and I start to crawl up the rattling shaft, foot by foot, knowing I'm not moving silently as the noise of my feet bracing against the tube echoes around me, but also knowing that right now, this is the only way in.

I reach a grate about halfway up the chute. Second floor, I think. A way in. The second floor of the building wasn't lit, so I might have some time to get my bearings, to breathe. I pull the grate towards me as gently as I can and I peer through; and there he is.

A police. He's pointing something at me.

A gun. I recognise it from the museum. But projectile weapons were banned after the chaos of the world's collapse. Not even the police are allowed to use them now. Not even soldiers.

And yet.

'Who are you?' he barks. I have to think fast. He has the hilt of his gun – a long one, a rifle – braced against his shoulder. It's not shiny, I note. It's grimier. It's been used a lot, it looks like, not like the rifle Rex and I stole from the house when we escaped Pine City.

He's not wearing a normal police uniform. His clothes are different: a solid black, covering him from head to toe. He's armoured. There are thick plates of something protecting his chest, shoulders, neck. All the way across his body. He has a helmet on, too, which I recognise is like the ones the police wear for riots or bomb disposal. A high tech visor on it.

'What the hell are you doing in there?' he yells. He reaches for me, grabs my shoulder as I'm climbing out. I feel his grip – incredibly tight, immediately painful, I can feel the bruise it's going to leave – and he hauls me out, forces me to the ground. I can feel the gun poking into the side of my neck as he pushes his free hand into the space between my shoulder and my neck, the muscles there. Squeezes really hard. 'Chan? What are you doing here?' He knows me. He must be one of Hoyle's team. I don't know who, but he recognises me. That's going to make the next part harder, I think. It's easier when you can't put a face to the pain you're causing.

'Hoyle told me to come,' I say. I grit my teeth. My voice sounds shaky through the pain. 'I knocked. Nobody answered.'

'Don't lie to me,' he says. 'Hoyle told us what happened.' He loosens his grip slightly; eases up on the pressure of the barrel against my body. I hear him flick on his radio. 'This is DS-one, on the second floor.' That's all he manages before I flip myself over, grab his head, pull it towards me. His helmet slams into the ground, and he stumbles backwards, pushing off me. He drops the gun, which clatters to the floor. I stand, grab his helmet again drive it into the wall behind him. It comes loose, so I pull at it, wrench it up and off. The fabric around his neck tears, and then I can see his face; and he looks scared, actually scared, but I can't let that stop me. Not now.

I grab the gun from the ground, and I swing the heavy end of it at his head; it connects with a horrible thunk, and he collapses to the floor.

There's silence, again, and then the crackle of his communicator, as Hoyle asks him if everything's alright.

I creep through the corridors. They're so narrow. Cells either side, most of the doors open. They're half the size of the berths on Australia. Maybe less. They have no windows, no light. Everything inside them is crammed into the tiny space, with barely room to walk. To live in. The beds look as hard as slabs of concrete; the toilets are miniature. Every room is filthy, for some reason. When the doors are closed these rooms must be hell to live in. Even in the corridor I feel trapped, that's how tight it is. Randolph told me they took bad people here: the worst of the worst. He told me the entire place was been designed to make the prisoners suffer. There are gates on the stairwells, no elevators that I can see. A locked door that I need an ID for.

I strap the gun across my back and go back to the police's body and drag him down the corridor. He's so heavy, all this armour. When we get to the door, I hold his hand up, and watch as the lock-light turns from red to green. I hear the click of the door unlocking.

As I go through, I lay his arm down to wedge it open. Just in case.

I hear the coughing before I see where it's coming from. The corridor gives way to a balcony, ringed in thick black metal mesh, in the middle of the building. It's clear from inside that the building is shaped like a cross, four points coming off a central spoke. And it's the central section that's lit up bright. The atrium, accessible by stairs. There's another gate at the top of them, and I can't see through it properly. There are shadows down there and the murmurs of voices. I can't make them out, not properly. I can't identify anybody, they're too quiet. But that cough. It's louder than the chat. Hacking, wet. Distressed.

Thud. The sound of something hitting hard, flesh and bone connecting. More of that cough. I get to the railing and peer down. The angle's wrong and I can't see much. I can make out shadows, people pacing.

And then I see her. Rex. She looks around, and I can see the pain on her face; I can hear the desperation in her voice.

'Tell him,' she says. She pleads. I remember her voice, back when we fought in the final moments of Australia.

Now kill me, she said. *Show me that you can.*

That same tone. Knowing an ending is coming, one way or another.

She's not being beaten. She's doing the beating.

She hits the person she's been brought here to end. I know how hard she'll be working them. I know what she's capable of.

'Wait,' another voice says. Hoyle. He's here, watching, supervising.

He thinks that having Rex do his dirty work means his hands are clean. He's wrong. He's just as complicit, just as guilty. More so. Rex is just trying to help me – me and Mae.

'Let him speak.' Hoyle's voice is dead calm. There's the sound of spitting. Of something – blood, I suppose, and mucus, brought up from deep inside the person – onto the concrete of the floor. 'Where are the others?' Hoyle asks.

The man Rex is torturing mutters something I can't hear. I know what it's like to be beaten by Rex. I know this man will be next to useless.

'We caught Mooney.' This is about that? 'You were working with her, weren't you?'

More murmurs. Another cough. Wet. The cough sounds familiar. It rattles, blood on his lungs, probably; or maybe just in his throat. Either way, he's in trouble.

'We've got holos of you together. We know. Don't make this harder on yourself.'

The man he's torturing murmurs something. I can't hear the words, but there's a defiance even to his grizzled noise.

'Go on,' Hoyle says, nodding at Rex. I watch her – I see her walk around the edge of the room, wrapping something around her mechanical hand, some sort of fabric, tight around the metal. To dull the blow, no doubt. They don't want him dead. Not yet.

I hear the noise of her hitting him. I know what happens when she's done beating him. She will kill him, and then they will kill her.

But Hoyle doesn't get to say how this story ends.

I do.

I strip the policeman of his armour. The pieces are attached to his body suit somehow, and I don't have one of those, so I stuff some of them down inside my jacket, my sleeves, the thighs of my trousers. I drag him to the balcony, where I was just standing, watching Rex and Hoyle. He's heavier than he looks, even without the protection. When he stirs, I put my hand over his mouth, press down, cut off his breathing. Just long enough to keep him unconscious.

I remember the gun. If he's got one, chances are they have them down below. I don't know how many of Hoyle's squad are down there, but if it's all five of them – four, now – I can't face those numbers. Not if they're armed. I saw what the bullets did to the birds when Rex was shooting at them before.

I wonder if the armour protects against bullets.

Standing at the gate, I can hear the prisoner moaning down below. I can't see why, can't see what Rex is doing.

I lift the police's arm up, to the scanner. Wait for the beep. The light clicks green, and the gate opens.

'Hoyle?' Rex asks. Her voice echoes. She calls his name again. Is he not there? Is he not—

I hear a click from the hallway behind me and dread clenches my stomach. I turn. There's a gun aimed at me. 'You shouldn't have come,' Hoyle says.

I wonder, as I leap towards him, if he'll be faster than I am. If he'll manage to fire before I reach him. I wonder if I'd even know about it if he did, or if the bullet would just end it straight away, me on the ground, blood seeping out, life going. Neither of us makes a sound. I know, as I slam the weight of my body into his, as I push him to one side and run through the gate, that he didn't actually fire. Maybe he couldn't. Maybe, when it came down to it, he didn't want to. Or maybe I'm just too fast.

He shouts after me, shouts to his men that I'm coming. I tear down the stairs towards the atrium, towards where Rex is. She doesn't look particularly surprised to see me.

'Get him away!' Hoyle shouts. 'Take her down, but alive!'

I get to Rex, grab her. 'We have to go,' I say, and she doesn't move, but her eyes flick down at the prisoner in the chair. I glance down at him. Unrecognisable, nothing more than a shape, a red mess. And then I know him. Then his features rearrange themselves, my brain making sense of what I see. The parts unswelling, unclotting, until his identity is perfectly clear.

Jonah.

He's in the chair, Unablers strapping his arms down. His eyes are swollen shut. His lips are torn, his cheeks stripped of skin in places, torn and bruised and beaten. Other signs of torture: patches of burn marks; of deep, slender cuts; his fingers bloody from where his nails have been pulled off.

I hear the bang of a gun firing before I feel it; but when I do feel it, I'm knocked off my feet to the ground. I can't breathe, and I scream, or I try to but nothing comes out. I see stars as I slam into the concrete, my legs slipping out under me, my whole body wreathed in pain. I still can't breathe. I can hear myself wheeze. I shut my eyes, because that's better, for a second.

'Alive!' Hoyle howls, near me. 'I said to keep her alive!' I feel his hands on my head. I cough. I still can't seem to draw in a breath.

Am I dying?

'Get away from her.' Rex's voice, and it's calm. Low, from deep in her throat. Deeper than normal. I know that voice. I know what it means.

Hoyle's other officers try to move Jonah. I can hear them untying him. He's too heavy, too weak to help move himself, and he drops to the floor, broken. Hoyle props my head up, and I watch, vision blurring, as the police rush to Rex. She destroys them. One by one they attack her, and she demolishes them. There's only one of them with a gun – the one who shot me – and she grabs his hand and crushes it in hers. Blood pulses from the mangled stump and he screams, falling to his knees. She claws at the throat of another, throws him against the wall. The noise his body makes as he crunches into it is sickening. The last, she wraps her mechanical hand around his jaw. Squeezes.

I don't see what happens, but I hear the crunch.

Then she comes for Hoyle. He lets me down slowly, doesn't shoot at her. He tells her to stay back, threatens that he will. Tells her that she has no idea what he can do. She doesn't balk, doesn't stop. Grabs the barrel of the gun as she gets close enough, crushes it in her hand.

She tells him that he doesn't know what she can do, either.

Then they start to fight. They swing punches. Hoyle is faster than Rex. His limbs move in a blur that I can barely keep up with, a speed that just doesn't seem to make sense. He hits her, and she reacts, and it takes more time for her to recover than it takes for him to strike her again. Again, and again. He's winning.

My vision clears. I reach into my jacket, pull the armour plate free. It's dented deep, the bullets having nearly broken through it. They'll have bruised me, that's for certain. Broken a rib or two, if I'm really unlucky. But the bullets didn't break my skin.

I need to stand up. Rex can't take him alone.

She's bleeding now. Hoyle hits her again, and hard.

He goes to hit her again. I'm on my feet now; I grab his hand. He looks back in surprise, but my grip doesn't stop him. His momentum drags me forward, and he turns, almost like he's surprised I'm still hanging on to him, and Rex takes advantage of his confusion, flexes her robotic arm. She gets her wind back.

There's so much power in their augmented limbs. I had no idea, not really. I've never seen him really use them to their fullest extent. But now I do. Rex slams her skeletal fist into his head, over and over, as he tries to shake me off, fight back. He can take her beating. If he was doing this to her she'd be dead. But she continues to beat him, until the skin on his jaw starts to tear, and he takes it, stays upright. That's not his real skin, not all of it.

I wonder if it hurts him.

She doesn't stop. She pummels and he trembles; he stumbles. He falls to his knees. I stand back, and I watch as Rex goes to town. She's not just using the augmented arm any more, she's using her whole body. Her other hand grabs his hair, slamming him into her knee. Forcing him to the ground.

I hear Jonah's voice

He says my name, and when I look at him, he's pushed himself upright, bracing himself against the wall. His hands have left bloody prints on the floor; his face is a mess.

'You came for me,' he says.

Then he falls towards me, into my arms; his blood on me, his face on my shoulder. I can hear him weeping.

When I have nightmares, they're always about the same few things. Australia, burning, tearing apart, destroying itself. My mother. Her cancer, which in my dreams becomes something that spreads to everybody I've loved, drying them out and rotting them away. Mae, dead; her face staring up at me accusingly because I was unable to save her. And Jonah, reaching for my hand, but I don't take it, and I let him fall backwards, away, tumbling into the distance as if he were just dust in a storm.

I've tried not to think too much about what he did; sacrificing himself so that Rex and I could escape. How I dragged him away from a place where he was happy, where he had a new life. I told him who he was. I forced him to confront it. And he wasn't happy, he wasn't grateful, didn't think I'd rescued him. But still, when all was said and done, he sacrificed himself for me.

I've hoped that Gibson and the Pine City staff took him back there. That they erased what he remembered, that they made him a new person again. But he ended up here, in another prison.

Maybe some scars run too deep to ever heal, and living on Australia was just one of them.

Hoyle is a motionless lump on the floor. 'We need to go,' Rex says. She walks past me, as I hold Jonah, down one of the corridors. 'The way out is down here.' She keeps walking, wiping her bloody hand off as she goes. I should check Hoyle's alright, but I don't. Not after this.

Rex throws the rag that was wrapped around her hand to the ground, and then grabs the bars of a gate that's in her way; she takes hold of the lock mechanism, squeezing it with her hand, crushing it. As it crumbles, it unlocks. 'Are you coming?' she asks.

I help Jonah move forward. He leans on me, staggering as he tries to walk. He's too heavy; I can't manage him by myself. I want to ask Rex to take some of the weight as well, but she's off already, working on the door at the far end of the corridor. The exit.

'Keep going,' I say to Jonah, but I know he will, he always does. He doesn't give up. Or, I hope he doesn't. I try and

remember any of the things he said to me, when I was struggling on Australia; when I wanted to end everything, to stay
down below. If he spurred me on, or if he simply supported
me, accepted who I was and what I was going to do. 'We
can do this,' I finally say.

'I can't believe you came back for me,' he whispers. Each
word takes twice as long as it should to leave his mouth; he
spits and stammers and lisps the starts and ends of words,
sounding barely like himself.

I look at him. His hair is matted with sticky blood. The
cut is shorter than before, close to the head, shaven, like
mine used to be.

'Hurry,' Rex says. So I do, so we do. I half-help, half-drag
Jonah forward and then as we get to the door, as Rex pushes
it open, finally, forces it, and it gives way, she takes his other
arm and we carry him out into the rain. It's pouring now,
but the sky is clearing in the distance, a beautiful blue and
white, the sun casting half the land in glorious light. But
here, it's still grey, wet, muddy. We struggle through the
puddles, the lashing rain blinding us. I point the way
towards the fence I came through, to where the road is. And
down the road, the boat.

I don't talk. I don't want anything to distract us. She will
feel as though she failed, I know. She came here to get
answers to a question, for me; and she might now think
that I ruined everything by stopping her. We support Jonah,
who is silent apart from the occasional grunt of pain as we
move him, as we make him take another step, or as hard
branches dig into him while we work through the
undergrowth.

We reach the fence finally, and I kneel down, grab the mesh where I pulled it up, try to pull it more; to make enough space so that Jonah won't have to crawl. I can't manage it. Rex passes Jonah to me and does it herself, her augmented arm making short work of the wire mesh, wrenching it apart; tearing a hole.

'Through here,' I say, and Rex steps to the outside, then turns to take Jonah. I pass him off to her, and I'm about to follow him when I see Rex's face.

She starts to speak. 'Hoy—' she says, and that's all there is time for. That's it.

Hoyle slams into me.

His weight drives me off my feet into the ground, into the wire mesh of the fence. It collapses under our weight.

'I can't let you leave,' he says. I look up at him. My chest is hurting again, from where I was shot. His body is steaming in the rain, the sweat from his sprint evaporating in the cold air. How fast is he? I didn't hear him come for us. I've never seen him run. Not at full speed. 'Not with him,' he says, looking up at Jonah.

'You were killing him,' I say.

'We were getting information. He knows about—'

'He doesn't know about anything!' I shout. Behind me, Rex is hesitating. She's wary to leave me. I glare at her. 'He was with us on Australia. He doesn't know anything.'

'I've read your book. Did you forget that? You think there's any other reason I only brought in Rex for this job?'

'Then you know what he means to me,' I say. He'll only know Ziegler's fictional version of a romance, but still. I cared for Jonah, and deeply. And Hoyle knows it.

'He's a terrorist,' Hoyle says, which I can't believe or even understand.

'He can't be.' I see Rex helping Jonah to his feet, backing off, away from us, slowly moving towards the road.

'Don't you dare,' Hoyle shouts at her, but I grab him, trip him, as he starts towards them, pull him down to the ground with me, to the mud and the tangled mesh. I scramble onto his back and I wrap my arm around his neck, and I pull, as tight as I can. It worked before, and it'll work now. I just need him unconscious, and we can be away from here, off in the boat, back at the camp. Somewhere else.

We won't have Mae. He won't have told us where she is.

But I can worry about that another ti—

'I don't breathe like that any more,' he says, and he pushes up, hunches his body until he's on all fours, like an animal, then throws himself up and back, surprising me. He rolls, trapping me beneath him, so we're face to face, my back in the mud, his hands on my hands, and he pins me down effortlessly. Pain that feels like heat roars through my ribs, and I cough back a breath of my own. 'You don't know what he's done. He can't be redeemed, Chan. He's done too much to be redeemed,' he says. As he talks I look at his torn flesh, where the dull metal of his replacement augments glistens in the rain.

'He's a good person,' I say.

'Mooney? What about her? Was she a good person?'

'She was a terrorist,' I say, remembering the holofile of the explosions she caused.

'He *worked* with her. We've got footage of them. They met in a facility, and she broke him out. His conditioning

145

didn't take, wasn't taking. Her people broke her out, and she took him, roped him into her terrorism with her.' I don't say that conditioning doesn't seem to take well with most people. 'He helped her. He was her accomplice, Chan. He helped her *kill* people.'

No, I tell myself. Jonah's a good person.

'They wanted to hurt the people who were running the conditioning prisons. He and Mooney, together. They didn't believe in punishing people for their crimes, wanted freedom for prisoners. That was their cause. That's what they believed in, why they killed innocent people.' He's shouting now, screaming at me. He looks distraught. 'Why would you help him? You told me the book Ziegler wrote wasn't real. Were you actually with him? Did you love him?'

I don't answer. I don't know how to answer that. Yes. Nearly. Sometimes.

'Jesus, Chan,' he says, still screaming. 'You might not get this, but you could have had a life here. You're not *like* the others. Rex? She came to me. She practically begged me to let her work for me. She *liked* it.'

'You used her,' I say. I can't see Rex and Jonah any more. The rain is turning lighter, settling as mist on the ground, obscuring them as they run down the road, away from here. I hope that they don't stop. That they don't wait for me. 'You got her to do the things that you wouldn't—'

'Because she was willing. That's what weapons are for. I was a weapon, once. So were you. Don't forget that.'

'I was a weapon for Alala!' I yell, trembling with fury. I push him off me, start to get to my feet. I'm unsteady, but so is he. 'We were both used, and we should both remember what it felt like. You would have killed Rex, when she was done.'

'No,' he says. 'I wouldn't.' His eyes are wide, innocent, and I almost believe him. 'She could have been sent for conditioning, back to Doctor Gibson. He's been itching to get another go.'

'You would have just changed who she was. Erased who she is.'

'Yes,' he says. 'But we wouldn't have killed her.'

'There's not much difference,' I say. I hit him, hard, in the side of his head. Catch him by surprise. My fist explodes with pain as it connects with the augmented bone.

He doesn't react, doesn't get angrier, or retaliate. I wish that I could hear him breathing. His unnatural silence, his lack of breath, is disconcerting.

'What happens now?' I ask. I can't outrun him. I can't outfight him. I've got no weapons. I'm wounded and he's stronger than me. He steps away, runs his hands over his head, touches his skin, where it's peeling. Then he fixes his eyes on me, stares hard and deep into my eyes. I don't know if it's a threatening look or not. I can't see any emotion in his eyes at all. 'Do we fight until one of us kills the other?'

Don't die, my mother's voice says, suddenly, from nowhere. And I think, I haven't heard that in a while. I haven't needed to.

'No. You go. Now. My people will wake up, and they will call what happened in. That's if they haven't already.'

'And us?'

'I say that you knocked me unconscious. I don't know how much of a head start that is.'

'You're letting me go?'

'No. I'm giving you a chance. You're going to be hunted. You're going to be pursued, because you're dangerous, you're all dangerous. And since you pulled that stupid stunt, broadcasting yourself all over the network, you're famous. On top of that, you're harbouring a known terrorist. But I'm giving you a chance. I care about you. I don't want you . . . I don't want the worst to happen to you.'

'So call them off.' I don't want to beg him, don't want to plead.

'It's out of my control. So you're going to have to run, and you're going to have to hide. Find somewhere else, another city. See if you can catch a ship going to another country.' The rain gets harder, heavier, even though I can see the blue sky over his shoulder. This is the rain at its heaviest. 'You won't have long. I'll tell them I don't know where you're heading.'

'You don't,' I say, but he nods, bites his lower lip.

'I made a promise,' he says, 'about the little girl.' As soon as he says it, I feel sick. Like there's an answer coming. 'The hardest part was getting her DNA. That was the only way to track her. That's how we pulled her file.'

'What?'

'We got her DNA and we found her. Now you have to do it, if you want to find her. Go.'

'What do you mean?'

His comm crackles to life.

He shoves me. 'Go, Chan. They're waking up. You have to go.'

'Where do I get her DNA from?' I scream, desperate.

'We took samples from everybody that got off your ship when you arrived in Washington,' he says. 'We found Mae by tracking her with her mother's DNA. You'll need to do the same.' And then he turns, starts to walk back towards the prison; and I grab his arm, and I'm saying something about how I told him that I'm not her mother, that I just care about her; that she's just somebody I made a promise to; and he swipes me away, like he's batting a fly off with the back of his hand, and then he starts to run, back towards the prison.

I've never seen him run at full speed before. I've never seen anything move quite that fast in my life.

As I stagger down the road, chest aching, clutching my arms tight across my body because that, for some reason, seems to help, the sky starts to clear. The clouds push away and the sun comes out. It seems impossible, given how cold and wet things just were, that the heat could be so sudden and so intense. But it is: choking and blistering. The water on the ground seems to evaporate as I watch; and I'm dry in moments. By the time I see Rex and Jonah in the distance, I'm thirsty and desperate for the rain to come back. I shout to them and wave, and they turn and wait for me.

'You're not dead,' Rex says.

'No,' I reply.

'You did well,' she tells me, and she gives me Jonah as though he's a doll, as though he doesn't weigh as much as he does. He's nearly passed out. 'He needs food and water,' she says. It hurts for me to support him, but he's in worse shape than I am.

'There'll be some at the boat,' I tell her, but only if Randolph didn't finish all the rations. Hoyle and the police will be coming, I know; and if they find us, there'll be no escape.

'They'll be tracking you,' I say. 'There's a thing, in your arm.' She looks at her mechanical limb. 'The other one,' I say. 'Where your ID is.'

I watch her pierce the skin of her flesh arm with her knife – she must have stolen it from a guard at the prison – and pull the chip out without batting an eyelid. As if the pain, to her, is nothing at all.

6

The boat is exactly where I left it. The beach looks different in the heat and the light; what seemed to be mud before is now golden sand, glorious and clean, the tiny beach giving way to the greenish hue of the water. It's not actually that colour, I tell myself. Water is clear. If you see any colour in it, it's either the mud that's been kicked up from below or it's simply reflecting what's directly above it.

'Randolph?' I see him sitting in the boat and I call out to him. He doesn't move, so I call again, but he's perfectly still. He won't move, I know, not any more. This was his journey and it's complete. When I reach him, touch him, he's warm from the sun, and his eyes are closed and he looks peaceful. I don't ask the others what we should do with him; there's no question.

We don't have the time, but I want to dig a hole. That's what they do here. They bury their dead in pits, under the ground. There they rot and decompose. It shouldn't be something that happens in the open. I take the oar from the side of the boat, the closest thing I can think to a shovel, and I start to lift lumps of sand up.

'Who was he?' Rex asks. She lowers Jonah into the boat and he winces, moans in pain.

'He helped me get here. You don't recognise him? He was one of the nomads.'

'I tried not to get too attached,' she says. But then she kneels, next to where I'm working, and uses her hands to help me dig my hole in the sand. It takes no time at all, not really, to give him what he deserves.

We struggle with the wind as it's blowing against us. We travel down the water towards the river mouth, out to the sea; and I point out New York on the horizon, just as Randolph did for me, and Rex stares at it, mouth slack, while Jonah sleeps, and I wrestle with the tarp we're using as a sail; and then, when we reach the sea, we fight the wind again, and I think how it would likely be quicker walking, once Jonah's rested. So we sail towards the land and pull the boat ashore, let him sleep, the sail pulled down as a tent across him. Rex and I lie on the shore, on the sand. She sleeps, but I can't. I'm terrified that now is when they'll find us. Hoyle said he was giving us a chance to escape, but I don't know how much help he'll be, once the higher ups get involved. They'll want Jonah back.

His injuries are bad. I don't know how bad, exactly. I ask Rex when she wakes up, as the first light of morning comes up across us, what she did to him.

'I hit him. Hard.'

'Did you break anything?'

'He was already broken when I got to him.'

'But did you—'

'They wanted me to interrogate him. They didn't mind if he died. I was not careful.'

'What did they want to know?'

'What he and Mooney had planned.'

'But he didn't know anything?'

She's hesitant. Chooses her words. 'He told me that he didn't,' she says, but that's not definitive.

We're both pretty good at telling when people are lying to us.

When Jonah wakes, we know that we have to move. We slip the boat back into the water, but can't put the sail up properly again, and the wind is still blowing against us anyway. So we row, Rex manning one oar, me the other. Jonah sits up at the front of the boat, wrapped in a towel that he found amongst Randolph's possessions, even though he's sweltering in the heat. There's a breeze from our travel, but the sun is violent. Jonah's skin looks sore. The sun and the wind and the beating he took, all of them have changed him.

I catch him staring at me when he thinks I'm not looking, not smiling or frowning, not anything really, apart from locking his eyes on me until the exact moment that I look directly back at him, and then shifting his gaze away.

That night we stop again. Rex and I are shattered, aching and burning from having rowed all day. It's impossible to tell how far we've gone, but we can't see New York in the distance any more. She sleeps almost immediately, lying on the shore, curled into a ball. I sit with Jonah, and I help him drink water. He nods and then his stomach growls at me, sounding to all the world as though it's furious.

We both laugh.

I take a stick from the shoreline, sharpen it on my knife, and then I wade out into the water and stand perfectly still. I wait until the fish swim up around me, until I can see them trying to nibble at my ankles, to see what I'm made of, if I'm edible; and when I see one that's big enough, I slam the stick down like a spear, skewering its body. I take it up to the shore and pass it to Jonah, repeat that again, and then I make a fire, hold the fish over it until the skin starts to crisp and blacken. I save some for Rex, for when she wakes up, and Jonah and I eat the rest in silence.

He's chewing when he makes this noise that's almost a snarl, and then he pulls a tooth from his mouth, from the back. Bloody and white, and he throws it into the sea.

'I knew you'd save me,' he says, his voice slow and measured, as though he's dragging the words out of his mouth. 'I knew that you would come and find me. It's what you do, isn't it.'

'Hoyle told me that you've killed people,' I say.

Jonah's silent for a while. I can't read his face when it's this swollen; it's so hard to see his eyes. Then he opens his mouth and he moves his lips for a few moments before he speaks, as though he's trying the words out before he says them. 'I didn't kill anyone,' he says.

'Mooney did.'

He nods. 'I didn't stop her.'

'Did you try?' I want him to have tried.

But he doesn't reply, doesn't look at me, either. 'After we left Pine City, I was angry with you,' he says instead.

'I remember.'

'You don't. You didn't know, I didn't let you know. I hated you, Chan. When we were getting away from that place, when you were telling me that I wasn't who I thought I was. I hated you. I was happy at Pine City, and you made me forget that. You made me forget who I was.'

'They did that. Doctor Gibson made you forget.'

'He did. But I was happy there. When we first left, all I could think was how I had been happy there. And you'd been happy as well, I thought. For a time.'

'They lied to us.'

'No they didn't. They gave us a second chance. We weren't new people, we were us, just . . . not as broken, not ruined. I was happy. And you took that away from me.'

'I'm sorry,' I say.

'That doesn't change anything.' His words sting me. It hurts, to know he's carrying such resentment around with him. 'We've done things wrong, Chan. We've done bad things, and we should be punished. That's what the Pale Women used to say to me. We had, all of us, done wrong. We should all be punished. We pile sin upon sin, and under their rules, we worked for forgiveness. Our whole lives were spent in the quest for forgiveness. Here? They do it instantly. They change you, make you forget. And we expect others to do the same: to ignore what we've done before, because we've been given this instant repentance. But we should have to prove we're sorry. We shouldn't be allowed to forget it. We should have to prove it. And if we can't, we should be punished.'

He's frustrated, angry, his voice croaking under the strain of his words. But he doesn't stop. 'Mooney had this plan.

She wanted the people who were being reconditioned freed. So I said I would help her. I wanted them free of people like Gibson as well.'

'What did she want to happen to them instead?'

'She wanted them to have another chance. Not in the cities, nothing like that. But to get them somewhere else, on their own terms. Free people, living free. Let them kill each other, if that's what ended up happening. But don't remove who they are.' He shuts his eyes for a moment; and I think about the times I've watched him sleep. How I liked being there; how safe we were, in those moments.

'She murdered innocent people. To free them, she killed people, Jonah.'

'She was a sinner, Chan. We've all sinned.'

'We haven't,' I say. I want to tell him that we on Australia were punished because of who our ancestors were; what *they* did, and their sins were passed down to us, their punishment heaped upon us, a legacy for the people of Australia. I want to tell him that now I understand that if you treat somebody like a criminal, they might be inclined to act like a criminal. Everything that is done to prisoners here is the same. Forcing a change to somebody's thoughts, their behaviours, rather than giving them a chance to change of their own accord? That's just as bad as what they did to our ancestors. Worse, in some ways. 'I've tried to do what's right. To save people.'

'And in doing so, you've hurt them. Committed crimes.' His voice is getting tired, croaking. 'Have you killed people?'

I have. I didn't mean to, but I have. The guard, who I

accidentally killed. Others, I'm sure, that I don't know about. People that I haven't saved, their blood is on my hands.

I tried to kill Rex.

I managed to kill my mother.

But I don't say those things.

'What makes you think you shouldn't be held account-able? And she,' Jonah says, looking over at Rex, 'she's a murderer. Doesn't matter if you've forgiven her; the families of those she's slain wouldn't. And not just on Australia. She would have killed me here, if they'd let her. And I have killed. I killed for you, on the ship.'

'I never asked you to.'

'But I did. I killed defending the Pale Women – that's what they needed from me – and I killed for myself. And now, I've killed to try and make a point. That's what Mooney taught me. That we can kill to force change.'

He goes quiet. I don't want to argue with him. I let him shut his eyes, lean back. He's tired himself out, I can see. I listen as his breathing changes to the calm that comes when you're sleeping. But I stare out at the sea, my thoughts turning over and over; I'm desperately awake and not even nudging towards sleep. That's when I hear Rex's voice. She creeps next to me, sits on the sand. Her body is in the same pose as mine, her head bowed.

'He's dangerous,' she says.

'He's confused,' I reply.

But I look over at him and I know that she's right. He believes something, and passionately. He's killed, and he could kill again.

Taking Rex's hand, though, I remind myself, he's not the only one.

Fiona doesn't seem surprised that Randolph isn't with us. She doesn't even ask where he is. She stands on the beach and watches as we approach, as I wade through the shallows, pulling the boat along in my wake. Rex is further up on the shore, walking on the grass. She doesn't mind the heat the way I do. I stay down by the waterline where it feels cooler. No matter if that's an illusion, it's how it feels. Sometimes that's more important, how it feels.

Fiona calls to the others to help us get Jonah out of the boat, ushering him up the warm beach. He trips, not used to the blaring heat of the sand. He'd obviously been inside for a while before we found him. Our journey has left his skin burnt on his shoulders and face; his scalp, I can see, is blistering. They give him a flask of water to drink, which he gags on, spits out – we're all dehydrated, we all need food – and then another, which he manages to keep down.

'You found Rex, then,' Fiona says. We all turn to look at Rex, up the far end of the beach, ignoring everybody else, trudging up to her tent. 'And this other one. I'm supposing he's not exactly going to be welcomed in Washington.'

'No,' I say.

'That's okay. We'll keep him secret with us. While we can.'

'Thank you.'

'What about the little girl? You find her?'

'No,' I say. Not yet. Fiona reaches out, pulls me close and wraps her arms around me. When she holds me tight and squeezes, it's wonderful, that single moment; a feeling that I don't need to do anything, be anything, that I am just being held, and that it's safe. Everything is safe, even if only briefly.

I wonder what Hoyle meant when he said I could find Mae. He said that I could find her if I tracked her DNA, that I would need her mother. Mae told me, when I met her, that she didn't know where her parents were. She lived alone, hid and scavenged. I saw her survive. I saw her hold herself together, not collapse. The things she was exposed to, they were worse than when I was her age. At least I had my mother, and Agatha. Mae had nobody. Nothing. Not until I helped her. I looked after her, kept her safe, until—

Until she was taken, by Rex, and kept behind: not used, not threatened, not dangled over the edge as a warning to me. Not actually threatened. But kept away from our fight.

I shut my eyes. I try to remember that day, that fight, exactly as it happened. Mae was taken to where Rex was and then kept safe. Rex said she wouldn't hurt her, wouldn't kill her.

When she nearly did, to hurt me, she drew her hand back. She couldn't do it. Instead, she said that she would bring Mae up to be just like her.

I picture Rex standing before me in that fight, in the clothes she wore then. Rags and furs and skins across her body. Her scars achingly visible for all to see, on show, on display. The letters carved into her chest: R, E, X. Jagged and shallow and bleeding.

Another scar. I saw it way back, when I first fought her. The only scar that stood out as being different to the rest: less ragged, less haphazard. We never questioned scars on Australia. Everyone had them. Rex is covered in them. I never asked her about that one, but—

One long, deep scar, low on her belly.

Not where something went in, not exactly. But where something came out.

I know. I do. I wonder if I've always known, somewhere inside me, but kept it buried, because it doesn't help.

But I know now.

Rex is Mae's mother.

I stand a few feet away from where Rex is sleeping, or trying to. The smell of food, of something rich and strong – probably one of the wild deer, I think – wafts up from further down the beach. The sun's gone down, and the heat of the day is dissipating. Nomads are emerging from their tents, greeting each other. There's a fire burning, probably where they're cooking the meat; and I can hear snatches of songs on the air, things that I've never heard. They're probably old. There's a lot of people here who want to hang on to the way that things were before, to a time that they never even knew, that they didn't live through. When their parents, their parents' parents were alive. Those songs, those books, those holos. They clutch these old printed texts to their chests when they sleep because they're valuable; and they keep the songs alive by singing them, all of them knowing the words.

But they mean nothing to me.

'Why are you watching me?' Rex asks.

'Are you okay?' I ask. First thing that pops into my head.

'Fine,' she says.

'Because, I wanted to check. They . . . Hoyle . . .'

'Hoyle was doing his job. I was doing mine.'

'You wanted to help me,' I say. 'To find Mae.'

'She is important to you,' Rex says.

Does Rex actually even know?

'You didn't have to do it,' I say.

'I did,' she replies.

We fall silent then, for too long; her lying down, me standing near her feet. A shout from the nomads cooking the food, that there is some for us, if we're hungry. My stomach growls at me, telling me that I am; and I turn away from Rex, and walk down the beach.

She doesn't move at all.

I take a small lump of the meat, along with a bowl of the small potatoes that the nomads have grown in the soil right up against the city wall. I leave them just next to Rex, where she's sleeping. She doesn't stir, not until I'm well away from her, when she thinks that I won't be able to tell that she is still awake.

'Do you want to talk?' Fiona asks me.

'What about?' Even as I reply, I know what she means. Nothing specific; just whatever is on my mind. Still, I don't want to talk. I'm not in the mood.

'We saw the holo broadcast you did, you know. Everybody saw it. Everybody knows who you are.'

'Doesn't matter,' I say.

161

'It'll make it harder for you to hide.'

'I don't care.' I want her to go away. I want her to leave me alone.

'We're here for you, Chan,' she tells me. 'You're one of us.' I let that hang in the darkness. 'We don't have homes either; not aside from this – from ourselves, from each other.' Then she walks away.

'Thank you,' I whisper, into the darkness.

'You're welcome,' she says, closer than I realised; listening still.

Caring.

I'm woken by the sound of engines, of birds flying in the sky. The brightness of their lights, shining through the tarpaulin over my head. And people shouting, screaming, the voices of the nomads to run, to get out. That they're here.

The nomads have always been left alone, to do whatever they wanted, no harm to anybody. Maybe some in the city are scared of them, maybe they don't understand why they wouldn't want to live behind walls, with the shops, with the work and the food and the everything that they have; but they let them be.

What's happening now isn't about the nomads. It's about us.

It's about me.

I run down the beach. Gunfire in the distance. The sound of police shouting at the nomads to stay down, to hit the sand, their voices muted by their masks and breathers. They're prepared. They've got equipment, and they've got training. This isn't a fair fight. I shout Fiona's name, and Rex's, and Jonah's, but my voice is lost in the chaos. I can hear everybody else shouting, their voices an indistinct mess of words and cries. In the darkness, in flashes of torch and blue light, I see nomads running, fleeing, hiding.

I see a figure lying on the sand, shivering. I run to him, and it's Jonah. Something's wrong. He's sick. An infection, most likely. He tries to say my name, but he can't quite get it out; I kneel next to him, help him to sit up.

'It'll be okay,' I say. That's a lie, I know, even as I'm saying it.

That was my mother's trick: lie to placate, to calm. How many times did she tell me that this life will get better, that one day, everything will be alright in the end, just go back to sleep. Jonah coughs, sputters, as the shouts and yells rip through the darkness, and the birds circle overhead.

'We have to get out of here,' I say. I pick Jonah up, jam my shoulder into his armpit, take his weight for him. I want to save the nomads – these people who were so kind to me – but I can't. There are too many. I'll die along with them.

I want to call for Rex but I'm afraid my voice will draw attention to us, so down the beach we go, Jonah and myself, just far enough from the camp that we can hide; out of the circles of light from the birds, away from the gunfire, away from the danger.

We keep walking. I want to keep going until the gunfire stops, but we can still hear it after what feels like hours of staggering down the seemingly endless beach.

*　　　*　　　*

Rex, soaked in blood.

I have seen her like this before, too many times. And every time it was down to me: either because I was forcing her to fight, when we were enemies, or because she's been trying to help me, to do what's right, somehow.

She finds me. Of course she finds me. She stumbles out of the darkness, chance or fate or good luck, I don't know which, and I see her. I am sitting with Jonah. I was cradling him as he shivered from the fever, sweat coating his skin in a thin film. The new day's sun is on his face. I was hoping the heat would make him feel better, but still he keeps on shivering.

I can't worry about him at this moment. Rex needs my help. I stand, run to her, leaving him lying in the sand. As I get closer to her, she tries to tell me what happened, but her voice chokes. She can't find the words.

'It's okay,' I say. I reach out to comfort her, run my hands over her head, to soothe her as much as I can. It's all I'm thinking of, until I notice the hairs trapped between my fingers, tangled. I don't know if I pulled them, or if they just came out.

I put them in my pocket.

I'll need them, I know, if I'm going to find Mae.

PART
TWO

7

Months after we left the beach, months where we haven't seen or heard from Hoyle or the rest of the police; months where the sun has risen every day, set every day, a clockwork motion that's all we need to judge the time; where Rex has recovered but retreated into herself, quieter than ever before; where I catch her staring out of windows, into the distance, at the sun as it does its arc, the only thing we know to be constant; in which she's pushed her body further than I've ever seen before, as far as it can go, beating herself up in some attempt to become stronger, as strong as it's possible for her to be; months in which Jonah nearly died, then came back to us, and then relapsed, his wounds turning to a sickening black on his skin that we were forced to cut away, that I was forced to raid hospitals in forgotten towns to find anything that might be able to help him, to cure him; in which he came back to us, but so, so slowly; in which, for almost a solid week he slept, not saying a word, drinking water and sicking it back up again, before finally the fever broke for good, and then his real recovery began; months in which I kept the twine of Rex's hair in the pocket of my trousers, and found myself playing with it nearly constantly, a tiny ball of knotted strands, trying to make it feel tangible before finally stopping myself for fear that I would make the hairs disintegrate under the strain; in which I thought about Mae every time I touched those hairs, about how they might be able to lead me to her, and every time I looked at Rex, her body sinewy in the sunlight, the sweat dripping off her onto the ground (mud or sand, in the heat it's hard to tell which); and in which I have been terrified, watching that same horizon as Rex and Jonah, for Hoyle and his people to come and find us.

It has been months of inaction. Of waiting. Of time passing and me being able to do absolutely nothing about it.

Jonah tells me that he's feeling better. He wants to leave the house today, to go for a walk. 'I'm going to be okay,' he says.

'I know,' I tell him.

'Will you come with me?' he asks, and he sits on the edge of his bed, holds his hand out to me. He wants me to help him up.

I take it, and I wonder when he will let go.

The heat is ridiculous. We're staying in a town called Sweet Valley; a stupid name, but when we passed it Rex stopped at the sign, and she stared at it. She seemed to like it, and I took that as a sign that we should stay here. It's big enough to be on the maps, but isolated enough that you don't have to pass through it to get anywhere else, which cuts down on the chance of somebody stumbling across us. The whole town is quiet. We found it after a few days' walk, when Jonah was feeling up to it. When he was feeling well enough. Rex scouted ahead, and I helped him. I walked with him. She found this place, then came back to fetch us. The best sign, the way we knew it was right for us? It was so over-grown. The plants, bushes, scrub, everything had spilled through open doors and smashed-glass windows. The wind, when it happens, howls through the shells of the buildings. The people who abandoned it wouldn't live here now. We could stay here forever, I think, the three of us. Hunting for food. None of us saying what's on our minds.

But the heat. Out here, so far from the city wall, the heat is unfiltered, brutal and damning. It comes at me the moment that the sun's up, and it's not gone until long after it's dark, and even then the ground radiates heat long into the night.

I tell myself it's better than being a prisoner again. Better to be here, in this heat, than to not be myself. And that's not even the likely outcome for me any more. Reconditioning was when they thought I could be changed. But we're dangerous, I tell myself. We're too dangerous.

We walk out of the house, Jonah and I. It's only one storey, but there's a basement. That's where we sleep, because it's nothing but cold stone down there, and there are no windows for the light to get in, so it's dark. The three of us will take ourselves down there. We don't say a word to each other, just curl up on the stone floor under blankets. Sometimes, you want to sleep under a blanket, even if you're sweltering. There's a certain quality to it; a safety.

Jonah's unsteady on his feet once we're outside. He squints at the sky until I lead him away, until I force him to walk. We had to cut a chunk from his leg, where it was infected; the wound is now fresh skin, raw and soft. It'll burn, if he's not careful.

'It feels good,' he says, 'the air.'

But the air is always like this. It's dry and close and hard to breathe; and it's the same air as inside the house. He acts like it's something else. Revelatory. Being outside doesn't change the air. It's all in his mind.

'Can you walk by yourself?' I ask. When we arrived here, he got worse. He made it here – like this body gave him the strength, just enough, and then as soon as he stopped moving it gave up on him, bringing the fever back worse than before, forcing us to act. Now, he's weak. Recovering, still. He leans on a fence, white faded paint, wood desiccating in the heat. The town must have burned once. There's a charring that runs over nearly everything, blackening the wood like a tar.

'This way?' he asks, looking out towards the fields in front of us. So we go. We walk slowly, at first, and then his pace picks up. He coughs as he moves, and he puts his hand to his brow to shade his eyes so that he can see better. 'How far does this road go?'

'A long way.' So far that I haven't walked it. There are mountains in the distance, and I haven't reached those. I don't know what would happen if I did. Would I climb them? Is that even possible? I point them out to him.

'Another day,' he says. He smiles. Rare to see him smile, even before this. Almost never on Australia. When we were in Pine City, then he smiled. When he'd forgotten who he was. 'Come on.' He reaches for my hand again, and I let him take it, and he starts moving faster, not quite running, but trying.

I don't know how I feel about him. Sometimes, he comes to me, feeling ill, or in pain, and he asks me to hold him, and I do; and I shut my eyes and our bodies together feel like something that might have once been able to happen. Once, on Australia, we were heading towards something together. We were in the same place. We were both trapped by our lives and we had a taste of freedom, of a future. But since then, everything's changed. We've come so far. He is a different person now, just like I am.

The things he's done: that's not the Jonah I knew.

'Do you think about home?' he asks. He clarifies, even though I know exactly what he means. 'Australia, about the ship?'

'In what way?'

'Do you miss it?'

'No,' I say, but even I don't think I sound convincing.

'I did, in the early days of Pine City,' he says, his voice wondering. 'At Pine City, when they were breaking us, I missed the control of the ship. Knowing that even if we were in danger, even if my life wasn't like it is for other people . . . I mean, we didn't know that, but . . . we were still able to control it, just a little bit.' We climb a hill, rocks sliding away under our feet. The dust is thick and gritty when I breathe it in; but there's something reassuring about that. Being able to tell when I'm doing something that's otherwise unconscious, that I otherwise take for granted. 'I remember that now. And I also remember that, after Gibson was done with my reconditioning, Pine City was all I wanted. I didn't care about the ship. I didn't remember that. I wanted the life Pine City gave me. Or, you know . . .' He's out of breath, his hand on his side, where he was injured. It looks like he's holding himself together. 'I wanted that version of who I was, who they told me I could be.' Then he looks at me, right at me. 'And I wanted you, still. But you had thought other things were more important.'

'That's not true,' I say. He waves the words away, smiles, like he doesn't mind. As if he understands.

'It's fine, Chan. I get it. I do. Some people change, but you didn't. You didn't soften and I did. I wanted to be softened. But I was still drawn to you, even when I didn't really remember you. I saw your strength, understood it and wanted it. You were like a rope, tying me to another version of myself.' We start walking again, or he does and I follow him, trying to keep up. He's picked up the pace, still clutching his side, moving like somebody who's angry, rather than driven. 'But I've been told who I am my whole life. I was told by the Pale Women, before I knew that there was even a choice. Told by Australia, really. We all were.' Is he right? 'Then Gibson told me who I was, or who I could be. And then you, by telling me that I wasn't that person.

'So, now, I know more about myself,' Jonah says. 'I know the things that I've done, and I can be held accountable for them. When I met Mooney, she explained to me that taking away the pain, taking away the memories, that doesn't

172

I tell Jonah that it will all be okay. I don't know what else to say, so I do as my own mother did and I lie. I tell him that everything will work out in the end; that he knows who he is, now, and that's enough. That's everything.

He nods as I say it, but won't look at me. We stare out at the land in front of us, behind us, all around us, and I lie to him, and he lets me.

That night, back in the house, he comes to me. He lies down next to me. I touch his neck, not even thinking, half asleep, arm wrapped around him; and he wakes me as he winces. But then he leaves my arm there, wrapped around him, huddled up to him for warmth even though we're not even cold, not even close.

'I think I loved you,' he says. His voice in the darkness, a whisper of the words so quiet I can't even tell if I'm meant to hear them.

I'm still thinking of whether I should say something back when suddenly the next thing I know it's morning, and I'm alone under my sheet, and the only evidence that he was ever here with me is a thin print of rusty brown along the line of my arm, blood from his neck imprinting my skin like a tattoo.

'I have to go out for a while,' I tell Rex. She's sitting down at the table in our house. The table is collapsing under itself. Some sort of insect has bored holes in the wood, leaving little marks you can see through. Chips of white paint remain on some of it, where it's been sheltered from the elements. We found it outside, and Rex said that she liked it, even though it's being eaten away. 'A week, maybe. Maybe longer.'

'What for?'

'Medicine. For Jonah. He's not well.'

'He's always unwell.' She doesn't seem too concerned, doesn't seem to mind if he's sick or not.

Doesn't matter: what I'm telling her is a lie.

'Where are you going?' she asks.

'Back to Washington,' I tell her. She nods. 'Can you tell Jonah for me? I can't find him. When he's back, tell him I've gone to get food or something.'

'You want me to lie to him for you.'

'Yes.' She makes it harder than it needs to be. I know where he is, but I don't want to have to do this myself. I don't want him – either of them – to know why I'm leaving, what I'm going to do.

'I should come with you,' she says.

'It's fine,' I say. 'Easier if it's just me. Harder to catch me if I'm by myself.'

She nods. 'You might find trouble.'

'It might find me, more like.' I smile at her. I want her to smile back, even if it's just once. I want to see if I can see Mae in her face, somewhere; because all I can picture of Mae any more is her smiling when I rescued her, when I showed her a place that she could be safe. Smiling or scared, those two looks are all I know of Mae. I've never seen Rex either smiling or scared. 'Do you want me to get you anything?'

'No,' she replies. I watch her squeezing the edge of the table with her augmented fingers. Is it still augmented if it's been entirely replaced? Either way, her fingers tighten on the wood, and it starts to squash, bend, so easily; as if she's folding paper.

I stand up, and she does as well. We face each other, as if there should be more to this. A goodbye. Saying good luck. A hug.

But there isn't, and then I'm gone, out of the house, down the road, towards the edge of the empty town. I reach into my pocket for the clump of hair that I've kept there, safe and close to me, for the last six months of our lives. This tiny ball that I've been worrying over, keeping safe, has become something else.

A totem.

'Books,' Rex shouts from behind me. I turn back to look at her. 'I want to learn to read better. Bring me some books.'

Still no smile, but it's something. Books is something.

8

Time changes any place. Or, maybe it changes you. Either way, the walk along the beach feels different now, as though the coastline I knew so well once has shifted. It's taken me days to get here, to the place where the nomads lived: a place, which felt like it was nearly a home to me, is abandoned, derelict. My legs ache. I've barely slept. There's no rest, now that I'm here. Only echoes of the settlement remain: torn fabric, clinging in scraps to the rocks on the beach; jutting stumps of tent poles; the scorched earth of the fire pits. But without any people it's lifeless; and it feels like it's always been so.

I stay back and watch the circling birds, flocking together in their patrol formations along the side of the wall, as they always did. I wait for a gap in their pattern that I know means they've got their eyes off the beach, and then I run, hurling myself into the sea, beneath the waves. The rope that used to guide me to the tunnel entrance is gone. I don't know where. Maybe the police took it down, to stop people using the sluice entrance. I can't even see the notches it was once attached to. So I have to swim alongside the wall and guess how far I've gone, and when I will need to dive under the waves to get to the tunnel into the city.

I find the tunnel easily enough, and then I'm in it, holding a lungful of breath. I know how long it will take to swim through, and how long to get out of the other side. I know how cold the water is, and how cold I will be until my body warms up. I know how long it'll take me to get into the city itself. I know how to get where I need to be, to travel the streets and not be seen, to hide away from cameras and birds and police.

This is the last time I'll ever come here, I think; and only now do I feel absolutely comfortable with how this city works.

Making sure that nobody sees me means waiting until nightfall, when there is a changeover in the guard shifts and I can sneak in. I take my time as I explore the city one last time; finding out exactly where he might be. I steal new clothes – all black, like before, like some sort of uniform I've fallen into wearing – to mask the dustiness, the wear and tear on my old outfit. I walk; I don't run. Running is great for getting away from danger. It's no good if you're heading into it.

When I get to the hospital, I make it past the nurses on duty, past the security cameras watching the waiting rooms. I find his name on a chart hanging on the wall. His room is at the end of a corridor and I can hear a faint beeping coming through the walls, carrying down the corridors as I make my way up them.

I watch him sleep. He doesn't have a clue that I'm here.

Time to tell him.

I put my hand over his mouth. The rough bristles of his beard scratch my palm, soft and chapped from the cold. My skin is too used to the hot of the outside now. His eyes open and he looks at me. He's confused for a moment, and then he works it out, what's going on. He makes a noise, a thin moan. A struggle.

'Don't say a word,' I hiss. 'You try anything, I'll keep my hand here. I'll push down, harder and harder. I don't want that to happen, okay? But I need your help, so we're going to get you out of here, and then I'm going to tell you what I need from you. You help me and I'll let you go. It'll be like I was never even here.' I take my hand away slowly, ready to slam it down. He doesn't see my other hand, on my knife, in case I need it.

'They told me you'd left the city,' Ziegler says.

'I did,' I reply. 'But I've come back.'

His clothes are in the wardrobe. He's not in here permanently, he says. Just until they're sure that his injury is healed. He tells me, with an almost desperate tone to his voice, that he should be dead. The wound should have finished him off. He doesn't seem as panicked by the thought of death as I figured he would be. I hand him his clothes, turning away for the moment he's out of his hospital gown and pulling on his underwear, then looking back at him. His body's thin from months of bed rest.

His throat is a scarred mess.

I think about Jonah's neck. What it will look like again when it heals.

If he ever lets it heal.

'They said that if it had happened anywhere else in the city, they wouldn't have gotten to me in time. That would have been it for me.' His voice is different. Coarser, harsh and gravelly. It actually suits him. It gives him an edge that he otherwise lacked, to go with the beard, with the plunging darkness of his eyes, the general roughness of his appearance. I expected some resistance, that he'd put up a fight. Instead, he's just telling me everything that's happened to him. 'They had to replace my trachea – the whole thing – put in an augment, which I'd always sworn I'd never get. I like humanity to be what it was, you know?' There are these gulps in his speech after every full stop. He's not used to talking, to using his voice. 'But if it's that or being dead? It's amazing how quickly you can change your stance. Now, from here to here,' he puts a finger under his chin, by the scar, and another a third of the way down his chest, 'I'm not entirely human any more. They said that when it takes, I'll be all-improved. I'll breathe better. It's tough because the body wants to reject the augments, but I'm getting out of here in another week.'

'You're getting out of here tonight,' I say. 'Hurry up and finish getting dressed.' I throw his coat at him, put his shoes down at his feet. He does the laces up and then wraps the scarf around his neck. His fingers brush his scar as he tightens it and he winces.

'The scarring is the last stage,' he says to me. 'They just go over the skin. Like, they smooth it out. Once they do that no one will ever be able to see the scar again.'

I think about Jonah and Rex, wearing their scars as a badge; a map to who they are, who they've been. Who they will be.

I remember the scar on Rex's belly. Long. Like a smile, I once thought.

A grimace.

'Where are we going?' Ziegler asks.

'I need information. You know people. So you're going to take me to somebody who can help.' I open the door to his bedroom. Nobody in the corridor. There are probably cameras so I pull my hood down tight over my head so my face can't be seen. 'Come on,' I say, and I reach for him, pull him along by the sleeve of his coat. 'Through here,' I say, pointing towards the fire escape. He wheezes a little, so I ask if he's alright and he nods. He coughs to clear his throat, and we're on our way again. Down four levels and then we're on the floor that I came in through: the laundry and the offices of the hospital. I check the corridors again, making him wait for me. He doesn't try to and run, doesn't shout for help. If anything, I'd say he looks like he's enjoying himself: the thrill of being a part of something, or maybe just being out of his bed. Maybe he's excited to be back with me; maybe he thinks this is research for his novel's sequel.

I lead him to the elevator, a much older one than any other I've been in. It grinds and clunks, and the only way to get in is to pull open a metal gate. I slam the gate when we're inside and press the button to go down to the very bottom of the building.

'Have you been alright?' he asks me, as the churn of the elevator's machinery goes on in the background.

'I've been fine,' I say. He nods. I don't ask him the same. The door opens to the parking lot. It's dark and quiet. We're at the back of the hospital. Nobody around. 'Shall I call my car?' he asks.

'No,' I say. 'They might be tracking it. We'll walk.'

'They? Who's they?' he asks.

'Hoyle. The police.' I look towards the exit. 'This way,' I say. I can hear the low-level rumble of the middle-of-the-night traffic.

I don't have to pull Ziegler along with me to make him cooperate. He follows me, always a few steps behind. I'm a fast walker, I know, even when I'm staying low key. It'll be harder to keep from attracting attention now that he's with me. But as long as we do what needs to be done before anybody notices he's missing, we'll be fine.

'It's good to be walking again. Outside, you know,' he says.

'I don't care,' I tell him.

'What do you want me to help you with?' He asks it like we're a team.

'Wait,' I say. Until we're out of the parking lot, and then along the road, across the next junction, down an alley between tower blocks, into a clearing, a courtyard between the buildings. A tree with benches beneath it. No cameras. The trees hiding you from birds that might be watching from above. Perfect.

I sit down, and Ziegler follows, taking the place next to me.

'You look well,' he says. He clears his throat again, but it sounds different. More for effect than because he actually has to. Then: 'I'm sorry. About the book.'

'Don't.'

'I hurt you, because I wanted to write a good story. And it was your story, wasn't it? I thought I had to make changes to it, to your story. To have it make sense, and to actually get people to pay attention.'

'Seriously, Ziegler. Shut up. I don't care.' I pull the hair from my pocket and show it to him. He squints at it, gets in close.

'Is that blood?'

'I need to do a test on this. Find out . . .' What? I know who it belongs to. I know that already. 'I need to find somebody related to who this belongs to. Does that make sense?'

'You mean you need the hair tested for its genetic markers?'

'Do you know somebody who can do that?'

'Yes. I mean, probably. I did.' He scrunches up his face, deep in thought. 'Valona. Used to live in the docks, actually. Long before you got here. She's a – was a – doctor. Went black market for augments, that sort of thing. She'll have the equipment you're after.'

'Where is she now?'

'Well, not the docks, not any more. She makes a lot of money.'

'I don't have anything to pay her with,' I say. He nods.

'You do,' he says. 'You've got your share of the book.'

The Girl Who Fell to Earth. I hated the title the minute that I heard it: so trite, and there's no power to it. Falling, like it was something I didn't have a choice about. Like I didn't have to fight to survive, or battle to try and find a way to save people, to get us somewhere better. As if I was just in freefall, helpless and out of control.

My name was in the book, and it might have looked like it was my story, but it wasn't. It was his. My story can't be told. I'd have to crack open my own head and pour it all out, and even then it wouldn't be *true*. That wouldn't be the facts. It'd just be how I see it.

Sunrise is coming so we walk quickly. Ziegler doesn't mind when I tell him to take a route other than the one he's used to, to stay off the main streets where possible; when we see police in the far off, he doesn't care if I tell him to sit down and keep quiet. When he asks if we can stop so that he can buy a coffee, and buy me one, I say that he has to pay with cash, that he can't use his credit. It's too trackable. He complies, digs out a crumpled note from his pocket, and returns with sweet pastries as well. Apricot for him, chocolate for me. He hands mine over with something like glee on his face.

I remember this, I think. We've done this before.

'They don't let you eat solids when you're recuperating,' he tells me. 'They want you to keep your body absolutely pure. Totally wholesome. Apparently it helps the healing process.' His mouth is full, the apricot in the heart of the pastry bursting as he chews. 'This is delicious,' he says.

We take a minute to eat and then we're off again. I'm hungry again as soon as I've taken the last bite. I tell myself there'll be time enough for eating when I'm out of here. We take the long route to where this woman is, staying away from the heart of the city. I wonder if any city has ever found a way to balance the needs of its many people and the needs of the few who run things, to make things actually fair. Maybe you'd have to start again, to build something from the ground up. But that's impossible, surely? Everything is destined to be what it was before, if you replicate it.

'This way. I think,' Ziegler says, leading me down a street. 'I'm struggling a little. My memory isn't what it was.' We are in an area where the houses – which are huge – are not attached to other houses, where the roads demarcate huge lawns, trees shading the sidewalks. It doesn't feel as cold here as in other parts of the city. It's not like it's warm exactly, but it's not cold either. Maybe this is the only place in the city where the temperature is just right. Like a story my mother once told me, something about a girl and three bears. Just right.

'If I called her . . .' Ziegler says.

'No,' I say. It's early afternoon now. We've been walking for hours and hours, and they'll know he's gone at this point. They'll have put out a missing person alert on Gaia, and the police – Hoyle – will have picked up on it. I know how it works. Everyone knows my connection to Ziegler. Hoyle will have been keeping tabs on Ziegler, or somebody will. They'll have wondered if I'd try to make contact. As soon as they find he's gone, they'll descend, looking for both of us. So I tell Ziegler to keep his scarf around his face while we're in public. I tell him to stay close to walls, keep his back to street corners where there are cameras. The software they use is intelligent, but not that intelligent. It picks up triggers and runs them – the software has facial recognition, some voice recognition. As long as we keep our faces obscured and don't speak, we're fine. They just won't know that they're looking at anything.

The houses are all set back, away from the streets and side-walks. Fences keep them separated. Each place is massive. Some of them are the size of whole blocks from the poorer parts of the city.

'This is where they all live,' Ziegler whispers to me.

'Who?'

'The people who run this city.' He shrugs. 'You've got the money, this is where you come, behind your gates, shut away.'

'Why wouldn't you want to be where the real people are?'

'Because people like the feeling that they've earned some-thing better. Everybody here's the same: they've done whatever they can to get here, and now they want to be around people like them. They don't want to have to see the real world. That's where they came from, and they pray they never have to go back there.'

'Would you want something like this one?' We stop outside one house. It's entirely white. The walls, the drive-way, the car in front of it – twice the size of most – the windows all white-tinted glass. We stare through the white gate, faces hidden.

'Funny you should ask,' Ziegler says. 'This one's Valona's.'

He assures me that she won't be on the grid. 'No way her security's run through Gaia. You know the sort of thing she does? It's off the books. Gaia would report people coming to see her, and she wouldn't want that. She'll be safe,' he says, but I feel uneasy. He approaches the gate, presses the buzzer. There's no screen there, no microphone. So we wait. 'What have you been doing all this time?' he asks me. I don't reply. 'You're not in the city any more. You must be wanted. You were working for the police for a while, weren't you?'

'Hoyle,' I say.

'You and Rex, you worked for them. It's fine, I would have. So what happened?'

'I don't want to talk about it,' I say. I want to tell him he hasn't earned it; that he betrayed me. He hasn't earned the right to small talk.

'So you've been living outside the city? Where? Are you okay?' I ignore him. Something's buzzing in the distance. I can't see it. 'Chan, listen,' he says. As if I have any other choice. 'I just want to say that I'm sorry.' The buzzing is getting louder. The problem with spaces like this is that little noises echo. Emptiness makes it harder to pinpoint where a sound is coming from exactly. 'I know I've told you already,' he begins. And then I see it. A bird, flying from the house, swooping down toward us, and fast. I grab Ziegler, pull him out of the way, dive to the ground.

The bird settles in front of us, hovering, twitching its head up and down, taking us in. There's laughter from it, human laughter, and then a voice: 'Ziegler? Is that Ziegler?'

A woman. She sounds incredulous, like she doesn't believe what she's seeing. 'It's been a long time!'

He stands up and dusts himself off. 'Valona. This is a friend of mine,' he says. He looks at me and the bird's gaze follows.

'The girl from the network! I saw the broadcast. From your book. You brought me a present! A real life celebrity!' She laughs. She knows me already.

'She needs your help,' Ziegler says.

'Okay then,' the voice says. 'You should come on in.' Behind the bird, the gates pull themselves open. The bird stays where it is and we walk around it, up the path. I look down at our feet on the pure white floor: the coating is not paint but something else, perfectly reflective from above, totally smooth and spotlessly clean. Against it, my shoes look even filthier than usual. The bird follows us, as if it's shepherding us up the path, making sure we stay on our route and don't deviate.

I'm not surprised when Valona opens the door and she's entirely dressed in white. Every piece of her clothing is white, and her hair's been dyed or augmented, and her skin is a peculiar pale shade that definitely isn't original but makes her look as though she's some sort of figurine, like something out of the museums, made of china or clay, or painted to be as pale as possible. Initially, she's hard to look at; the effect is so jarring and unnatural. But you can tell she likes that. As soon as she sees my face – I don't know what my expression is, but I can imagine – she laughs again.

'This much bodywork, you're thinking, it should be il-legal, right?' she says, gesturing at herself. 'Should be, could be, is. Doesn't matter. Come here, come inside.' She ushers me past her, and then leans in to kiss Ziegler on both cheeks. She makes the noise of the kiss out loud, into the air, not actually touching him. 'It's been far too long. What happened?'

'You know how it is,' he says. He sounds sheepish, drops the volume of his voice a little, as if he doesn't want me to hear.

'I know. You go legitimate, it changes things.'

'I was always legitimate.'

'Sure. But sometimes you wanted illegitimate things.' She looks at me. 'Open your jacket,' she says.

'Why?' I'm annoyed at myself for being defensive, but still. She's going to find my knife, and she's going to try and take it.

'I need to check you. I can check you or you can leave. Your choice.'

I open up my jacket and she reaches her hands in around my back. Her face is close to my neck, and I can smell how sweet her skin is. It's not a perfume but another augment: like the smell from the top of the pastries that we ate earlier this morning: sweet vanilla.

'You like that?' she asks. Her hands rub my back. Not quite scratching, but searching. 'It smells exactly like you want it to. It's personal to whoever's smelling it. Everybody is different. Most expensive augment I own. Highly illegal.' She brings her hands out, catches one on the handle of my knife as she comes. She pulls it from the sheath. 'Even smelling it is illegal, you know. You've broken the law, tut tut.'

'Don't mess with her,' Ziegler says. 'She broke the law well before she met you.' He says it like he's almost proud.

She holds the knife up. 'So you came armed?'

'Prepared,' I say.

She turns the knife over in her hand, holds the blade and passes it back to me. 'I don't care if you've got a weapon. A weapon is sensible. I'm a bad person. I just want to check you're not police.'

'I'm not,' I tell her. She turns, smiling, and walks down the perfectly white corridor into a room. Massive, like I imagine every room in this house to be. The white dominates, but there are flecks of grey accents on the furniture and objects. Massive sofas. And then, against another wall, holos: images of Ziegler and myself, reports, information from Gaia.

'So the network said,' she tells me, 'But sometimes the network lies. It says that you're wanted by them. You've done something you shouldn't have?'

'She needs your help,' Ziegler says.

'You said that already.' I notice that Ziegler's book is on one of the tables. I can see the spine, peering out at me. His name, my story. Or a version of it.

Ziegler smiles at Valona. The smile of a man who wants something. 'You've still got medical contacts, I assume. Access to the databases.'

'I've got as much as I need.'

'Chan has to find somebody. She's got a sample.'

'I'm looking for somebody related to this person. The person the sample is from,' I say, pulling the hair from my pocket. I say it so fast it's as if the words are crowding each other, jostling for space.

'Related? Related isn't always good enough. Lots of genetic markers are shared, you know.' Valona brings up a

191

screen. A piece of software. She doesn't have to hack her way in; she's simply got access. I don't want to know how. At the top of the screen I can read the phrase *United American Medical Database*.

'It's from her mother,' I say.

I see Ziegler's eyes widen, but he doesn't say anything.

'Then let's see what we can find,' Valona replies.

The sample of Rex's hair and blood goes into a metal tray and Valona scans it with something that looks like a pen, which she pokes into the hairs. She doesn't explain herself as she goes. She knows what she's doing and doesn't care that I don't. It only takes seconds for the screen to fill with letters and numbers, a garbled mess that I can't understand. A code of sorts. She swipes at the screen. Sections of the code highlight, blocks form. She taps at those, selects them all then swipes again, and the screen clears.

On it, four identification numbers remain.

'Which one are you looking for?' she asks.

'I don't—'

'The first one, that's the perfect match. That's all of them. It's the sample. The second one, that's closest. The daughter, you say.'

Mae. That's Mae.

'What about the other two?'

'Relatives. Further away. One of them,' she points at the third, 'recently deceased. The D at the end of the ident –' she points to a letter on the screen – 'that's how we know. The other is alive. Maybe a grandparent. Could be a cousin, strong bloodline links. A cousin whose parents were a little too close.' She laughs.

I want to touch Mae's number. It's the closest I've been to her in . . . how long? A year? Find out where she is.

I ask if I can take over and Valona stands back.

'Be my guest.' I touch Rex's number. Her picture fills the screen. She's on record. Hoyle did tests on us, checked our blood for diseases. Now we aren't informants, we're in Gaia, just like everybody else. Her page has all her details. A guess at a date of birth, one that she made herself. Her injuries. Her last known location. The job she did; the fact that she was an informant for the police. The fact that she isn't any more and is now wanted by them for questioning. Everything they know about her is right there on the screen. 'This isn't who you're looking for, though,' Valona says.

I swipe back, and there's Mae's identification number, waiting for me.

Come on, Chan.

I touch it. I don't hesitate, because I feel sick, my stomach churning; and I don't want that to get the better of me, to delay finding my answers. I don't know what I expected to feel, if I thought that this would be a relief or sadness or joy, but it's all of those things. There's a picture of a girl, and for a second I think it's somebody else entirely, that this system is wrong, and that it doesn't know. It's made a mistake. But it's not. Mae's older, that's all. It's just time. It never stops, and neither has she. Her hair has been left to grow long, out of the shaven style everybody had on Australia, now that she lives in a place where lice isn't something people have to worry about. Her eyes are a fierce green-brown, and they're shining – not tired, not sad, not lost. She's smiling, her mouth full of white teeth. A different smile than I ever saw from her. Straight teeth now, just like everybody here. Her skin is clean and clear. No scars that I can see. She once had little scars – nobody escaped Australia without them – but they're gone, brushed away. Augments maybe, or likely only just time helping them to fade to nothing.

But it's Mae. It's absolutely Mae, and I wonder, in that moment, how I could have ever forgotten this face.

'That her?' Ziegler asks.

I nod. I scan the holo for information about where she is. Nothing. There is a blank where her date of birth should be. I doubt that even Rex would know that. We didn't exactly keep strict time on the ship. 'How do we find her?' I ask. My voice is soft.

'Medical records. Let me,' Valona says. She takes over again, swiping, typing on another screen, inputting Mae's identification number and her name, and that's when I notice that she's got a new one. Mae Blackwood.

'Where did that come from?' I ask. Names weren't like that, not on Australia. They were simpler. Mine was – is – Aitch. It took me months of being here to realise that it wasn't a real name; it was a pronunciation of a letter. Chan H. My actual surname, lost to time and whatever else came between me and it, however many generations. They stripped away the name, and left the prisoners with that abbreviation. Mae's was never Blackwood. Rex's wasn't Blackwood. I've never heard that name before.

'She was adopted,' Valona says. Every second feels like it's being dragged out, and I'm being dragged along with it. I want to be, but also because I can't help it. The new screen changes, loading up with Mae's information. Another photograph. Older still. Not smiling, but I know that doesn't mean anything. Or maybe it does. Maybe it means she's unhappy. Maybe. 'She spent a month in a relocation facility.'

'Did they change her?'

'Change her how?' Valona stops and looks at me. She's intrigued, as if I know something that she doesn't.

'I was in a facility. Have you heard of Pine City?'

She nods. Smiles. This isn't like when Alala used to smile at me. She was placating, fascinated and amused, but she was always going to screw with me. Valona's smile is because she knows what happened. Hers is the smile of having the upper hand, but still being intrigued. One neat white eyebrow set against the same colour of skin, raised to show her interest.

'I know about that place,' Valona says. 'Don't worry. They don't change the little children, not if they don't need to. The brain is too delicate when they're young. It keeps developing; you can't mess with it.' She turns back to the holo. 'Not officially, at least.'

'So what's relocation?'

'Finding her a home. They searched, to make sure that somebody appropriate took her. Takes a long time. They want to make it perfect.'

'The services?'

'It's an art, you know. You can't just give a child to anybody.'

'Where did Mae end up?' Ziegler asks, like he's impatient, like he's the one with a vested interest in her.

'With the Blackwoods.' She flicks through to a file of information about them. A different database, just as easy for her to access. 'The wife, she's high up in the services. Says here that she started the program – one of the leading lights in it. The husband, he was a politician. Dead, now. Died a few months ago.'

Oh God. Terror, in my gut: that Australia ruined Mae more than I thought. That she is Rex's daughter and Rex is a killer, a murderer, was a bad person for so long and now she's something else, but I'm still not sure what; and can that be passed on? Does it run through the blood, like a disease? 'How did he die?'

'Cancer. Rare, now, but according to the files, it was a particularly malignant one. All over him. Everywhere. Maybe they could have taken enough away, augmented him to save him. Likely they caught it too late.'

I think about my mother. My mother's own blood.

Ziegler interrupts my thoughts. 'So she's with the woman. There an address?'

'New York. Manhattan. They're – Blackwood – she's important. Big building.' Valona taps the screen again. 'Here.'

'The Prestige? Jesus.'

'What's The Prestige?' I hear myself asking, but my voice is strange. It's a question I should ask to keep myself in this place, in this time. Here and now.

'New York doesn't have as much land as we have. The islands are small, so that means that they built up, not across. Houses like this,' he gestures at the stark white mansion, 'don't exist there, not really. Everyone lives in towers: and they're *impressive*.'

196

'Like where Ziegler lives.'

She laughs. Ziegler looks affronted at her reaction. 'Ziegler always acted like he was the big I Am. Honey, listen. Ziegler's a fraud. A phony. What he has isn't money. It's pocket change. Real money? That's something else.'

'Money's what you've got,' I say. 'Why you're like this, why you live like this.'

'Yes,' she says. 'Not dissimilar. Your girl is in New York. The Prestige, Apartment 35D. It's not quite a penthouse, but not far off.' She swipes through other pages on the medical records, but quickly. I see one of them, at a glance: a list of the times that Mae's been to see the doctor. The things that were wrong with her, the medicines she's taken, the diagnoses.

Then Valona shuts the holo down.

'I need to pay you,' I say. 'I don't have—'

'I don't care. Don't worry about it.' She takes my hands. 'I've got money. This? It's a story. I was visited by the girl who fell to Earth. That's enough, I'd say.' She stands up, pulls me with her. 'I've got a client coming soon, so I'm going to have to ask you to leave.' To Ziegler: 'I think we'll see each other soon. You should be in hospital.' And then, to me: 'You and I, we won't see each other again, will we?'

'I don't think so.'

'Then let me say that this has been a pleasure.'

'Thank you for helping me,' I say; and she smiles, as if the thing I asked for help with is all par for the course. As if nothing I could ask of her, ever, could be out of the ordinary.

*   *   *

'Where are we going now?' Ziegler asks as I walk down the street, away from her house.

'You're not going anywhere,' I say.

'Chan, come on. I helped you get here, didn't I?'

I stop, turn, grab him by the neck. One swift movement. He winces, which I knew he would. I knew it would hurt. Even if it's not a tangible physical pain, it's where he was cut. Wounds can hurt long after they've healed. He's spent months nursing his wound, worrying about this specific part of his body. My fingernails digging into the scar tissue is going to make him afraid, make him panic. 'You put me in this situation. You betrayed me. You could have helped me before, way back, and yet you used me for your own gain.'

'We couldn't have found her back then! There wasn't any way.' His voice croaks even more through my grip.

There was a way. There was Rex, right there. If I'd only known.

'You are not a friend of mine,' I say. 'But I'm not going to hurt you. I'm not.' I loosen my grip. He stumbles, falls forward, feels his neck. He's checking for blood. It's been months since his throat was slit, and the skin's been grafted on top of the wound, and it might be raw now, but of course he's fine. 'I'm grateful you brought me here now, Ziegler, but this is it. This is where we end.'

'Chan,' he says, something like defiance in his voice. He's not accepting it. 'Chan, listen. I wrote the book in your best interests. I wanted your story to be told.'

'It wasn't my story.'

'I told you, I just wanted—'

'Even before that, I needed your help. I was in trouble. You were the one who put me in touch with Alala. You didn't warn me about the sort of person she was. And you knew! You knew she would use me.'

'I told you to be careful—' he begins. But I don't let him finish the thought.

'You told me she shouldn't be trusted. So I didn't trust her. I did trust you, though. I trusted that you wouldn't abandon me when I needed you, when I was desperate. But you ran. You're a coward. I don't have time for cowards.'

I start to walk. He's on his knees and he looks pathetic.

'What about if they come looking for me? If they ask me where you've gone?' I stop. He's right. Hoyle – or whoever's above Hoyle, whoever is in charge of finding Rex and me – will make him tell them. That's their job, and Ziegler? He's weak. 'That's not a threat, Chan. I'm not saying I'll tell them. This is yours. But they'll find me, and I know they'll get it out of me.' He won't hold up to torture. They'll break one finger and he'll tell them everything.

I'm sure he can see, in my eyes, that I'm thinking about what will happen to him next.

'You take me with you, let me help. I can be an asset, you know that. I know things, and I know people. And I can help you.'

'So, what? So you can write about it?' He doesn't say anything, doesn't promise that he won't. My life now is just another story to him.

'And what can you do?' I finally say. 'You'd just slow us down.'

'I've got a car,' he says. 'I can drive us. I can take you to get Mae, to New York.' Like he's haggling, as if he can change my mind. As if his help will, what, redeem him?

But he's right. And I want Rex to come with us. I need to see this through with her. It'll take me ten days to get back to her and Jonah, if I go at the same pace I took to get here. That's ten days there, then I'll have to rest. I don't know how they'll react when I tell them I'm leaving again. Jonah might argue. Rex might argue.

'I can call the car now. Should be easy to get it. We take it, get out of here.'

'You can't call it,' I say. 'They might have tracers on it. We need to check it in person.'

'So we go to it,' he says.

'You'll have to drive me to collect Rex first.'

'Okay,' he says. 'Whatever you want. Car's at The Royal. Let's go.'

The Royal looks to be in far worse shape than I remember. Even from a distance, it seems as if it's dingier. It's not as amazing to me as it once was. It was once so exciting to come here, to know that Ziegler was there to help me; or, at least, I thought he was. I watch him as he stands on the sidewalk that rings the building, hands in his pockets, coat pulled tight, looking up at the tower he calls home. He seems to feel the cold outside, certainly more than I do.

'I was an only child,' he says. I don't reply. 'Did you know that? Just me. I had parents but they died. They didn't want any more than me. I was enough.'

'Why are you telling me this?'

'Nobody came to visit me. In hospital, I mean. It's funny, I seem to have a lot of acquaintances, but apparently no friends. There was a thing about me on the news, I've seen it. It's not like nobody knew where I was. But they didn't care. Do you know,' he turns to me, his back to the building, 'you were the first visitor I had?'

'Maybe if you didn't betray your friends they'd be more inclined to bother,' I say.

He smiles, half impressed, half sad. 'Nobody will have cleaned the apartment. It'll be dusty. They say that you can't go home again, but, well, here we are.'

'Who says that?'

'They. Some author, once.'

'That's ridiculous,' I say, but I'm lying to myself. I can't go home again.

I never really had one to begin with.

'I don't know. This is my house, maybe. I don't know if it's home any more.'

We walk across the tarmac in front of the tower, and then to the front door. He presses his hand to the security panel and it beeps. Gaia welcomes us – welcomes him – home. I cover my face and sneak in past the gate.

We've made a mistake. The gate here, it'll be on the main-frame. It doesn't matter that I kept my face hidden, that we didn't call the car, that we stayed away from birds and police; they'll be watching Gaia, waiting for him to register somewhere. All the hiding we've done, and now we've made this mistake, right at the last minute. Ziegler feels me hesitate, looks at me, and he gets it then. He doesn't even pause. He grabs my hand.

'Quickly,' he says. We get into the stairwell, run down the stairs. Then we're in the garage, lights flickering to life as we move through it. 'Where are you?' he shouts, his voice echoing, and his car flashes, a blue light splitting the darkness of a far corner. We run over as we hear it warming itself up. 'Get in,' he says.

'It's still off the network?' I ask, and he nods.

'I didn't change it,' he tells me.

'Where shall we go, Mr Ziegler?' the car asks.

'Take us out of the city.'

'I need a destination.'

'I don't care,' he shouts, 'just go. Baltimore, anywhere. Go!' The car processes that, brings up a map. 'We can change the destination when we're on the road,' he says. 'It's the right direction. As long as we're heading in the right direction, as long as we stay out of their sight, stay ahead of them, we'll be okay.' Out, and into the brightness of the day. Up the ramp, onto the road. Away from The Royal, and I look out of the rear window, and there's a bird in the sky, high above, far away. Far enough that I don't think it can spot us.

'Come on,' I say, under my breath, willing the bird to soar away. But it's not the bird we have to worry about. Parked in the middle of the road, waiting, there's a car; and then, like magic, another appears at our side, from an adjacent road. The windows are blacked out, and I can see the police symbols painted on their sides. Hoyle would have known there was a chance I would end up here. All he had to do was station cars, birds, men, whatever, and have Gaia do the rest. The cars are programmed to box us in.

Unmanned cars, meant for brute force. No one will get hurt if there's a collision; except for us, of course.

'Hold tight,' Ziegler says, and then, to Gaia, 'Give me control.' A holo appears in front of him, swipe controls to move left and right. Crude graphics, not actually a part of the system design. They look like they've been made by an amateur. Where everything else in the car is sleek and perfect, these are pixelated and glitchy. But they work. He swipes left and we leave our lane, darting into the other, where oncoming traffic is forced to divert, to stop, to pull over. Gaia's control will try and save the other people, and we can take advantage of that. 'It's been a while since I've driven,' Ziegler says. He pushes us back to the right and we slam into one of the police cars. Sparks and grinding, and the car seems to tilt up on its side. I scream.

Ziegler swings the car around, slams into another one of them. We collide hard, and I feel it in my teeth: an ache, a pain in my jaw from clenching so tight.

'I didn't think I'd ever need the manual controls,' he says. 'Just a precaution.' But he drives like he knows exactly how they work, like he's done this before. The other cars on the road move out of our way. They find their path altered and the passengers panic – as one car swings past us I see them staring at us, jaws gaping, eyes wide at Ziegler's hands flashing around in front of the holo controls, at my no-doubt terrified face. This is the sort of thing that happens in the movies, on the news, never in real life – and the cars avoid us. More police come in after us. I see that some of the new cars have people in them. The police are wearing helmets, steering manually like Ziegler is, but I can see from this distance that they're much calmer than he.

And one of them is heading right for us.

I wonder if my mother ever had a clue what my life would hold. She told me that when you've got a child, you think about what you want for them, from them, for the rest of their lives. On Australia, it felt like we had no future, but she taught me to learn, to grow. She wanted things for me. I understand that's true here, too. Parents here encourage their children to learn, to grow, to develop, to reach and to become something special. Something extraordinary.

On Australia, my mother didn't have that luxury. Perhaps the most extraordinary thing she ever dreamt of for me would be that I would one day be somewhere that wasn't that ship; that one day, I would be somewhere with land beneath my feet, actual ground, with other people who hadn't grown up there, who weren't going to try to hurt, kill, eat me. She dreamed of a life without danger for me.

And here I am, on earth, in a car speeding into the face of oncoming traffic, people trying to ram us off the road, to catch me, to kill me, and I can only think that my mother could never have predicted this.

Ziegler swings the car around a corner, throwing us both to the left. The police are too late to react. They overshoot us and go screaming past, buying us some time. Not much. Not enough.

'They'll start shutting the entrances, seal the city off,' he says.

Everything is closing in. The walls, the gates. Everything. But I've been trapped before. 'So we wait it out,' I say. 'We hide, and as soon as they open them again, we get through.'

'They won't let us.' His voice is ragged, panicked. We careen around corner after corner. This is sensible, a clever tactic. Same as I use when I'm running from people. If you can get out of the line of sight of your pursuers for just long enough, you have a better chance of slipping away. They can try and predict where you'll go, but they won't know. 'We might have gotten through if they weren't on high alert, but now they'll—'

'We're not going to give them a choice,' I say. 'We'll hide, then when this has all died down we'll wait for the gate to open, when there are deliveries or mass passage vehicles. And we take that opportunity.'

He's quiet a moment, processing what I've said. Then, swinging the car down an alleyway, he says, 'It's a good plan. Better than anything I've got.'

We pull out of the alley and onto a quiet street. I can hear car sirens ringing out in the distance, but I can't see their lights. Nothing directly behind us, and only normal traffic in front. 'Darken the windows,' he says to the car, 'and get back in pattern.' The car falls into line with the rest of the traffic. I look out at the sky. There are birds a few blocks over, circling the streets, searching for us. But we're not on Gaia. Every car looks like this one, pretty much, apart from the scratches where the other cars slammed into us; and accidents happen. For now, we're as close to invisible as we can possibly hope to be, given the situation. 'So we need to find a place,' he says. 'Got any ideas?'

'Maybe,' I reply. I bring up the map, and I point. 'There.'

He nods. Doesn't question. 'If you say it's safe,' he says, 'I'll take your word for it.'

The fence is unguarded when we arrive. Everybody has gone for the night. Some nights there's a watchman, but even when he's here he's usually sleeping. If you don't disturb him, he'll let you be. Likely it's not worth the trouble, him looking into every little noise he hears. I've wondered why they even bother with him; it's not like this place is worth being in. An artifact from a failed space program and a load of overgrown abandoned buildings. It's not like there aren't better things the land could be used for.

As the darkness settles, the streetlights and lights from the wall spark into life above us. Ziegler pulls the car to a stop in the underbrush by the fence. We get out and start pulling back the mesh, making a wide enough gap to get the car through. Then, as I hold the fence back, Ziegler gets back in and drives through. I check the area, to make sure there's no security patrol, and when I'm sure it's clear – the doors to the main building locked down tight, the lights off, no sounds coming from the hangar – he gets out of the car and we sit on the cracked concrete, and we talk.

It's cold here, so close to the wall, and every word we speak, we can see our own breath.

'There's a tunnel not far from here, in the wall. Under the ice.'

'That's how you get out to the desert?'

'To the sea. It's not all desert out there, you know.'

'Just most of it.'

'Just most of it,' I agree.

'And that's where you've been living?'

'With the nomads,' I say. He nods. Smirks. Like he knows everything, like he knows those people, who they are and what they did for me. What they stand for.

'They're good people,' I tell him. 'Everybody says that they don't have a place here because they—'

'I didn't say anything.'

'Just because they don't want to live here doesn't make them—'

'I wasn't saying that. I was thinking the opposite,' he says. 'This city: we think it's everything. Amazing. We tell ourselves that we've learned from our mistakes, that the things we've done in the past are forgotten, forgiven. We were given a chance to start again.'

'You were.'

'Ah, but we're still human. We still act the same way. I betrayed you. I could have helped you. Should have. But I didn't. Because at the end of the day I was worried about my own life. I had a nice life, and I didn't want to lose that. I've lost enough, but then I lost you. I didn't know it would hurt, that I didn't want to lose you too.'

'What happened to your little girl?' I ask. I remember the pictures of her, in his apartment. He never spoke about her, so I never asked.

'What?' He seems shocked. He didn't expect this question. He probably forgot I'd ever even seen her picture.

'You had a picture of her. Not a holo.'

He nods. 'Samantha.' He sighs when he says her name. 'I haven't said her name in a while. I haven't needed to. It's sort of been in my head, and that's it – like it's been mine, only.'

'She's dead.'

More nodding. Over and over. Like doing it just the once wouldn't, somehow, be enough. 'She was sick. She died. Nothing anybody could do. Her mother left straight afterwards. Wasn't my fault, wasn't hers. It just happened.' He looks at his feet. He's been worrying a hole with the heel of his shoe, grinding it into the chipped fragments of concrete and thick brown soil. 'Sometimes things just happen, and then they're done. And afterwards, you're still here, and you have to deal with them alone. If you can't deal with them, you run.' I feel like I should tell him that I know what running feels like. And I've had my share of loss. And yet, I know that my situation is not the same. I've *had* to move on. I can tell, looking at Ziegler now, that he hasn't. Or, at least, he hasn't been successful, if he's tried. 'Samantha,' he says again, her name elongated slightly, and I can hear the relief in his voice – I think it's relief – to say her name. I think how, once, I would have reached out to him, tried to comfort him.

'I'm sorry,' he finally says to me. 'There's nothing else I can say, but I am sorry. I'll prove it to you. I'll take you to where you've got to go.'

'You'll help me to get Mae back,' I say.

'I'll help you do what's right,' he says.

And then we sit in silence. We listen to the cars on the distant street quieten down, then get hushed entirely as the night closes in and the city goes to sleep.

*   *   *

'What is this place?' he asks me. We're both lying on the
ground now, thinking about sleep but unable to find it. I
don't know how tired I'd have to be before everything else
fell away and I managed to pass out. I'm not tired enough.
Not yet.

'Some sort of government facility. They don't use it
anymore. There's a warehouse, where they store the ships.
Or, at least, the lander part. Like the bottom bit of Australia
that we came down here in – the part we found underneath
the pit that let us control things.' That let us escape.

'What?' He sits up. 'There's another ship?'

'Not the whole thing, just the part that landed here or
took people up; where the guards lived. But it's got a name
printed on it: The New World.'

'Jesus, Chan. You didn't think to frontload that bit of
information?' He scrambles to his feet, rifles around in the
car. He comes back with a holo tablet, brings up a window.
In the darkness, the bright blue of the light is almost blinding. 'The New World. There were rumours about it – that
it was the first one they made. They made it for ordinary
people after it was decided that the prison experiments
had been successful. Well, I say *ordinary*. For the
government.'

'They thought the prison ships were a success?' I want to
show them Australia. I want to show them what my life was
like. Let them tell me it was a success.

'You know what I mean. As far as they were concerned,
it was viable. Sustainable, if they needed it.' He shows me
a site on his holo: information about The New World, all
the usual mishmash of information and unformed thought

that his beloved conspiracy websites serve up. Not real journalism, just piecing together a story from fragments and a lot of guess-work. 'But nobody ever knew if it was real. It was all rumours. I mean, now, people don't care any more. We don't care if we ever landed on the moon or not. People stopped caring if The New World was real or not as well.'

'Well, it is. I've seen it.' At least, part of it.

'Didn't you say those things have beds in them?'

'Yes, but—'

'And we're sleeping out here?' He grabs my hand. 'Come on. Show me. Give me a tour of it. I spent months showing you this city when you first got here, now you can repay the favour.' He pulls me to my feet before I can protest and we push through the bushes, back to the path that leads through the complex. 'Which way?'

'Over there,' I say, pointing to the warehouse. Dark windows, no lights. Still no security here. We might be lucky. This might be one of the nights that they don't bother even showing up.

The front door is locked, and there are no lights on. No security, I'd guess; not like the first time I was here. I look around, above the doorway. A little way down the wall there's a vent halfway up the building's height. I grab Ziegler's arm and rush him around to it.

'There,' I say. 'Hoist me up.' He kneels down and I step up and onto his shoulders; and then he stands, pushes up to his full height. He shakes and I can hear him gritting his teeth as I stick my knife into the edge of the metal grate. The vent is filthy with black dirt and coughs up a cloud of dust as I prise it loose. I hand it down to him and pull myself up and into the hole.

'Thank god,' Ziegler says, sighing, rubbing his shoulders. I climb in and crawl through. The ventilation shaft curves and then carries on; but there's another hatch, which I force open, and then I drop to the ground, clumsier than I'd like but without hurting myself.

I think about how many times I've fallen down in my life. I wonder how many times I've got left.

I'm in a corridor with doors off to one side. There's a large glass window looking into the darkness of the main room on the other side of the corridor: the warehouse where they're keeping the ship. I peer through, but the lights are off; and then the sound of somebody – Ziegler, I tell myself, to stop from panicking; it's only Ziegler – banging on a door, a window.

I find the door and unlock it. It swings, Ziegler's hand already pushing it.

'No alarms?' he asks.

'There was one, I think. But I don't hear it. I can't hear it.' He looks around the door frame. 'They could be silent. But if there isn't a box . . .' I watch as he checks behind the door, checks the ceiling, checks the corners. Nothing. 'We're clear, I think,' he says. 'Okay. Where is this thing?'

I take him into the main part of the warehouse. Lights flicker on as we walk, catching our movements on their sensors. Then, we're at the lander. It looks older than all of the other technology in the city. A remnant of a past time. I remember how incredible it was when I first went through the hatch in Australia, how clean and neat and smooth everything was inside. From the outside, it's clunkier than I imagined. There's only the one corridor, then beneath it engines, some sort of exhaust thing that Ziegler lies beneath and peers up into. The outside is smooth; not unlike the metal skin of the birds. Makes it better for flying, I suppose. It's shaped like a saucer. Like a frying pan.

'It's amazing,' he says, but I'm not sure I agree with him. It's dusty, certainly. *The New World* is printed on the side in bold letters. Looks a bit like the font that the police use on their cars; official and strict.

'Hold on,' I say. 'There's an alarm.' The first time I was here, there was an alarm.

'It hasn't triggered though,' he says.

'Not yet.'

He scrunches his face in thought. An idea. 'Wait here,' he says, 'don't move a muscle,' and then he's vanished into the hall, and I hear the sound of the door slamming behind him as he goes out into the night. Seconds later, it slams again, and he's in the room, holding something out in front of him: an EMP, just like Alala gave me. 'We short the electrics,' he says. 'They'll go off. They probably won't come back on until somebody manually trips a switch.'

'Okay,' I say.

'I really want to see inside that ship,' he tells me. The grin on his face is almost manic. 'You ready?'

'Sure,' I say, and then I realise why he's so excited: as he rolls the EMP forward, towards the computer console that sits against the side wall of the warehouse, I realise that there's still a part of him that didn't believe me, didn't believe my story. This is the proof that everything I said was true, the proof he was always after. Rex wasn't proof, not really. Maybe we were both liars, or insane. Maybe we invented the story of Australia as a way of justifying something to ourselves, of making our own lives that little bit more exciting. There was no concrete evidence, not really. But this lander? It's undeniable.

The EMP flashes, a blue light that bounces off the surface of the ship, and then all the lights go out. Every single one. The room is plunged into darkness, so black I can barely make out the outline of the craft right in front of us.

'Light!' Ziegler says, and a beam of bright blue-white light shoots from his glasses, so bright it's almost blinding when he glances towards me. 'Down a few levels,' he says as I flinch, and the light dampens, until it's more of a haze in front of us, a glow that we can see by. 'Shall we open her up?' he asks, but I know it's not a question.

There's a ladder on the edge of the lander, indents in the metal for foot and hand holds. We climb up, me first, and then I walk around until I find the hatch, just like the one I knew on Australia; and then I kneel, take hold of the lock, turn it. It hisses, expelling the gases from inside the cabin. The air is old and stale, having been trapped for a long, long time. We both cough at it, step back and wait. Ziegler peers down inside, the light from his glasses shining into the hole.

'Anybody home?' he asks. A joke. He laughs at himself, and I can't help myself from laughing a little too. It's so ridiculous, for some reason: the thought of anybody living here.

He lets me go down first. The coldness of the metal rungs stings my hands; and it feels so strange to be climbing down this ladder, so like the one on Australia, the touch of it exactly the same. I feel almost the same sense of relief as I put my hands on the bars. Through the light of Ziegler's torch, I see a place that's absolutely identical to a place I once thought of as a sanctuary. Even the carpet is the same. I ease my tired feet from my shoes. My feet stink from having been in them through wet and dry, heat and cold, but I don't care. Better than the smell of the old dust in this place, the stale, tired air. At least a bad smell such as this feels like life. And the softness of the carpet underneath my feet! No stains on this one. I think back to the fight we had on Australia: the blood that must have been spilled. How it must have soaked in. How it would have dried, and the carpet wouldn't have been soft any more.

I lead Ziegler down the corridor to the rooms, and I open their doors. The beds are exactly as I remember them. The mattresses aren't much if you've lived in this city your whole life, but for us they were a revelation. I remember how I couldn't get used to them. How I slept on the floor, sometimes. And here: a kid's bedroom. Animals on the walls. A box of toys, which I open, under the light of Ziegler's torch, and I remember Mae playing with ones exactly like these. I wonder if she's too old for toys now. I pick up a doll with thick brown hair, and I pocket it. She might want it, when I find her. It will remind her of what we went through; of who she was. Then Zeigler and I go to the kitchen. We pass a room that, I'm sure, is the twin of the one that Agatha died in; not the same room, of course, but in the same place, a proxy for it – and then to the room off to the side, with the controls, the computer system; the screen that first showed us how we would get back to Earth. The single button: controls for people who aren't engineers, who weren't specialists or pilots. Everything automated.

'Jesus,' Ziegler says. 'This place is incredible. It belongs in a museum.' He strokes the top of the monitor. 'No dust. The vacuum from the door must have held, all this time.' He sits in the seat in front of the monitor. 'This is where you sat? This is how you brought your people home? Jesus.'

He leans forward and touches the screen, and it comes to life. Not just that, but the lights in the corridor, flicker on. A background hum grows underneath us; a subtle vibration in the floor that I can feel on the soles of my feet.

I know that vibration.

The screen shows the same thing it showed when I first saw the screen on Australia. Icons, rows of them. Things that, at the time, confused me. I didn't know what they were. And now? Now I know. One of them is for cameras, one for files, another for music, another for maps, navigation.

Ziegler stares, and laughs.

'Don't press anything,' I say.

'Just—' he starts to say, but he's reached over and tapped the icon for the map before I can stop him. I swat his hand away but it's too late. The screen's changed and now there's a picture of Earth, greens and blues. 'The map's out of date,' he says, but then he reaches to the image, for something above the image of Earth. He stretches it out.

Above the Earth, in orbit, there are ships. little specks, moving in the sky. One of them reads *Aus*. The other *SA*. Australia and South Africa. Abandoned, left for dead. But there's a third, as well. *TNW*. The New World.

'Huh.' He zooms in as much as he can, making the icons slightly less fuzzy on the screen. 'It says the main New World ship is up there.'

'It can't be,' I say.

'It says that it is. They launched it. It's up there waiting for this thing. They never told anybody.'

'And nobody worked it out?'

He shrugs. 'Not many people bother looking up at the stars any more. If they did, who's to say that they'd even be able to see anything? Anything that's left up there they'd just think was debris. If the lights are off on The New World, if there's nobody home, there's a good chance that we just didn't ever spot it. Or that the people looking don't care. There's a lot of debris up there, from when we were obsessed with space. It didn't take, so we left things in orbit. These are just more detritus.'

'What about South Africa?' I ask. 'Do you think they're—'

'Don't think about that,' he says. 'Chances are they died a long time ago.'

'We didn't.'

'I think you were lucky.'

'Or not,' I say.

'Or not,' he agrees. He stands up and walks into the kitchen. 'That's everything?'

'That's everything.'

'Okay.' He shines his light down the corridor. 'Then all we do now is wait for the morning deliveries to come through the city gate. I'll set an alarm for first light, then we leave, we drive close to the wall, we wait and see what happens. You good with that?'

'What do we do until then?' I ask.

'We sleep,' he says. 'Those beds looked pretty comfortable, from where I'm standing.'

When I shut my eyes, lying here, it's almost as if I am back there again. I can feel the exact same tremble of the ship, the slight tremor of its power – or, it feels the same and I know it isn't, I know it's not even close, but it's comforting, somehow, to think of it as being the same thing – and I can taste the same air, even though the air here is stale and dead. There are no sounds until I close my eyes, and then everything that was on Australia comes back to me: the screams, the cackles, the shouts from the fights.

In those memories, everything is terrifying, unsettling and brutal.

And yet, it's the best, easiest sleep I've had in as long as I can remember.

I wake to darkness. I'm confused, that half-sleep befuddlement where I think that I can feel the shape of Mae in my arms, wrapped up around my body, and I'm holding her, keeping her safe; and then, as I force myself to sit up, the spell is broken and it's only a blanket, a duvet, clutched into the same shape. A comforter, that's the word. Babies have comforters; something to keep the artificial feeling of safety going while they're sleeping alone.

I leave my room – the room, not my room, no matter how much it's the same as where I slept in Australia's version of this ship – and I look down the corridor. In the main room, light. Light coming from the small cockpit. I hear Ziegler in there, muttering to himself.

'Are you okay?' I ask him. He leans back, stares at me. Glasses off, his eyes red and tired. 'Did you sleep?'

'I've slept a lot the last few months,' he says. He yawns as he says it, though, stretching his neck, leaning back. I can see where there's no stubble coming through on the scars on his neck, where the healed skin is still so fresh.

'So what have you been doing?'

'Nothing, really. Reading the files about this ship. And there are documents about the others, as well. Stuff from the archive about these ships, this project. About Australia.'

'What sort of documents?'

'A passenger manifest.' I step into the room and look at the screen. He minimises something, or closes it, really quickly, and then opens another document. 'So, a list of names of everybody who was on Australia originally. Men and women. No children, obviously. Maybe you could find somebody that you're related to?'

'They're dead. There's no point.'

'It might be worth it. Might be worth seeking them out, if anyone's left alive. Rex had somebody alive, right? A relative?' He pauses. He's testing me, I know. He wants to get me to talk about this thing I am definitely not talking about with him. 'Aside from Mae,' he says, and he watches me to see how I react. So I don't. I stay still, and calm.

'I don't know,' I say. And I don't know if I care. They're not who I am now. I don't want to have to explain myself to them. Besides: what's some cousin, a few branches of the family tree removed, going to want to have to do with me?

'Do you know what your surname was before you were on the ship?'

'No,' I say. He smiles sympathetically and closes the document.

'Maybe we find out another time, eh?' He stands up. 'We should go. It's nearly time. Sun's coming up.' We walk down the corridor, towards the hatch. The hatch is still open, the ladder dangling. Up there, there is no mulch of dead bodies, of decomposing flesh. Outside, there's the living city.

'Did you find out anything else?' I ask him.

'No,' he says, but I can tell that he's lying. I wonder what he knows, what he's keeping from me; and I wonder if I even care.

We drive the car out of the fence, same way we came in. It's barely light, and the streets are quiet. Ziegler keeps the car's lights off, and then we're on the road, driving back towards the city gate. He keeps his hands hovering over the manual controls. He's ready. We stop around the corner, and we wait. As soon as something comes through, as soon as there's a truck or a delivery or a coach, something that'll distract the guards, we can make our move and get out of here. We can't wait here for too long: sooner or later, a patrolling bird will spot us, come down for a closer look. Best case, they'll think we're loitering, try and move us along. If we don't, the police will descend. Then hell would break loose again, and we'd be right back where we started.

We don't talk. We keep our eyes on the road. The police are not on alert any more. There's no way that the police will think we'll want to take the car out of the city. They'll think we abandoned it, left on foot; that we're already gone, snuck out somehow.

Or, at least, that's what I'm counting on.

So we wait.

Four hours, and still nothing. And we're both nervous about someone stopping to check on us. We're waiting in a parking bay, but still. There's only so long you can stay still somewhere and not expect to draw attention.

'Who's that?' Ziegler asks. He points at three figures approaching us. Not the usual guards. Police.

Hoyle. I can tell by the way he moves.

'I don't know,' I say. Ziegler doesn't know Hoyle. I don't want to let on. I don't know what he's doing here, how he found us. It doesn't change our plan.

He let me go once. He told me to run. He could have stopped me, but he didn't.

I wonder if he'll try and stop us now.

'What's that noise?' Ziegler asks. We're quiet, totally hushed, and then we both hear it: the rumble of a much larger vehicle than ours, then the echoing noise of the gate, starting to open. Something's coming through. 'Do we wait and see if they're stopped?'

'I don't know.' I haven't done this before. I don't know what to do. 'We wait, maybe. Give it a moment—'

I'm interrupted by the engine of whatever vehicle it is kicking up a gear, and then the nose of a lorry roars onto the street. The body of the truck is articulated like one of those weird insect creatures you see in the outside of the city: small sections knotted together to allow it to snake its way around tight corners. The lorry angles its own way towards us, and I scream, '*Now!*' and Ziegler slams his hand forward and we accelerate, and he steers us up along the inside of the lorry; one side of our car, two wheels, going up onto the pavement, then around it, and the gate starts closing because we're too late. We're not going to make it through. The guards stare at us as we rush towards them; I can feel Hoyle's eyes on us.

He hits the emergency barricade. Thick metal bars rise from the ground, designed to stop anything in their tracks. They're as thick as my body, I reckon, about as tall, and I scream at Zeigler to go faster, because we're nearly clear of them, and we're nearly going to make it out of the gate, just in time.

The rising plinths slam into the underside of the car, throwing the back of the vehicle up into the air.

Even Zeigler screams.

Then we're down again, and there's a crunch, something almighty in the body of the car breaking, but we're still going, still speeding forward. 'Please ensure care,' Gaia says to us, 'Please ensure care,' over and over, and suddenly, unbelievably, we're through, and I look behind us as we clear the gate entirely, as we're out on the road, in the outside world. He's distant but I can still feel Hoyle watching me.

If he started running he could catch us
He doesn't run.
But before this is over he will, I know. And soon.

'Please ensure care,' the car seems to almost sing. We're stopped a few miles out of the city, far enough that the wall is small in the distance 'Please ensure care.'

'I can't shut it up,' Ziegler says. I'm standing next to the car and he's underneath it, lying on his back, towels from the trunk of his car stretched out on the tarmac to protect him from the heat. He's trying to find the source of the damage. The volume isn't working, we can't turn Gaia down, and the car isn't responding to his commands any more. 'Hand me a rock.' He reaches one sweaty palm out, fingers covered in thick grease. I find a suitable stone – sharp edge on one side, blunt lump on the other – and give it to him. The rock is so hot I can barely hold it, and he hisses when it hits his palm, drops it, blows on it, then picks it up again. Amazing how only a day or two away from the heat can trick you, can make you complacent. It's blistering. I can see Ziegler's skin already getting burnt, and his is darker than many others in the city. He's not as used to the sun as I am.

I stand back and listen to the sound of him hammering the rock against metal, trying to fix the voice or break it entirely, I'm not sure which. I suspect that he doesn't know – or care – either. There have been no drones, no cars, no Hoyle chasing us. We're out. We're free.

'Please ensure ca—' the Gaia voice says, and then there's one more almighty blow of the rock, and the voice is gone. Silence. There's no bang or fizz, just the silence of the desert.

Neither of us says anything; and it isn't until I hear the wheeze of Ziegler catching his breath that the quiet is punctured.

We drink the water that he keeps in the car. 'Better to be prepared,' he says, as he hands me a bottle. It tastes stale and warm already, but I don't care much. There are energy bars as well, and we eat those, one each. He lets me pick my flavour first.

'The solar panels'll keep us charged for a few hours,' he says. 'They don't get much use, but still. Enough to get us to – where are we going?'

'Sweet Valley.'

He grins. 'Hang on. Sweet Valley? What sort of place . . .'

'Don't laugh at me,' I say. 'It sounded nice.'

'And is it?' He's laughing. I work out that it's not at me.

And I sort of laugh as well. 'It's awful,' I say, and that just makes us both laugh even more.

'Where's it near?' he asks, when he's pulled himself together.

'Near a place called Scranton.'

'Scranton? You walked to Pennsylvania?'

'We had to.'

'Yeah, well. Thank God we don't.' He looks around at the landscape and wipes sweat from his forehead. The sand and the shrubs and the burn marks on the ground from whatever fire they last had here. 'I haven't been out here in years,' he says. 'Not this far from the city. I came outside to speak with the – what did you call them? Nomads? I spoke with them a few times. They were good for stories, some-times. But this far out? Who lives this far out?'

'I do,' I say.

'We used to come here with my father. Years ago, before it was as bad as it is now. He would want to drive out to the towns, the ones that were abandoned, and see if we could find anything interesting. You wouldn't believe it. Everybody was pretended it was all okay, that it was all just some fun adventure, and it didn't matter that we'd had to abandon whole cities. We were allowed to forget about them. But my father, he wanted to come out and find the things that people had left behind. So that's what we did. And my father would treat it like a holiday. We went to abandoned towns and looked around, took what we wanted. He made it a fun thing for me. I didn't even know it wasn't normal, you know. That was how we bonded.'

'The heat gets so intense you can't be out in it,' I say. 'Not at all.'

He nods. 'That's what I remember.' He pats the roof of the car. 'We should go,' he says. 'The navigation systems aren't working any more, so you'll have to guide me. You think you can remember?'

'I think so.'

He drives, hands held in front of him. The car doesn't adjust for the road, so every now and then we hit a pothole or a crack. The car doesn't know to avoid them any more. When we bounce around, so do his hands, and then my teeth rattle, until we're back and steady.

He puts the radio on. Songs that I don't recognise – not that there are many I do. 'Do you know these?' he asks.

I shake my head.

'They've been around basically longer than anything. I

mean, some of the books have been around longer. Some of the buildings, like the museums. But something about songs, about music, endures.' He turns the radio up. The songs are catchy. They don't sound anything like the music that plays in shops around the city, that you sometimes hear coming from cars. Those things have tweaks in them to alter your moods, to play with your hormone levels, to make you buy things or feel a certain way. The song Ziegler's currently listening to sounds pure, somehow. Clean.

'Songs are like the best stories,' he says softly, reflectively. 'You tell them, over and over, and they endure. We make the same mistakes again and again but somehow we do some things right, as well.'

After I get the hang of it, and Ziegler starts singing, I try to sing along as well. I feel like I know all the words, some- how; as if they're a part of who I am, as a person. As if they're already a part of me.

Morganstown is printed on a sign as we roar past. We don't stop. In the far off, I can make out something: a lump of fabric, like a tent, that stretches the length of a city block. As we pull closer, I can see that it's a single giant cloth, sewn together from what must be hundreds of rags and bits of fabric, a quilted-together mess of different colours.

'Look,' I say, and Ziegler pulls the car over to the side of the road.

'Nomads,' Ziegler says.

He's right. My nomads, maybe.

My heart leaps. One fabric catches my eye. The one that Fiona gave to me, for my tent. I know it.

Then I'm out of the car, running across the sand, scream-ing Fiona's name, hoping that she'll hear me.

A corner of the tent lifts and I see a mass of people inside, huddled together in the shade. Hundreds of eyes stare at me.

Fiona steps out from somewhere in the middle of them.

'I wasn't sure we'd ever see you again,' she says. She's missing an eye. The skin around her socket is dark and wrinkled and scarred, and there's a black pit where the eye once was. I didn't see it happen, but I know when it did. A fist, beating her, over and over. I remember the sound of her crying out in the night, and me not being able to do anything. That fist, forcing her to the ground; the police not letting her stand up again. I look at the others, peering at me from underneath their temporary shade. Broken arms, on some, makeshift slings holding their limbs to their chests. Some legs in splints. Injuries that haven't yet healed, and it's been months. They haven't had the chance.

'I think I was always going to find you,' I say. Fiona comes to me, and she holds out her arms, and I meet them.

It feels good to be held, even if just for a moment.

The nomads have draped their fabric over trees, over rocks, turning it into this shaded haven. We sit in the middle where it's coolest, and we eat bread that they've made: ragged, torn-off chunks, dipped into oils and vinegars, that they share with us. It's heavenly. Ziegler sits at the edge of the tent, scratching his burnt skin as he eats their bread.

'This is really good,' he says, mouth full.

'Made it myself. Well, we did.' She gestures around. 'A load of us.'

'Well, yeah. It's good bread. You could sell this in the city.'

'We definitely couldn't,' Fiona replies. She turns to Ziegler and stares at him, like she's sizing him up. 'You used to come out, speak with some of us. Lots of questions, if I remember correctly.'

'You do.'

'And you look as though you've been through the wars yourself. You'll fit right in here, should you want to.'

'I'm sorry,' I say. I can't help but glance at where her eye should be. 'It was my fault. I brought them to you.'

'Don't be stupid,' she replies.

'They were looking for me, and Rex.'

'No they weren't. They were looking to cause some damage. You didn't really matter.'

'I could have given myself up.'

'You think we'd have let you do that? We'd have fought to get you back, and then God knows where we'd be. Not here.' She takes my hands, squeezes them. I can feel the slickness of oil on hers, giving a softness to her skin. 'Nobody died. We're all okay. Wounds heal. That's just a part of life. And think: we got one heck of a story out of it. Next time somebody comes to us, a stranger who's lost, we'll have this tale to tell them.'

'I'm still sorry.'

'And that's why we wouldn't have let them take you.' She looks over at the road. Squints. I wonder if she's used to looking through the one eye yet. I wonder if she'll ever get used to it. 'So where are you off to?'

'A place called Sweet Valley, somewhere near Scranton. Chan's set up shop there, sounds like.' Ziegler's taken another piece of bread. Usually, he's got manners but now he speaks with his mouth full. My mother told me to never do that. Even with all the madness on Australia, she still told me that it was rude.

'We've heard stories about Scranton. Don't go there,' Fiona says. 'I mean, I don't know if they're true. But it doesn't sound like somewhere you'd want to visit.'

'We won't,' I say. I can tell that Ziegler wants to ask more about Scranton – he's always after the story – but I don't care. I want to move forward. That's all that matters now.

'You found your little girl?'

'I know where she is.' That's not the same thing. I know where she is and I know what her name is, now. And I know who her mother is, even if her mother doesn't.

'So you're going to get her back?' I nod. 'Finally. That'll feel good, I reckon. It's a relief, to put people where they're meant to be. That's what my life feels like it's about, now. Finding someplace for us to settle.'

'Have you been moving since you left Washington?'

'We couldn't stay there. Some of the young 'uns were worried that the police would come back, maybe even bring the services, take the kids away.'

'Kids?' The crowd parts, and there's a woman. I know her. I recognise her from somewhere. One kid, who's a toddler, clings to her leg, sucking its thumb. Another baby, wrapped in pale yellow cloth, hugs tight to her breast. 'You didn't have any children with you when I left.'

'Usually, we tend to skew a little older. But then, we met Judith, just after we left Washington. Found her wandering around a small town right outside, as we passed through.

And there's been word of mouth, I reckon. We've got families coming here, now. Some of the people you brought to us, they're having children. Starting anew.'

There weren't children with the nomads before. There were stories – about the services descending, just as they'd done to those who lived in the docks – but it was also so hot. I got the impression people who were pregnant and had nowhere else to go wanted to be anywhere but in the blazing heat. 'We need somewhere where we won't be threatened. Maybe it won't be a better life than we had outside Washington. But we have to try. We keep moving, hoping we'll find it.'

'We heard what happened to you,' Judith says to me. 'That they changed you at a prison, or tried to. I don't want to be changed. I don't want anybody to change. When June was born, they took her away,' she touches the head of her elder daughter, who's tugging Judith's skirts. The little girl looks up at me and her face splits into this amazing smile that's absolutely pure and totally perfect.

'I was living rough,' Judith says, 'and people said I should have muted her. I didn't. I said, I can't, because she shouldn't have to change. So I left. I came here. I found Fiona.'

As she speaks I remember how I know her. I saw her in the docks. I tried to help her, because the services were coming for her and her baby. The baby – that was June, then an infant – was crying, and I wanted to give Judith a hand. Help her out.

I don't say anything. It doesn't matter if she remembers me or not.

'Fiona told us your story,' Judith says. 'So, we know it, and we've decided that we don't want that. We don't want to be put in a spaceship and sent away, or have to go to prison. If being free means living out here, finding something else – something new – that's better than the alternative.' The baby pulls on her hair, aimless hands tugging it over her face, and she smiles. 'I nearly lost my girl. I would have lost her.'

'We'll need somewhere to go, when I've got Mae,' I tell Fiona. 'A new home. Can we come with you?'

'We'd be devastated if you didn't,' she tells me.

She hugs me again, like that's a full stop to the conversation. And all I can think, right here and now, is that these people are my future.

We make our apologies. It's time to leave. There are things we have to do, and of course Fiona understand. 'Time waits for no one,' she says.

'I want to find you. When this is over,' I tell her.

'I can't tell you where we'll be. That's the life we've got. We only move at night – it's too hot to do anything in the days – but then you'll be able to see us, when we've planted ourselves. We'll find each other again, I'm sure.'

That's not good enough for me. 'Can we make a plan? Somewhere we can meet? I'll help find somewhere for us all to live.'

'We'll stumble on that place,' she says, gesturing at the other nomads. 'We'll know it when we find it. It's just about being in the right place at the right time.'

I'm always in the wrong place at the wrong time. It's as if the structure to the world is different for me, the rules aren't the same.

'Listen: we'll find each other, I swear,' Fiona says, gently. 'You're going to Sweet Valley. The way your friend tells it, that's not too far from here.'

'Mae's in New York. We have to go and get her from there.' Fiona raises her eyebrows, then laughs, then the laugh breaks into a cough in the dryness of this air we're breathing.

'Jesus. Right. Big city, that. I don't want to make assumptions, but I'm guessing you're not going to like it very much.' She stands up, and starts to walk with us towards the car. Out in the sunlight, her hand shades her remaining eye. 'That's been through the wars as well, I reckon,' she says, indicating the car. 'Oh, wait.' She turns back, shouts with her hands cupped to her mouth. 'Somebody bring out the crossbow!' Judith runs out, baby still strapped to her, Rex's crossbow in her hand. 'We found that,' Fiona says. 'Figured your friend might want it. It's not been used. None of us fancied it.'

'She'll be very grateful,' I say.

'You'll find us,' she says. Then, 'But maybe we're not the important thing. You'll find what you need. That's the first. Get closure. When you're ready to stop running, then find us.'

She doesn't hug me goodbye. She and Judith turn and walk back to the tent. I watch Fiona lift the fabric, letting Judith in first, and then she ducks through herself and the flap drops shut.

'You ready?' Ziegler asks.

9

'Wait here,' I tell Ziegler. We're parked the next road over from the house that I've been sharing with Rex and Jonah. The car looks like hell, like it's been through hell. 'I need to tell them that you're here.' That's not really true. I need to see them first by myself. I want to. I want to tell them that I'm okay. After that comes dealing with Ziegler; they've heard my stories about him, they know that he betrayed me. They'll question my decision to trust him, to bring him here. Rex doesn't take kindly to people who she thinks are a risk. He could betray me again, she'll say. I won't say that Rex could, as well.

Or that I could betray her.

Ziegler doesn't protest. He shrugs and stays seated in the relative coolness of the car while I walk down the street towards the house. The sign that reads *Sweet Valley* is planted in the hard dusty soil, a sign that we saw the first time we arrived here: beaten and battered, but otherwise intact. I think it's the only thing in this town that survived whole.

'Rex?' I shout. 'Jonah?' But there's no reply. There's only the hint of movement from the shrubbery, as whatever lives in there scurries away from the sound of my voice. 'I'm back.' There's silence throughout the town. I hear the faint whistle of the wind rattling through the derelict buildings. I search for them, shouting their names. I go to our house, the three bedrooms we took as our own. It's the best kept place here, and while it's a wreck, it's our wreck. That's what I said, when we found it. It's ours, for as long as we want it. Everything looks in order: the beds are intact, sheets pulled over the mattresses, coverings over the termite holes in the walls and windows, to stop the light getting in. There are bottles here, of water that's been drawn from the river, turned so hot under a beam of light that I can barely stand to touch them, let alone think about drinking it.

I was quite happy drinking the bottled water when I was here last. I've been spoilt by being away from this place. It's amazing how quickly you forget; or, maybe, adapt, to something different. Somewhere else.

There's a bang. A huge, roaring noise, a crack like thunder that comes through the air and seems to echo everywhere, ricocheting off every wall. A gunshot. It must be. I run out into the street. No idea where it came from. No idea who was shooting, or what – who – they were shooting at. Could be nomads – the dangerous sort, the sort you don't want to mess with. Could be police, but didn't sound it. One shot, and it was too ragged. Police weapons are neater, quieter, made to sound like they're safe. This was angry.

'What was that?' Ziegler asks. 'Are you okay?' He's out of the car, running towards me. Out of breath again. He's not cut out for this kind of life.

233

'I told you to wait for me,' I say, but I don't mind. I'm worried about Rex and Jonah, grateful to have Ziegler here with me. He peers into the distance, down the street in front of us.

'Look,' he says. He points.

Somebody's walking towards us. I can't make them out entirely, with the sun behind them. I squint, and step closer. They're carrying something in one hand, hanging at their side. A gun, I'd guess. Long and dark, glinting in the light.

And they're dragging something big in their other hand. They're struggling with the dead weight – it's a body, I can see now, from the shape of it, being pulled by its leg or arm.

Rex is the one walking towards us. I didn't recognise her; she's shaved her head again, taken the hair right back down to her scalp, like it was on Australia, and she's got new clothes. She must have found them somewhere. She's dressed all in black apart from a white vest – or, what would have been white, but it's smeared in blood. She's got new boots as well.

I don't see Jonah.

I can't tell what she's dragging, but it's big and heavy and dead.

She stands still when she sees us. Raises the gun. Points it at us.

'Who is he?' she asks.

'Ziegler. You met him.'

A pause. 'With the throat?'

'Yes,' I say. 'He helped me. Where's Jonah?'

She looks behind her, at the body. I still can't see it exactly, not with the sheen of the blood reflecting in the sun.

'Oh no,' I whisper, under my breath, wondering why she's so casual.

Then he appears. He's walking behind her, dragging something himself, and I can see it now: some sort of animal, big and dead, its head lolling on the cracked road behind him as he walks.

As I get closer, I see them better. Goats. Sparse fur on their bodies, skin poking through in bald patches. They don't look like they were in the best health. 'We've been hunting all over,' Rex says as I get close enough. 'Jonah felt stronger. Less sick. I found these,' she holds the gun out in front of her. It's like something from the museum, old and grey, the metal tarnished, the wood on the handle chipped and scarred. 'I thought I should teach him how to shoot.'

I hug her. Jonah stands back and watches. I hold her until she drops the gun and holds me as well; even if it's only for the briefest moment.

After Rex has taken her knife to one of the goats, skinned and gutted it, we build a fire in the middle of the road and drag benches from a house opposite, and we stick poles torn from a metal fence through the carcass and prop it up over the flames. We turn the roasting carcass every so often, and sit around and smell the meat as it cooks, listening to the sizzle of fat as it drips into the flames. It's so hot around the fire, but I don't care. The smell of the food alone is enough to make me want to stay here. Rex doesn't ask what happened in the city – not why I'm with Ziegler, not why I don't seem to have the medicine that I told her Jonah

235

needed, not why there's a car parked down the road – so I don't tell her anything about it. It's easier for both of us.

I smile at Jonah, who smiles back. He seems peaceful. His neck is covered, so I can't see if it's healed yet, but he seems better. Stronger. When the meat is ready, Ziegler asks for a knife and I hand him mine; and he carves chunks of meat off the body, puts them onto plates that are nearly intact, found inside a cupboard; and we eat them with potatoes that we've roasted at the base of the fire, which are charred to black but soft inside. When we're done, Rex takes the bones and throws them behind the house – 'for the vultures,' she explains, to pick the meat off them – and Jonah takes my hand as I tell Ziegler I'll show him where he can sleep.

Jonah's fingers, warm, twined through mine. He says, 'I'm glad you're back.'

I say, 'So am I.' But I mean that I'm glad *he's* back; that this Jonah, smiling at me, reminds me more of the person I knew on Australia than the one I left here in Sweet Valley. His hand squeezes mine.

'There's a house with a fine room this way,' I say to Ziegler, and I pull myself away from Jonah. Not now. There's time enough for us when I've got Mae back. When this is all done. Ziegler stands, and we start to walk towards it.

'Are we staying here?' Jonah asks.

'No,' I say. 'We have to leave tomorrow.'

'To go where?' Rex asks.

'New York.' She looks blank. It means nothing to her. 'It's a city to the east. That's where Mae is. We've got the car, so it won't take us long to get there. A few hours. We should leave at first light.'

'Fine,' Rex says. She and Jonah stay seated, not talking. Their frames are silhouetted in the fire as we walk away.

'Do you think she knows?' Ziegler asks me.

'I don't know,' I say.

'Are you going to tell her?'

'I don't know.' He's silent. 'Do you think I should?'

'Depends what you want to get out of it,' he says. 'Depends on what you think's going to give you the best outcome.' He looks up at the house I've led him to. The second-best preserved building, which is still a crumbling wreck. 'There's no place like home,' he says, and he walks up the steps to the porch.

The wood breaks as he treads on it, the stair giving way underneath his weight, and he falls in up to his shin, collapses back onto the ground.

He's not hurt. He laughs. As I pull him out, he asks, 'Are you sure you want me coming along with you?'

'I'm sure,' I tell him. 'Positive.'

I lie in my own bed and think about how quickly my story could end.

There is a route to Mae, assuming we get into the city easily enough, and then I find her, and then she recognises me and she asks me to take her with me. So I do. I am pursued, hunted by the police, Mae's new mother unflinching in her own desire to get her back – but we'll escape. I won't stop running. We'll run forever.

I don't know how Rex fits into it. That time she took Mae from me, back on Australia, might have just been a coincidence. Mae could have been any child; it was what she represented to me, Rex's enemy, that mattered, not who she actually was.

There's a knock on my door; the soft sound of the hinges as it opens. It's Jonah, his frame visible in the darkness.

'Are you asleep?' he asks.

'Come here,' I whisper. He lies down next to me, and I wrap my arms around him. I can feel a bandage around his neck, or a scarf; something that's there to protect the skin. He winces when my arm touches it, as I pull him close, but then the pain is gone, and he's comfortable.

His arms wrap around me, and I can only think how warm he feels and how much I missed this feeling.

'You're okay,' I say, and I only hope that he believes it.

Rex stands by the car, examining it. Ziegler shouts for it to unlock, but it doesn't respond.

'I forgot that I broke the systems,' he says. He goes over, touches it, and the lights blink on. The door slides open, and Rex peers inside.

'It's small,' she says.

'This size car is called a compact,' Ziegler tells her.

'I do not see how we all fit inside it.'

'It'll be cosy.'

'I do not like small spaces,' Rex says. 'You should have owned a bigger car.'

'Bigger ones cost more money. And this is efficient!'

'Were you poor?' she asks.

'No, I wasn't. Are you? I don't see you—'

'Ziegler?' I shout, interrupting them. He's exasperated. He walks over to me, out of Rex's earshot.

'She takes some time to get used to,' I say.

'She's—'

'She takes some time.' That's it. I get back to putting the things I want to take with me into a bag. I don't have much. The doll I took for Mae; a copy of *The Girl Who Fell to Earth*. Even now, as I flick through the pages, I wonder if any of it was real. Sometimes it's as though it's only ever been this book, and my memories are just a half-remembered dream; like when you wake from a nightmare and you don't know for those precious first few moments if what you're remembering is reality or not. If those things actually did happen, and the world you're living in is drastically different to the world you went to bed in. The first line: *My story begins on the day I killed my mother.*

Almost like it happened, but not quite.

Still, it's sort of my story. It comes with me.

From the trunk of the car I pick up Rex's crossbow. I hand it to her and she takes it, smiling. She doesn't say anything; she puts the sling over her body, and it hangs close to her. Then she runs to the side of the road, comes back with a gun in each hand.

'Do we need these?' she asks. She's holding them by the barrel. They look so ineffective, so basic. No fizzing lights or special technology. Strange to think the damage that they can do. 'We have ammunition.'

'Bring them,' I say. I don't want to have to use them, but

we might. Still, 'No killing, though. Seriously, Rex. I don't want anybody to die for what we're going to do.' In reality, it's about Mae. In her new life, there'll be no killing. There'll be no fighting, no violence. There will be peace; the best thing I can give her.

I don't want Mae to live the same life I have. If we have to kill to get to her, to rescue her, to free her, she's going to know. She's going to feel it, and she's going to regret it. I can't have that. In order to start over, I have to start now. No more killing.

Rex throws the guns into the car. 'If I shoot somebody and they die, that's not my fault.'

'You know how much damage they cause,' I say. 'You know. You saw what happened when you shot the goat. Aim for the legs, if you have to use them on people. But try not to. If they shoot at you, then you shoot back. Try to take them out of the game. Go for augments, if you can. No killing.'

'Hoyle,' Rex says, growling his name under her breath. Still.

'No killing,' I reiterate. Not just for my sake, or for Mae's, but for Rex's as well. I know that Rex has killed, but killing changes you.

I still dream of the face of Barney, the worker from the archives.

I still see him falling down that stairwell.

Everybody who dies, I see them falling. Even if that's not how their life ended.

I don't want that for Rex any more than I want it for myself. For Mae.

Never again.

'I've got a present for you,' Rex says, walking up to me, her voice brusque. She's not good at approaching in any way that suggests calm and tranquillity. 'Come with me,' she says, and I follow her, back to the house we've vacated.

There's a small cardboard box on the floor. She stands by it, picks it up, holds it out to me.

'For me?' I take it from her and open it. I don't know what to expect. I don't know what Rex would think was a present. Perhaps it's a head. Hoyle's head, in a box.

I open it, and it's a pair of shoes. Nothing like Rex's. Sneakers, they're called. Fancy ones. Pure black, apart from this flash of white on the side.

'Where did you get these?' I ask.

'I went to Scranton, while you were gone.' She pauses, weighing up what to tell me. 'It was a bad place,' she says. 'I went because I had to get new boots. I found these too.' I make a note to ask her about Scranton later. That story will keep.

I sit down and pull my old shoes off. There's that familiar smell, the sweat of having spent days and days on my feet. The shoes I take off aren't yet falling apart, but that's not the point. I push my feet into the new ones, and they're immediately comfortable and soft, and they fit perfectly. Better than the others. The sore parts of my feet don't feel nearly as sore as they did only moment ago. The blisters aren't rubbing. 'I thought that you would like them,' Rex tells me.

I stand up and hug her. Her arms hug me back.

I have to tell her about Mae. I have to. I just don't know how to.

*　　*　　*

We pull away from the town. Crammed into the tiny space of Ziegler's car. Rex sits next to Ziegler, and I sit next to Jonah. He takes my hand. Rex stares out of the window, and I think about what comes next: the three of us – and Ziegler, if he wants – living somewhere else, taking the nomads somewhere we won't be found, won't be caught, and I can help Jonah overcome what he's going through, find himself again, and Rex and I can raise Mae, taking it equally, two mothers being better than one; or, maybe she won't want to, and she can be Mae's Agatha, older and wiser and more distant, but the one who'll show Mae what to do, how to survive if anything should ever happen to me.

We're in the desert, and we're on the road, and we're off, away.

Finally, in the distance, I can see New York. The towers on the islands.

I can see the end on the horizon: because Mae's there, somewhere. And come what may, I am going to get her back.

PART
THREE

PART
THREE

10

We can see the buildings stretching up towards the sun, like trees craning for sunlight. They're all different shapes and sizes; some pointed at the top, some flattened off, each unique to the last, except for one thing: all of them have so much glass. They all reflect and shine, the haze of the day a halo around their edges.

The road diverges into many. Only the central lane has been maintained, the tarmac replaced. I think about how it was once my job to work the roads, back in Pine City. It was only ever used for deliveries and convoys. Nobody drives out of the cities any more.

We look for somewhere to stop, so that we can make our way closer on foot. We don't know whether the police will be looking for us specifically, but it's better, safer not to risk it. The car will do nothing but draw attention, given how beaten up it is now. We take our things, put the guns in the bags, abandon the car. Ziegler tells it he'll come back for it. He's so alone in the world that he wants to reassure his car that he won't forget about it. He won't leave it behind.

He pats it on the hood. 'I'll see you soon,' he says.

I feel so sad, that this goodbye means something to him. And I tell myself that when this is done, I'm going to make things right for him, help him out, if I can.

There's no gate to get into New York. No fence, no wall. The city is six islands surrounded by water. At the edge, on the mainland, there are the bits of the city that were here before it was turned into islands. Ziegler points these out as we walk towards their encampments. He says they're run down now, inhabited by people who can't afford to live on the islands, like the nomads outside Washington. They're doing their best, trying to make it a home, but they don't have the coolant the rest of the city does. Even at this distance from the islands, the towers of the buildings are mammoth. I can't really understand them, what they'll be like close up. In Washington, the wall limits how high the buildings can be built. Here, there's no limit to what can be erected. Ziegler points out struts around the buildings, nearly as big as some of the towers themselves. He calls them buttresses; supports.

'Of course,' he says, 'they won't help if something happens. If there's a quake or a tidal wave or whatever, maybe they'll be fine. But we only protect against the things we've survived before. If something new happened . . .' He mimes the tower falling with his arm, makes the noise of it crashing down into the ground. 'Think about how many people live in one of those things. I wouldn't dare live that high. I wouldn't risk it. But it's status. The higher you live, the more money you have.' I think about how we've lived much higher, Rex and Jonah and myself.

We keep walking. The city gets closer, but somehow still seems like it's the same distance away; it's just becoming clearer in our vision, the towers bigger, the lights brighter. It's like we can never really reach it.

Rex walks with Ziegler, in front of Jonah and me. I see them talking about something – or, Ziegler talking. Rex doesn't say anything, merely nods her head every so often at whatever it is he's saying, and he points and gesticulates while she keeps her hands to her side, fingers clutched into fists. That's her resting position. She's not preparing for anything, it's just how she is. Always ready.

So Jonah and I walk together, in step. Our feet tread the ground at the side of this smaller road – tarmac that has been left untouched since this part of the city was abandoned. I can see the faintest traces of lines drawn down the middle of it in a faded yellow paint; and I can read the chaos of history in it: how the road was once perfectly straight and now it's bent and jagged, twisted into a tangle. Jonah watches my new shoes as I walk, while I watch his boots. A shared moment, as we both do the same thing.

'I want to help you,' he says, from nowhere. 'And Mae.'

'Do you remember her?'

'I think so.' He describes her to me, and how I met her, and what she was like, but the words he uses aren't his own. They're mine. They're how I talk about her. These aren't his memories, but I'm not going to tell him that. I don't want him to feel like he doesn't remember, like he's lost that part of himself, too.

'Are you worried about her?' he asks.

'No,' I say. But that's another lie. I can't keep lying. 'I'm worried she'll have forgotten me. I'm worried that she will have been changed by them.' That's true.

'Like they tried to change me?' I can hear the spit of anger in his voice.

'They tried to change all of us,' I remind him. 'They tried to make us all forget who we were. Everything we knew.'

'She'll remember you,' he tells me.

'She might not.'

'I did.' He smiles at me. That's when I realise that he's making himself smile. It's forced, awkward. I can see the difference. He's always had the same thing that gives him away when he's lying. His hand, creeping to his neck, to feel the wreckage of skin there. 'I remembered you. I knew that you were a good person. I think when you feel something about a person, it's stronger than memories. It's embedded deeper.'

'Maybe,' I say. Maybe that's true. I've thought about this a lot: why Gibson found it harder to get me to accept the new future – the new reality – that he was offering. And why Rex rejected it outright. I think we'd been through too much to simply erase everything; and maybe there was even a part of us that didn't want to have it gone. The past that makes us who we are. Maybe sometimes it can't be taken away without destroying the person entirely. We're the sum of our memories.

I don't hear my mother's voice as much any more. But I remember her. I remember how it felt when I was with her; a feeling, a perfect feeling. I can never lose that. And Rex? She was the same. She had a purpose; a reason to fight. She might not have liked herself, but she was formed by scars and violence. That made her who she was.

Jonah's different. His childhood was a different sort of bad. He never knew who he was, not entirely. His childhood was one of penance, of being forced to harm himself, to punish himself; and as much as it made him who he is, he simply didn't want to be that person. When I met him on the ship, he wanted a way out of that old life. He was healing and soothing the sick because it was right, not because he was told to by the testimony books he was forced to read. He did it because he believed in it. When he helped me, it was because he wanted to. He wanted out of his own past, not to be trapped by it. Gibson's techniques offered him a way past the life he had lived, and he took it. How could he not?

I think now, his desire to be punished for what he's done, for who he is? That's the old Jonah coming through. The true Jonah. Torn between wanting to forget, and wanting to embrace.

'She'll remember you. She will. She'll know what you did for her.' Jonah takes my hand. We're both too hot to hold hands, sweaty palms and tired arms, but still I hold on; there's something so reassuring about the feel of his touch. 'I remember.'

Yes. I took him away from people who, in their own twisted way, cared about him. I took him to fights, got him injured, got his life threatened, brought him to a place where he's a stranger, a convict, unwelcomed and unwanted; I had him nearly killed by somebody who, long ago, would have willingly done it of her own accord. And now he's expected to trust her. And now here we are, trudging towards a city we don't know, where we don't know what will happen; and all so I can fulfill a promise I made to a little girl who might not even remember me.

Be selfish, my mother's voice says to me from nowhere at all, and I know that I am. I absolutely am.

The first part of getting into New York proper involves a boat. There's a bridge further along, but Ziegler thinks the boat will be easier. The water is less likely to be patrolled. It's mostly only used by tourists and visitors, come to visit from the other big cities. Ziegler says it's expensive to be a tourist; more than most people will ever manage.

At the cleanest part of this stretch of mainland, there's a crowd waiting at what looks like a dock. Ziegler points towards them. 'We hide in that group of people. They only scan you when you're getting off the boats, and there are other ways past the gates, then. We can get down onto the beaches, make our way along there. Climb up another time.' As we wait, I look back at the buildings behind us. There are people at the windows. At a glance, these blocks and towers look abandoned, but people live here. They make do, and they do what they can. The buildings remind me of the run-down towers in the poorer parts of Washington – like where Dave, the guard that I—

I stop myself. I have to stop thinking about that. I have to move on.

Or, maybe I don't. Maybe being haunted is better than forgetting.

Not being able to move past it might mean I've learned from it.

The streets are grimy, the concrete buildings a filthy grey from the dirt that's piled up on them, and there's lichen growing on them as well, the hard green moss that says you're somewhere too wet and salty, too pounded by water over time. Like the rocks on the beach; like the outside of the Washington wall. I can almost feel how slimy they must be to touch.

'When that group gets onto the next boat, we go with them. The cameras are obvious, or they were. Just don't look at them. Keep your heads down, or stare out to the water. You see a bird, look away. Don't look at anybody with a device, so no one catches an image of us. We just have to get into the city without being spotted, and then . . .' He shrugs.

'Are there cameras in New York?'

'More than anywhere else. We won't be able to avoid them once we're on the island.'

'So what will happen then?' Rex asks. 'They will come for us.' Her augmented hand twitches to her bag, to the gun that's hidden inside. That's what it's like when she's priming herself for a fight: already halfway to acting.

'I don't know. They're on Gaia, but it's not the same police force. Depends if they think we're a big enough threat. They've got their own crimes to deal with; we might be further down the list here than we were in Washington.'

'Three of us are wanted for crimes. One of us was going to be killed, and the other was going to do the killing. I'm fairly certain they'll see us as a threat,' I say.

He smiles. 'So they'll try and catch us. In which case, I suggest you do what you do best,' he tells me. 'I suggest you run.'

'Heads down,' Ziegler says. The boat is coming across the water towards us. There's a cold wind coming off the water. It's not hard to act like we want to huddle together when that wind hits. I tell myself that I know one thing I want, when I finally find out where I should live, stay, settle down, make my home: I want to know what the temperature is going to be. I want to have it be the right climate, all the time. I miss that aspect of Australia. It might not have been perfect, but at least the temperature never surprised you.

The boat is a glossy, glassy oblong, thin and sharp at the ends. It is enclosed by a glass shell all the way around, and the central part has been ballasted in some way, so that whilst the boat bobs about in the water and the whole thing rocks as the waves crash up against it, the people standing inside remain absolutely level, the deck is perfectly balanced. The boat pulls up to the dock next to the jetty that protrudes across the water, a thin walkway of black metal that feels altogether too familiar; it reminds me of the walkways on Australia. I hold the railing while we shuffle onto the vessel, the rocking of the boat making me unsteady on my feet.

We stand with the crowd inside the boat, staring at our hands or our feet or each other, not making eye contact with the strangers and trying to be as inconspicuous as possible. Rex pulls her augmented arm close to her body to hide it; Jonah reaches for my hand and I take it. I'm working so hard not to be noticed that I don't realise when we start to move out into the water, and then across towards the island of Manhattan.

On the glass around us, holos begin. A smiling woman, either not real at all or so augmented she's barely got any of her original skin left, starts talking. 'Once a solitary island off the coast of the mainland, Manhattan is now six smaller islands, supported and joined by a network of bridges. Flood barriers have been created to protect the city from the water. These are ready to rise up like walls at a moment's notice.' There are pictures and videos to accompany what she's saying, but her voice is so bland I find it hard to pay attention. I lean in towards Ziegler.

'Do you know where we're going?' I ask, my voice barely more than a whisper.

He nods. 'The Prestige isn't exactly hard to miss.' He cranes his neck, peers over the heads of the tourists, out the windows towards New York. 'Look,' he says, pointing. My eyes follow his finger to a cluster of buildings right in the middle of the first island, so close together they remind me of fingers on one hand, reaching upwards. They're so close it's as though they're almost leaning on each other for support. 'The one with the halo.' It takes me a second to notice what he's talking about, and then, finally, against the sole cloud in the distant sky, I see it: a ring of yellowed light, spinning around the top of one of the buildings. 'The building doesn't have its name on it, or at least it didn't. That's how you know it's expensive to live there. The residents don't advertise. The building is aspirational, because everyone knows it's the most expensive place to live. Everyone wants to live under the halo.'

As we draw closer I can just about make out the darkened pockmarks of windows on the Prestige; some lit, some darkened. Rows and rows of them. I wonder how big the apartments are. I wonder what sort of space they've put Mae in. Is it a room, like she had in the final days of Australia? Are there a variety of animals on the wallpaper, toys in a box? Or is this more like being at Pine City, under Gibson's watch: tiny, bare grey rooms?

I reach into my pack and touch the doll that I brought for her. Under my thumb I can feel its hair, soft and lifelike; and I think about lying in bed with Mae, telling her that everything will be alright, stroking her hair, and her going to sleep, calmed by my touch.

'We won't have long after we get off the boat. They might not see us, but they might. There won't be alarms that we can hear, because they won't want any panic, so we have to move and keep moving even if we don't think there's anything wrong,' Ziegler says, softly. 'If I need to, I'll give myself up.'

'What?' I ask, shocked.

'I haven't done anything actually wrong. Worst case scenario, they have to let me go.'

'Worst case scenario, they say you were helping me.'

'Which I was,' he says. 'But you didn't force me to. You might think you did, but you didn't. I did this because I wanted to. And I'm not sure I've done anything wrong enough to land me in permanent trouble.' He smiles, but it's sadder than I'd like it to be. 'Besides, I've lived a life worth writing about now, haven't I?' He looks back at the shore. 'The city's quiet this time of day, so we can move fast. There won't be crowds, or not so many of them. You just keep moving. Get to the building, then work out how to get up to where Mae is. What floor are they on?'

'130.'

'Okay,' he chuckles, 'so you're not taking the stairs. You get in, try to use the elevator. It'll be Gaia-run if you're unlucky, private systems if everything's going in your favour. Some of the moneyed places keep their facilities off the grid, because rich people like that. It'll mean tighter security than Gaia, but also more human. Humans can be worked with. They can be compromised, coerced.' I can't help but notice that he glances at Rex as he says that. 'The elevators won't run the entire height of the building. That's a stability thing. Likely they'll go up to the halfway point, so floor ninety? Something like that. Then there'll be another elevator. Get to the right floor, find the door to the apartment.' Again, to Rex. 'The more expensive floors might have private security. If there are guards up there, you'll have to deal with them. They're not just going to let you in.'

'Prepare for docking,' the holo intones. 'We hope you enjoyed your trip.'

'Okay,' Ziegler says, 'get yourselves ready,' and we hear the clang of the boat docking and then Ziegler's face drops – I'm shocked by how drastically and dramatically it changes – and I glance at what he's seeing: the black of a mass of uniforms that stand, poised, waiting for us on the dock. I don't know what's going on, if it's an ambush. Unless—

'Get down,' I shout, as the fizz of a striker breaks the silence, and one of the other passengers – one that I'd assumed was a mother, larger calves that are pure muscle, like she's walked a lot in her life – spins, holding the weapon out in front of her. She aims for me, first, and then, upon seeing me duck, turns her attention to Rex, who hasn't flinched. Rex's augmented hand shoots up and grabs the striker in mid-air. The blue electrics course down her arm. I see the pistons work, these delicate analog mechanics trying to apply the pressure that she's telling them to. The striker goes dark, the light extinguished, and then cracks in two. The pieces fall to our feet.

Rex is blindingly efficient. I don't even have to fight, not here. I save myself and watch her plough through everyone else on the boat, everyone I thought was just an innocent stranger. The lack of kids in the group should have been a giveaway. She grabs the one who tried to strike her, hauls her easily over her head, throws her into the other passengers. The boat doors haven't opened yet. I watch as the pilot and crew run down the jetty, away from the water's edge.

Then I see him. Hoyle. He's standing in the middle of the jetty walkway, and he's waiting for us. I know that he won't let me go a third time. He can't, especially after I've done what I'm here to do.

'Break the windows!' I yell at Rex, so she grabs another of the fake tourists and slams him hard against the glass. Up close, the force of the impact makes cracks spread out like cobwebs. Not enough. This stuff's designed to withstand waves pounding against it. It needs more effort put in. I grab another of the ambushers, hurl him away from Rex. He thuds to the ground, cracks his head – helmeted, but still, the noise of it makes me wince and feel sick and worried and somehow elated, all at once – and I pick up his striker. I flash it on, feel the vibration of it in my hand, through my palm. I ignore the other attackers, because Rex has got them taken care of – they're matching blows, but she's unstoppable, unflinching, wiping blood from the corner of her mouth with one hand while she cracks their noses with the other – and I start whacking at the crack that's appeared with the striker. We need an exit, but I'm not making fast enough progress.

I glance over at Jonah and Ziegler. 'Find something to help!' I shout. Jonah looks as though he's unprepared for battle. He doesn't look scared, he's just letting us take care of the problem, understanding that we're better than he is at fighting now. Either we've done it more, or he's done it less. He's not cowering, but wary, hesitant. I think about shouting at him to fight, but I don't. It's easier to let Jonah be who he is. I don't want to make him go back to what he was on Australia.

Ziegler's terrified. Arms raised, fingers splayed, ineffectual, so I shout it again. 'Find anything! We need to smash the glass!' I hear the sound of the door being forced open. If they get it all the way open we'll be delivered straight into the hands of the police and Hoyle.

'Chan,' Rex says, out of nowhere. She's silent when she fights, usually, but at my name I snap my attention back to her, and I see her struggling. The one she's fighting is stronger than she expected. He's avoiding Rex's augmented hand, swaying and swooping like he's trained. A boxer, maybe. He kicks out, plants his boot into the side of Rex's head, and she crumbles in a way that looks like she's actually been really hurt.

I throw myself at his back, my legs around his waist, hands on his head, and I haul his helmet up and off, then jab my fist into his temple, over and over, until he goes down.

Done.

I'm about to shout at Jonah again, to break the window, when there's a bang so loud it makes everything in the boat ring at the same time, chime with the echoes of it; or maybe the noise is just in my head, but it's deafening and painful, and it seems to play with my vision as well, almost dizzying me. The glass shatters. I look over at Jonah, gun in his hand pointed at the glass, the end smoking.

'Yes?' he asks.

'Yes,' I say. 'We need to get out of here.' I look through the hole he's made. It's a short fall. The water's choppy. I hope that they can both swim. I check Rex is alright.

'I can stay,' Ziegler shouts, 'I can delay them.' But that's ridiculous. There are too many of them. They're in armour, so they won't be able to swim. We can, though. Fleeing this way is our only choice.

'Are you okay?' Rex tries to stand. I help her to her feet. 'Lean on me,' I say. There's blood running down her face, a cut deep into her cheek.

'I'll be fine,' she says, even as she's shaking her head that the opposite is true. She doesn't feel fine.

'We have to go now,' I yell. I glance back at the doors and they're fully opened. Through them I can see the police advancing down the jetty, coming fast, stacked tight, in a formation that leaves us no option. Hoyle is behind them.

We lock eyes. This is it.

'Chan,' Jonah says, peering down the side of the boat, into the water.

'Jump,' I shout. 'Jump!'

'Chan!' Jonah screams.

'What?' I look at the thing Jonah's showing me. A lever on the side of the boat. *Pull this for emergency lifeboat. It will automatically inflate. Fireproof. Engine capacity . . .* He doesn't ask if he should. He grabs the lever, yanks, and the thing unfolds from a panel I didn't see in the side of the boat like a piece of clothing that's been bundled into a ball, turning itself flat on the water. He climbs down onto it, and I see how rough the water is, how unsteady his footing is, but he reaches up and takes my hand, helps me down; and then Ziegler, then Rex. 'Hold on,' he says, and he hits the button that makes the boat start, and we're pulling away as the police pile into the boat we just left, as they stare at us, shout for us to come back, as if that's something we'd do.

I can only assume that these police haven't had much experience in the way of combat. I don't give up. I fight or they run. There's no other option. There never is.

This smaller boat moves faster than I thought possible. Behind us, the police release the birds. Suddenly things feel very familiar: we've been here before, I know – tearing away from police, our guns primed to shoot them down – but that time we had everywhere to run to, really. Every possibility. Here, there's a finite amount we can do. And we need to get onto the island. We need to get to Mae.

Above the city, the halo of The Prestige swirls.

'Give me a gun,' I say, and Rex passes me one.

'It only works up close,' she says, so we both aim, and we wait for the birds that are tearing through the sky to come up close to us, so close that they're priming their whips, that same blue electricity fluttering through their innards, ready to reel us in.

'Fire,' I say, and we hear the roar in our ears, and we see them clatter and crumble out of the sky, smashing into the water, lost in our wake.

'Here,' I say. We're under a bridge, a sharp green colour across our heads, throwing us into the shade. There are people camped out beneath the struts that anchor it to the land. This part of the city seems like one of the few places that the buildings aren't jutting up against the water. The people under the bridge stare at us as we pull up onto the sand. They're scavenging, I realise, pulling things out of the water, shaking them off. Debris, rubbish. They're not looking for food. They're all wearing the same clothes. A uniform. They're keeping this place clean.

'We need to move,' I say.

'The police aren't following us,' Jonah says, but Ziegler knows that's not the point. Just because we can't see them doesn't mean they're not there.

'They'll be setting up guards anywhere they think we could plausibly have made it off the water. They'll be watching the streets, locking down as much of the city as they can. Makes sense to pay attention to the bridges as well. If they don't know we're here already, they will soon.'

'Take everything, leave the boat,' I snap. I sound angry, I know, but I don't care. I am. We have to go. And there are too many of us. Four people is too many. Would have been easier if it was just me, I think. If I'd refused to let them come with me, maybe we wouldn't have been attacked. If I'd been a little bit more selfish—

'They're coming,' Ziegler shouts, as we clamber onto the road. I swing my gaze down to where he's looking: a car in the distance, screaming towards us, lights flashing. So we run across the road, darting through the traffic. Ziegler is behind the rest of us, panting and tired, but I can't stop. I can't wait and check that he's alright. If he falls behind, I have to leave him.

'This way,' he shouts, directing us off the road, down an alley between buildings. It's too narrow for cars. Everybody here is dressed well, but there isn't the time to take them all in, to really notice them; and they stare at us, because we're the only people running. They look at us now, and some of them point at me, at Rex.

'The girl who fell to Earth!' I hear, and I think, I should stop for an autograph, and I almost laugh at the thought; I would, if I didn't need the breath. 'Hey,' the same voice shouts. They'll tell the police. It'll help them find us faster.

I can't care about that right now. I can't care about the people, about the cameras, about Gaia or the birds or the sound of the sirens. Now, there's nothing but running, and what happens when we get to The Prestige? Do they follow us up? Do they chase me, until my hands are on Mae's, and then drag me away from her? Is that how my story actually ends? Doesn't matter. Just keep going. Keep running.

We don't stop. There's no moment to catch our breath, no time to hesitate.

Ziegler trips, falls.

Jonah grabs him, drags him to his feet. Then they're moving again, the two of them now far behind us, and getting further away.

Through more alleyways, down more streets. More cars to avoid, more people staring, pointing. Through the sirens and calls from onlookers who stop to gawp I can hear the flapping of birds that I can't see, can't stop to look at, can't even pause to think about. Rex's feet, slamming against the pavement even harder than mine. I can hear the sound of them echoing around the buildings as we go. Hear her panting.

A bird, low flying, comes at us from a side street. It slams into her, right into Rex's side. She reaches out, grabs it, crushes it with her augmented hand as if it's nothing, and then she discards it. But there are more coming. Not up in the sky, not like they usually do, but screaming along the streets. Aimed directly at us, to try and knock us down, corral us some way. And they will, they will. There are too many of them.

I stop, wait for Jonah. 'Take him,' meaning Ziegler, 'and go the other way.' I want them to go away from The Prestige. 'Stay safe, and lose the birds, and we'll meet you under the bridge when we have Mae,' I gasp.

He nods.

I kiss him. It's like our first kiss, back on Australia. It feels like it felt then; that, somehow, it could be our last as well. But no: this time, it's different. It's not passionate; it's knowing. It's sharing, and understanding. It's hoping.

Then he's gone, and we're gone, and I know that they are slower than us, that they might be caught. *Be selfish*, my mother says in my head. *Don't die.*

I am being selfish. If they're caught, they will be taken away. Ziegler will survive. Maybe they'll change him. Maybe.

Jonah will . . . I don't know. I can't think about that, not now.

I have to be selfish. I have to rescue Mae.

As we get closer to The Prestige, avenues turn into alleyways that feed into plazas, paved plateaus of concrete and trees and manicured bushes and vines that cling to the bases of the structures as though this place is some strange jungle. Ziegler said that the people who rebuilt New York wanted it to feel, as much as it could, like a part of the old world; so they filled it with plants. Rex and I drop to a walk as soon as we lose sight of the police, as soon as there's no sign of the birds. The sirens still scream in the distance, but we can't see anything near us.

The halo is a beacon, so we walk towards it, heads down apart from when we glance up, to check we're still on the right track. The buildings become more luxurious as we go: red carpets spill down to the street from their fronts like walkways, people in uniforms – long black coats, hats – waiting to hold doors for visitors and inhabitants, taking bags from hands and bowing to everyone. The people who live in these buildings are dressed in furs and tech-augmented outfits that seem to shift and change as they walk, altering their forms and colours and finishes as we gaze, astonished. I've never seen anything like it.

And then Rex stops mid-tread, as if there's something underneath her shoe, about to be crushed. She catches my gaze and then stares upwards, and I follow her eyes.

'This must be the place,' she says.

The Prestige. There's no sign. The door is a brass and glass revolving portal. Through it, I can see people wearing strange smock uniforms that remind me of the outfits that the Pale Women wore: flowing to the ground like coat-dresses. The staff all have the same expression on their faces: a half smile. Unaggressive, unintimidating, welcoming but blank.

I stand stupidly outside, gawking, because I don't quite know what to do next. Mae is inside here. God knows what's happening to her. This place is so hostile to strangers, so unwelcoming. Everything is so strange.

I promised her I would come for her.

I promised her I would save her.

I step up towards the door, and the doorman pulls it open for me, and, finally, I step inside.

11

'Do you want me to call up to somebody?' the woman behind the counter asks. She's got the same friendly half-smile as the rest of the staff, the same blank expression. And yet, she's the least threatening person I can imagine. 'You're here to visit an apartment?' Her accent isn't American. It's something else, more like Alala's was, but polished to a shine. A perfect version of it.

'Yes,' I say, but then I don't know how to continue. I don't want to say it. I feel like, if I say it, it becomes more tangible. She doesn't have a surname. Never did. 'Blackwood.' The word almost hurts as it comes out of my mouth. 'Mae Blackwood.'

The woman nods. There's no screen in front of her, no holo or Gaia interface. Instead, her eyes flicker, augments like I've never seen before going to work as she does whatever it is she's doing.

'The Blackwood family are listed as being at home,' she tells me. 'Are they expecting you?'

Wait. 'I want to surprise them,' I say. She tilts her head, awaiting clarification. 'I'm from out of town. They don't know that I'm here.'

'I'm afraid that won't be possible,' she says. I can sense Rex behind me getting antsy, moving from foot to foot. They aren't scanning us here, or maybe they are. Maybe she is. Maybe she's trying to delay us.

I can feel bile in my throat. My pulse in my chest, my neck, my ears, a thumping inside my skull.

'Call them,' I say. 'Tell them that we're here from the Services. The adoption team. We're here to check on how Mae's getting on.' My voice sounds shaky, unconvincing, even to me. I don't have identification, I don't have anything.

She speaks, quietly. There's no headset that I can see, and I can't hear her.

Run, I think. Get out of here. This is going to get worse before—

'They said to go right up,' she tells me. She smiles. 'We need to check, you understand. We can't have strangers in the building.' I sag with relief. It worked. I don't know how, but it worked.

She indicates the elevators, down to one side. Deep red carpet – the colour of blood, I think, the actual colour of actual real life blood – and mirrored walls that seem to be intentionally tarnished, like time and the elements have beaten the sheen off them, and plants that seem to grow from the wall itself, organically organised intrusions into the space. 'I've programmed the elevator for the correct floor. You'll change on floor 89, and then it's left down the corridor, second door facing the atrium.'

'Thank you,' I say, remembering a distant lesson from my mother about manners.

I walk to the elevator, Rex behind me. It's waiting for us.

We step inside – it's carpeted, and I wonder what it would feel like between my toes, because it looks so expensive, so clean and so new – and the doors slide shut behind us, a satisfying swoosh as they close. And we rise. I can feel the strange sensation of being whisked upwards in the pit of my belly, momentarily replacing my fear. But only for a moment.

Music plays as the elevator moves. It's a version of one of the songs that Ziegler played in his car. There are no lyrics: just a twinkling version of the original, turned into something else. The same, but different.

Rex pats her hand on her thigh, in time to the music. She doesn't know she's doing it, but I notice.

I'll tell her about Mae when we're done. When we're somewhere else, settled down; when we can share the responsibility. That's when I'll tell her the truth.

We reach floor 89. When the doors open my jaw drops. We're facing a garden that's open to the sky above. Even though the sun is beaming down, it's cool here. There's a wind, but it's soft and gentle. Trees stretch up from the garden into the sky, vines climbing and swinging between them, and there's a stream bubbling along between the roots, lined with soft grasses and flowers and places to sit. People are using the space, as well: a woman with a holo beaming up from her lap, gesticulating as she speaks into it; two kids – twins, I'd guess, a boy and a girl, their hair identical, their clothes nearly so – playing something, chasing each other around a tree; a man and a woman sitting on a rug on the grass, eating food from a hamper, drinking something from glasses that sparkle in the light. It's so much like the arboretum on Australia, or what the arboretum could have been, that it makes me ache: it's tranquil and cared for. It feels safe and good.

It feels like a sign.

There's no ceiling. The apartments are ranged along walls that face the arboretum, one on top of the other, impossibly high up. Even looking up at them makes me feel slightly dizzy.

'We should go,' Rex says.

We walk down a pathway between trees to a second bank of elevators, these fronted with glass. As we stand inside them, as the glass doors close and we start to rise – and as that music comes back, a reprise – I watch the arboretum (the atrium, the woman on the reception desk called it) – drop away below us; and I think, I have seen this before. It's like Australia, but not.

A soft bell in the lift dings. Behind us, doors we didn't notice open out onto a corridor. It's lighter than the ground floor; one wall is a window, looking out onto the sky above, the garden below. Doors on the other side of the corridor are made of a polished dark metal, like some sort of mirror.

'This is it,' I say. We walk down the corridor slowly. Me first, Rex behind me. I take my time. I look in the mirrored doors: will Mae recognise me? How much have I changed? I can't even remember. My clothes are different. My hair has grown out, so I pull it back, away from my face. I tie it off. I'm still me.

She'll know me, I tell myself. She'll know me, and—

And she'll know Rex. The last time Mae saw Rex, Rex

had taken her. She was going to hurt her, probably. Maybe. She was trying to kill me.

She might not want to see Rex.

'You should wait here,' I say. 'Just until I've . . .'

'She'll be scared of me,' Rex says.

'Yes.'

She nods. 'I'll stay here.'

She sits on the floor, propped against the wall. I hear the rattle of her bag, as the guns clink against each other. We might need those as we leave here. Whatever happens, I know leaving here won't be easy.

And then I'm there. The door to the apartment where Mae lives now.

I stand outside the door. I feel exhausted, and sad, and excited. Everything is a muddle that I can't even begin to understand. I push it aside.

I reach for the door to knock on it, to let Mae know that I'm here. As I stretch out my fist, the door opens, as if someone's expecting me.

'Hello Chan,' Hoyle says. His hand is on my throat faster than I can react, hauling me backwards, pushing back, till I hit the window opposite, so fast I can barely tell what's happening; and then I'm slammed into the ground. He starts spitting words at me, reading me my rights, like he does with other prisoners. 'You shouldn't have come here,' he says, when he's done, pressing my face to the carpet. 'I gave you a chance to run. You should have taken it. You should have—'

Something thwacks into Hoyle's body, makes him flinch and loosen his grip on me. My vision's blurry from the shock of his grip, but I can see Rex coming towards us, crossbow aimed at him. She fires bolts off, and Hoyle swats them away. She fires two quickly: one for him to catch, the other to hit. It thumps into his eye with a dull thud, and then she charges, runs as fast as she can; she leaps, augmented fist raised, brings it down into that eye, breaking the bolt in half, driving the point further into his head. There's a fizz of electronics, of something failing.

He screams, grabs for Rex, spins her off him. She flails; is thrown into the glass wall that overlooks the atrium, and then Hoyle starts punching. Aggressive, hard, punishing her. Still gasping I creep forward, push myself to my feet, and then I'm behind Hoyle. I grab his arm, to stop him hitting Rex, startling him, and she sees her opportunity and takes it. Goes right back to work on his eye. The fake skin starts peeling away, and I can see no light from the augment – I didn't realise the eyes were backlit until this moment – and as I watch, she hits him until the metal of his face starts to crumple.

I look down at the atrium. Police. Only a few of them, clearing the grass. Those twins being led away. The police are armed.

Rex kicks Hoyle's legs out from underneath him, and he falls to his knees. Her boot slams into his head, and he topples backwards onto the floor. A sliver of the metal bone in his cheek falls out. His jaw's hanging badly. He scrambles backwards, to the wall, using it to get to his feet. He stares at Rex. 'You stupid bitc—' She charges at him.

'Go!' she yells to me. So I do. This is what she came here to do. To help me get Mae away from this place. Now it's my turn to act.

I stagger towards the door, and behind me I can hear the

sound of their fighting; their fists driving into each other. They slam their bodies against the walls, the floor.

I slam my hand against the door to Mae's apartment. Three beats, and it rocks open. A woman. She's older. My mother's age, probably, when she—

Behind me, the sound of the fighting intensifies. I can't worry about that. I can't. I turn to the woman. Her eyes are huge, terrified. She cringes away from me, cowering. She's wearing a thick white jumper, light blue trousers. No shoes. Immaculately augmented toenails, matching fingernails. Hair in a modern style that looks like she spends a lot of money on it. 'What do you want?' she asks.

I glance around the apartment. High ceilings. Shelves of books, like Ziegler and Valona both had. I know that's a kind of mark of wealth in this world, to have the actual thing here rather than relying on a holo. A piano in the corner, and a beautiful one at that. Art hangs on the walls: not adaptable holo frames, but real art. Gilt gold frames. Certificates hanging on the walls. Everything in here is physical, tangible. It's as if it's been taken from a time before, like the artefacts that they have in the museum.

I step forward through the doorway; and she steps back, hands out in front of her, wary of me. Afraid. There's a certificate on the wall closest to me. Marina. Dr Marina Blackwood. Next to it, a photograph of her and her husband, I'd assume, when she was much younger. I could say to her, We're the same. We've both lost somebody we loved. They died the same way. Please don't fight me. Let me do what I have to do. Next to it, another photograph: the two of them again, but her husband looks sickly here, his hair thinned and white, his cheeks sallow; and between them, grin on her face, teeth missing, is Mae.

From behind me, there's a smash. The sound of glass breaking. I look back to the hallway and watch as Rex drives her shoulder into Hoyle's gut, forces him to the window overlooking the atrium, again and again and again, and then it finally gives way, and he starts to fall.

He grabs her. He pulls her down with him. As I watch, the two vanish through the broken window, to fall into the atrium forty floors below.

'Mom?' Mae asks. Her voice. Her voice.

Oh God I remember her voice so perfectly, like it never left me.

I whip around and there she is, behind the woman. Held back, the woman's arm stretched out, keeping her safe.

I see her; and she sees me.

In that moment, a kind of echo rings through my head.

I remember how she sat on the edge of the walkway the day we met, however many floors up. I don't know, exactly, not any more. We were high. And around her, there was nothing: no chaos, no violence. A patch of quiet solitude on the ship, where people left her alone. I didn't know what happened to her before that, and I didn't know – how could I? – what would happen to her after it. I knew that she was in danger, or I thought that she was. I was searching for Bess's son. But I found her throwing dolls down into the pit. As much as anything is fated, that was. Her dolls fell; and I fell. She rescued me just as I rescued her.

Her smile, when she trusted me.

I reach into my pack, bring the doll out that I took from The New World's lander. I don't ask if she remembers me, because she has to.

I hold the doll out in front of me. 'Do you remember this?' I ask Mae. She's wearing clothes that look like smaller versions of the ones that Blackwood wears. White top, blue denim trousers. A necklace around her neck, and the pendant is a bird. It's shaped to look like a real bird, that is. I crouch down, so that I'm eye-level with her. I've done that before. She'll remember it, just as I do. Only, she's taller now. It's not quite the same. 'You know me,' I say.

'You're Chan,' she says, her voice soft, uncertain

There are tears in my eyes. When did I last cry? When my mother died? I don't think so. She told me to not cry.

Don't cry. Don't die.

'You remember me?' Repeating myself, but I don't know what else to say. No, I do. The doll. 'You remember this?'

'Get away from her!' Blackwood says, her voice strangely muted, and Mae buries her face in the woman's body, so that she can't see me. So that I can't see her.

'You used to throw them off the—'

'Don't talk to her,' Blackwood says, but I don't know who she's aiming that towards. Me or Mae. Willing us both into silence.

'I'm taking Mae with me,' I say. I look at Mae. 'You remember what I promised you? That I would come back for you. This place, it's not for us. It's different, and we're

273

different. We didn't grow up here, and they don't want us here. They don't.'

I reach for Mae. She pulls her body tight away from me, but I get my hand on her arm. She'll thank me for this, I know. She's not made for here. She's made for—

'Don't take her!' Blackwood screams. She swats at my arm, at my face, my chest, to get me to let go. But I won't. I don't. 'She's my daughter!'

'She isn't,' I say, because I know who her mother is, and it's not this woman, not here and now. It's not. I pull Mae, and she cries as I drag her toward me.

I want to ask her why she cares so much about this woman. What Blackwood's done for her; what she's given her.

'I'm taking her,' I say. My voice is measured and calm and logical, because I am those things. I promised her. I have fought to get here. This is—

Be selfish.

This is me being selfish.

I pull her to me, and Mae thumps into my body, and I wrap my arms around her. She calls for Blackwood – 'Mom! Mom!' – and I think about how we never used that word on the ship, because we used Mother, or Mummy. Blackwood tries to hit me, but her blow is soft as I pick Mae up, shush her, head for the door. Blackwood comes behind me, howling something: that Mae is her daughter, that she loves her. So do I, though. I love her as well. She was there for me, and I was there for her. And she's the reason why I've done everything I have done on this planet; she's what it's all been about.

Blackwell spins me, slaps me, and then my cheek stings, so I push her back, and she stumbles, hard. Trips over her own feet, slips on the ground, on the polished floor. Her head smacks into the shelves behind her. The picture of the three of them falls, the glass smashing on the ground next to her.

Blackwood blinks at me, astonished. Her eyes. I hadn't noticed them before. They're the same colour as Mae's. I wonder if anybody else even knows that she's adopted.

I turn for the door again, holding Mae as she screams for her mother – for Blackwood – and Blackwood calls for her, begs me. Don't take her. She's my baby. She's all I've got left.

Standing in front of me is Rex. She looks like hell. I don't know how she saved herself – if she fell and somehow survived, or if she clung on to something, pulled herself up – but she did. I can hear the rattle of her lungs as she heaves air into them, as if each breath takes incredible effort from her. Her skin is beaten and bruised.

'Put her down,' she says. How long has she been listening to this?

'She's coming with us,' I say.

'No.' Rex stands firm. I can see she's hurting, that even keeping herself this steadfast against me – feet locked in place, the same width as her shoulders, fists balling up – is costing her. 'Put her down.'

I let Mae go, set her onto the floor. She runs to Blackwood. Rex is distracted, so I take a swing, and—

She's ready for it. She reaches up and grabs my hand from the middle of the air; she stops me before it can connect. She uses the augmented one, the one that can grab drones from the air, crush metal girders, that never tires and doesn't feel pain – and she squeezes my hand so hard that I can't even think for a second.

'She stays,' Rex says. 'Don't do this. You do not want to do this.'

'I do,' I say through the pain, 'I do.'

'No,' she says. 'This is not you.'

I shut my eyes. I think about who I am, who Rex thinks that I am. I imagine how a fight between us could end, in that moment: her robotic fingers wrapped casually and snugly around my fist. In my imagination she doesn't just squeeze, she crushes until I hear the crunch of bones. I jab at her again with my other hand, twice, three times, right into her face, into her eye socket, and I feel it crunch, give way beneath my fist, and then her eye is full of blood, and she's screaming as she holds onto me; then we keep going, beating each other until there's blood everywhere, and Mae and Blackwood are screaming; until we're not standing any more. We're equally matched because she's broken and I'm driven; and we're on the floor, beating each other until we pass out, or kill each other, and then whatever happens, happens: our bodies, taken by Hoyle and his police, or gasping their last, or something other than the fight.

I am not that person.

I want Mae to be happy. I want her to have the life I never did, that my mother tried to give me. If she could, she would have sacrificed everything. She would have given it all up for me. She did in the end. She might have had more time. I don't know. I'll never know. She sacrificed herself so that I could have something better; something that would be more than survival.

I have to do the same, for Mae.

Be selfish.

'I have to tell you something,' I say to Rex.

'You don't,' she replies.

'It's important.' She needs to know. I can't tell if saying what I'm going to say is the right thing to do, or a last ditch attempt to get Mae. I don't know. I can't feel what's right, inside me. 'Mae is—'

She reaches up her hand. Her augmented, gnarled hand. The metal dented from all the fighting.

'Please don't say it,' she says.

Her eyes are wet.

I've never seen her cry.

She knows. We both know.

Nothing more needs to be said between us.

She loosens her fingers. My wrist sings with pain, and I know there are broken bones, heavy bruises, but I'll be fine. I'll heal.

All of this will heal.

The woman that Mae calls her mother stares at us, shocked and unable, or unwilling, to move; and the way that Mae clings to her, the girl's tears dripping onto the woman's skin, makes me ache inside. A deep ache inside of me. You can tell how much Mae cares for this other woman because it's the same way that I cared when my mother died, and then when Agatha died. It doesn't matter who gave birth to you. What matters is who is there for you. Who's doing the right thing, trying to make your life better. There's nothing insidious here in this apartment. Nothing that would suggest a hard life, a life of pain and struggling. Blackwood hasn't taken away who Mae was, or still is: she's left her exactly the same, but added to her. She's made her a better person. More complete. I wonder what Mae would have been, had she stayed with me. Had I saved her from that first landing on this planet, when the services took her away. We would have been on the run together. And think of the things that I did, the things that I saw. Living in a place that was barely better than the ship really: Alala tricking me, using me, and the drugs and the violence and the biting cold, and the services coming to steal babies who—

No. Not steal. Judith told me. She told me what they did. The children were taken, given to families who would give them a home that their parents couldn't.

Like Blackwood with Mae. A piano, clothes, education. Love. A life without violence and fear.

Mae is better here than she would be with me. It hurts to say that, but this is how she gets the life she should have. She deserves to be happy.

Really, truthfully, her being happy is what we both deserve.

I look at Mae. At Blackwood.

'I'm sorry,' I say. 'This is where you belong.' I can feel the wetness in my own eyes. They used to say, on the ship, that crying was a weakness. Crying's when they heard you, when they got you. But it's not a weakness here. Here, it's truth. It's power. 'You're doing well, and you'll do better. Just . . .' My mother's voice. *Be selfish. Don't die.* Advice for another place, and another time. Not what Mae needs. 'Just, be yourself.'

That seems enough.

I turn away from her. I didn't get what I wanted. Or, I did. I wanted her to be safe, her to be happy. I wanted Mae to have a future.

So did Rex.

And so she does.

We stagger out of the apartment, back towards the elevator, and I don't know what happens now. We go somewhere; we find somewhere. We leave this city, and—

'Chan.' Hoyle's voice. Something's broken about it, like the part that makes the sound is twisted and it comes out garbled. I didn't know he was augmented even in his voice box. I don't know how those parts of the body work. I press the button and listen to the whirr of the building's internal mechanisms, and we wait. 'You have to come with me.' The voice stretches itself, like it's slowing down, then speeding up. He doesn't have control over it. He's made his way up here again. He looks *destroyed*. His skin is hanging off limbs that look, in turn, as if they're barely even attached. The eye that was blinded isn't lit; that whole side of his head has caved in, collapsed in on itself. He doesn't want to fight. He couldn't survive another fight. Neither of us can.

'You fell,' Rex says.

'You let me fall.' His voice is so hard to listen to; barely even human.

Rex smirks. Through the pain, through all that's happened, she smirks.

'I'm leaving,' I say to Hoyle. 'Don't worry. You'll never see me again.'

'You've done too much damage. I told you to leave. I told you to hide.'

'You knew that was never going to happen.'

'Somebody needs to be held accountable for the way you've acted, the things that you've done,' he says. 'This city – this world – won't stop hunting you. It needs somebody to blame. Somebody to punish.' His face twists itself into what might have been pity, were the skin there, were his eyes able to emote. 'I'm going to have to take you in.' He looks at Rex. 'Both of you.'

I glance at Rex. She looks towards the glass doors of the elevator.

I shut my eyes.

Okay.

I hear Rex's arm flex, draw back. She slams her fist into the doors as hard as she can manage. The first time she hits them, the blood on her knuckles makes a print on the glass; the second time, the glass splinters; and then the third, it shatters, the shards falling harmlessly away down the shaft, and Hoyle is screaming at us to stop, trying to run towards us, not full pelt, but fast enough. So Rex grabs me, and she steps through the hole she's made. She takes hold of the cable that runs down the middle of the shaft and then there's a breathless moment where we're suspended in mid-air and then we fall, Rex holding me with one arm and using her mechanical hand to hold the cable, to slow our descent down the shaft. We're plummeting, but safe, and she grits her teeth – I wonder if she can feel the cable burn her augmented hand; if pain still works that way for her – until we land with a horrible thud on the roof of the elevator. It's heading up still, and quickly, so she squats, grabs hold of the other cable, the one that's working the mechanism.

'Hold on,' she says, and yanks the cable. I've never seen her strain so much, but the metal rope buckles and twists and contorts, and the elevator lurches to a stop. I look down and there's a hatch.

Of course there is. There's always a hatch.

I heave it open, and there's nobody inside, so I jump in, landing hard, trying to brace myself with my bad hand, but I forgot how useless it is, the damage that Rex has caused. Still: some things are more important than pain. I hear something crunch above me, the twang of the cable giving way, snapping, and then Rex is inside the elevator next to me, and we're falling, so fast it's ridiculous, so fast I don't know how we'll survive the impact.

We will. We always do.

Neither of us screams. We've both fallen far, far too many times to start screaming now. I feel her take my hand instead.

We wait.

There's a screech of brakes, and the elevator shudders as we're slowed and finally stop. I hear a terrible grinding of gears, but we're fine. The doors don't open, so Rex starts to prise them open with her hand.

Something heavy lands on top of the elevator. A part of the machinery, falling after us? I look up. Two dents in the ceiling. The imprints of shoes, of feet.

Hoyle.

'Run,' I shout, and Rex yanks the doors open, and we're fast out of the elevator, stumbling into the soft grass of the atrium; but so is he. He tackles her, slams her into the ground, presses his metallic knee into the small of her back, and she howls.

'Leave!' she screams.

But that's not what I do.

I grab a handful of soil from the ground of the atrium, hurl it at Hoyle's face, hoping that the open, metal, mechanical parts of him don't like grit. He swipes to get it off him, lets go of Rex, falters. I kick him in the chest, hard as I can manage.

He staggers, and Rex is up, and she grabs his left arm at the shoulder. She gets purchase with her other hand, digging her fingers into where his arms join with his shoulders, and then she pulls; they both strain, but her augment beats his.

It was stupid of them to give her the best they had, the best they'd made.

His mechanical arm comes off clean in a hiss of sparks and tearing cables. He falls back, shocked, leaving himself vulnerable, wide open.

Rex swings the arm like it's a club, slams it into his head, the metal of the biceps colliding with his chin, taking his jaw nearly off. It hangs on by threads of metal and silvery wires.

His body hisses as he slumps to the ground. Not dead, but out.

At the other end of the atrium the second elevators, the ones to the ground floor, open. All of them open at the same time, the ping noise that signifies their arrival chiming out. The music from inside can be heard from here, and the doors stay fixed open as the police – their armour and masks glinting and with their weapons raised – pour out, rushing towards us. So many strikers, blue lights flaring. So many guns, muzzles pointed.

'No shooting,' Hoyle says, pushing himself up, trying to get to his feet. 'Take them alive,' but Rex hits him hard in the mouth. His jaw clatters to the ground next to him, and he collapses again. The police circle, take aim. They're ready.

We go at them, and we go hard. We hurl ourselves like we're weapons. We kick and we punch, and we ignore the sounds of bones breaking, of helmets cracking, of weapons getting destroyed. Rex crushes the guns when she can, bending them into uselessness. I grab a striker, and we both lure some of them into the stream that runs through the gardens; then I ignite it and drop it as we jump out, electrocuting three of them.

We count how many are left, shouting the numbers out loud. They don't stand a chance. We might be beaten up and bruised and in pain, but we've fought tougher than this lot. We've done this before and we've survived. We're nearly at the doors to the elevators now.

I kick one into a tree and he hits his head. He tries to crawl away, so Rex boots him in his face. Another gets both arms broken – the crunch is disgusting, and I'm used to disgusting – as we both take him at exactly the same time. Another, we toss through the glass at the side of the atrium, but he doesn't fall all the way through; he's left hanging, his head through, his body limp. There's no blood; he'll live. They'll all live. Rex knows better than to kill them now. She knows, just as I do, that it's not worth it.

It's not what we do.

We're down to three when Hoyle makes it to his feet. We don't notice at first. It's not until I hear the click of a gun, feel the metal pressed to my temple, that I know. His voice is low and quiet, in my ear.

'I didn't want this,' he says. I freeze. I don't think he'll kill me, but I don't want to test him. Maybe Hoyle thinks he could live with himself if he did kill me. I don't want to find out. 'I didn't want to hurt you, Chan. I really liked you. I thought that we had something.' The other police are done. Rex is mopping them up: one choked unconscious, another tethered with his own whip, the last crawling away from Rex as she prowls towards him.

'I liked you too,' I say. 'I just had to do what I had to do.'

'I knew how it would go. I knew how it would end, and that I would have to stop you,' he says.

Rex has finished with the police. She's not looking at us yet. She's breathing, her shoulders rising and falling as she stares at the floor, at the carnage.

Hoyle follows my gaze. 'She's done,' he says. 'Damaged beyond repair. But you're not. That's why I left you out of what we had her do. I wanted you to be better, Chan. All I could do to help fix Rex was physical, give her that arm. But you? I knew I could fix you in a whole other way.'

'I don't need fixing,' I say. 'I'm not broken.'

'You could have had what I had. You could have lived in the city, been a part of everything, fitted in.'

'I've never fitted in,' I tell him. I say it loud enough that Rex can hear. 'I don't belong here and I never have. It's fine to act like I could change, to make myself fit. I could change, Rex could change—

'Rex can never change,' he says. 'And I suppose I was wrong about you.'

'You were,' I tell him. He means it like it's an insult, but it's not. 'This isn't my home. It was never going to work.'

'You should have let us have our way with her,' he says, looking at Rex. 'Let us make her the killer she is. All she's ever going to be. She's a waste, and she's made you the same. Now? You're broken like her. Ruined.'

Rex stares back at him. She rolls her shoulders, cricks her neck, and walks towards us. I can feel the gun pressed to my temple, but I don't care. I know what will happen, and so does she.

He waves the gun at her, then puts it back on me. 'Stop!' he shouts, but she doesn't. She is, as much as anybody can be, unstoppable. I can almost feel the thud of her boots on the ground, even though I know that's impossible; but each step seems to shake the floor we're standing on, shake the whole damn building. 'I will kill her,' Hoyle says to Rex, but she is only six feet away now, and I know that he won't. We both know that he won't. If he were a killer he wouldn't have needed Rex.

When she's close enough that I can feel her breath on me, she reaches for the weapon, pulls it from his hand, tosses it to one side. 'Nobody dies here,' she says. He takes his hands off me and I step away. Rex stands in front of him and he quivers. He's weak, scared. He can't do anything.

Rex looks back at me and he takes a swing. He means to punch her, but she grabs his fist. He struggles; he's too weak.

But she lets him go. She stops holding him and he drops his arm to his side, seemingly exhausted, perfectly still. Defeated.

We walk away. 'Neither of us is ruined,' I say, as we go. 'We're fine.' I take Rex's hand. I feel the wetness of the blood on it but I don't care. We step into the elevator, and the music plays as I press the button for the ground floor. There's something triumphant to it: the sounds joyous and happy, even as we know that this isn't quite over, not yet.

We run out of the building. The police have reinforcements, cars blocking the road. Birds in the sky, but there are also the civilians in the streets, on the sidewalks, going about their lives. 'Head for where it's busy,' I shout. We dash through streets full of people, yelling at them to get out of our way, and they do. The police follow on foot; the birds ripping through the sky, trying to keep an eye on us. We race through alleyways, darting into shops that have visible exits, doubling back on ourselves, winding our way towards where we need to be. And we're running, but the birds keep up, and the police keep coming, pursuing us, and—

A car screeches to a halt in front of us. Big and black. Wheels visible, like the derelict cars you find lying at the roadside in the abandoned towns, only this one isn't rusted to a shell, this one has its paint and it's clean and like new. A door opens. Inside it, there's Valona.

'Don't stare,' she says. 'Ziegler informed me where you were going.' The inside of the car is perfectly white, so abnormally close to the shade of her skin that if she stopped moving, shut her eyes and her mouth, I think she might fade into the background altogether. 'I told him you'd need me.' She looks out of the window, her hands gripping a wheel – a physical wheel, not like the hack-job in Ziegler's car – and yells at us to get in, which we do, because I have no reason not to, and being with her – even if this is a trick, somehow, another betrayal – is better than being out there; and she slams the car into reverse, peers behind her, swerves and manoeuvres and then grabs the handle at her side and pulls it upwards, and we spin as she turns the wheel, the tyres screeching, as the engine screams and we race away.

My guts rise into my throat. If ever there was going to be a time to scream, this is it; but if I open my mouth, I worry about what will come out.

'Strap yourselves in,' she says, and there are buckles which we fasten around our waists while she accelerates, smashing the wheels and the controls around in a way I don't understand but that makes the car swing around corners, swerve around other cars, go up on sidewalks and down alleyways. The police cars – manned, unmanned, it's hard to tell – pursue, ramming things out of the way. They really want to catch up with us. 'Where's Ziegler?' she yells.

'I thought he called you!' I yell back. I have to shout over the sound of the car. It's so much louder than Ziegler's, louder than any other car I've been in. It's more like the roar of the bike we stole that time. Or even, like the noise that came from the engine that kept Australia going. A rumble; a growl. I love it, in a way.

'He did, but he was on the move. He said that you'd know where to meet him.' She sounds impatient. He'll owe her for this, I know.

'They're waiting for us under a bridge. Where we came in.'

'What colour bridge?'

'What?'

'Red or green or black or yellow? What colour bridge, there are a lot of bridges.'

'Green,' Rex says, and Valona nods, swings the car around another corner. The car growls as she makes us go faster. 'Who is this?' Rex asks.

'Valona. Valona, meet Rex,' I say.

Valona nods, a smile curled up on her lips. 'The one who you tried to kill?'

'That's her,' I reply.

I notice that Rex is smiling too. Only slightly, but it's there, for a moment.

Valona drives the car off the road, smashing through a fence, and then we're down onto sand, racing along the beach at the edge of the island. There's no sign of Ziegler and Jonah at first, and I wonder if they were caught, lost. Then, from the shadows under the bridge, two figures wave. Hiding in the freezing cold, icy water lapping around their ankles; the only place the police won't have searched for them, where there's no Gaia tech to find them. I roll the window down. 'Come on,' I yell, 'they'll be looking for us,' and I watch as Ziegler and Jonah pull themselves out. Soaking wet, they shiver, shaking the water off as they approach the car. Ziegler gets in the front, next to Valona.

'You'll ruin the leather,' she says to him, annoyed; but I think she's only joking. I think she doesn't much care.

'You can bill me,' he says, teeth chattering as he turns the car's heating system up, blasting us with warm air; and then we're gone again, back onto the road, swinging around, falling into line with the traffic on the bridge. Vines wrap themselves around the girders of the bridge, so thick in places I wonder if they're capable of bending the metal, if they'll wrap themselves tighter and tighter until the bridge buckles and collapses, falling into the water beneath. There's no getting around the other cars, so we slow down, shuffling along in slow progress.

'We hid in the water when they came,' Ziegler says. 'Swam out a ways.'

'Are you okay?' Jonah asks me.

'I'm fine,' I say. He reaches for my hand, sees the state of it. I'd almost forgotten that Rex crushed it. My fingers are slightly crooked; there's bruising all over it, all down the back; it's already starting to go a deep purple. I don't know if it'll ever recover, not to what it was. No more grabbing ledges to stop myself from falling; no more throwing punches with it. I'll need to reset it, I know. Break it back into place, bind it tightly. And yet I'm certain that there are no more hospitals in my future.

Jonah looks around at us. 'You didn't get—'

'No,' I say. 'She was . . . We found her. She was fine. She was happy.' There's silence, as I breathe. As I let the decision breathe. 'It's better this way,' I tell him, and I really mean it.

'If it was the right choice, it was the right choice,' he says. He nods. Sage words that mean nothing, but they're comforting.

I look over at Rex and wonder if they're comforting to her as well. She stares out of the window, eyeing the cars on either side of us, watching for police. Leaving Mae was her choice. It was hers all along. I know her story; I don't even have to ask. Rex is only a couple of years older than I am. Mae must have been born when Rex was only just able to have a baby. I don't need to ask; I know she gave Mae up because she wanted a different life for her daughter. She was scared, so she did what she thought was best, and handed her over to the ship. It was not a good life, but it was better than being a Low. Being a Low meant death; being outside that at least gave Mae a chance of survival. The children on the ship without parents were taken in by somebody who cared, usually; given families, parents and brothers and sisters, and sometimes they grew up to be parents themselves. Giving them the best possible chance. That's what Rex gave her daughter then, and that's what she gave her now. That's what *we* gave her. The thought makes me swell inside; at what Mae could grow up to be. The good she could do; the things she could change.

'Where are we going?' Valona asks, as we reach the end of the bridge; as the road diverges in front of us. 'What's next?'

'We find the nomads,' I say. 'They're back towards Pittsburgh.'

'That's a long drive.'

'We can walk,' I tell her, 'or there's Ziegler's car, some-where on the road.'

But she laughs. 'That piece of crap? Won't get you there,' she says. 'No, I quite like driving. Find it relaxing.'

'Chan,' Ziegler says, 'there's something you should know,' and he's about to keep talking when Rex interrupts him.

'Something's coming,' she says. I look out of the back window of the car and there it is. A cloud, in the sky: a mass of birds, a shadow darker than any I've seen before, blotting the sky. The formation is coming towards us.

And, on the ground, something else. A bike? A car? On the road, a bird flying low? Faster than anything else.

'What is that?' Valona asks, glancing in her mirror.

'It's Hoyle,' I say. 'It's The Runner.'

The cars behind us move out of his way, Gaia pushing them to the side. I shout at Valona to go, to drive faster, and she shouts that she is, she's doing everything she can, but it's not enough. We dart, drive between cars, then the road gives way to the cross-country roads, to potholes and cracks and thick branches of gnarled dead trees jutting from the concrete, and we go, but still they come. The cloud, advancing; The Runner, Hoyle, a blur of grey metal now. I wonder if it hurts him to run like that. I wonder why he hasn't given up, yet; and then I realise that I haven't either. When you get it into your mind to finish something, you do everything you can.

Everything gets one final push.

'Get the guns,' Ziegler says, and he and Rex lean out of the windows, aiming at the cloud of birds. They take shots and the cloud disperses. Some fall down; the rest make new formations. They get closer and closer, and Valona tries to keep us on the road, but then they start diving, slamming themselves into the ground around us, aiming for the car itself.

'They're suiciding!' Ziegler shouts. 'To drive us off the road!'

'Or they're just trying to hit us,' Valona says. She sounds astonishingly calm, as if this is just another day in her life, another story she'll casually recant at a dinner party.

'Aim lower!' Rex shouts, as they dive-bomb us, and she and Ziegler take more of them. I watch Hoyle avoid their carcasses as they smash along the road in front of him. His control is incredible. His name suddenly makes sense. In all this time, I've never seen him open up; let go, use his body to its fullest. Rex aims at him, but I grab the gun, move it away.

'You'll kill him,' I shout. He's moving too fast. I picture him rolling, crashing along the ground, tearing himself apart.

'I was aiming for the ground at his feet,' she says, 'to make him pause.' She and I both know that she's good but not that good. She takes more shots at the birds, but one gets past the gunfire, slams into the roof of our car. There's a window there and it shatters, raining glass down on us, but the bird doesn't make it through. Instead, Jonah aims at it, pulls the trigger, and it's blown away, off the roof in a fury of sparks and metal. More birds hurl themselves at us, hitting the metal around the windows on the sides of the car, denting it. More and more. I can hear the sound of their whips, fizzling and coiling in through the windows, and we fight them off, cutting and shooting and breaking them. One of the whips snakes in through the open window next to Jonah, and he grabs it, tries to shake it free, but it takes hold, driving upwards. It pierces through, and then we're being lifted clean off the road, wrenched upwards. There's a horrible metallic creak as the roof starts tearing off; Rex aims upwards at the dent, and there's a scream of metal, a hole made, the bird exploding, the blast powerful enough to take out our windows, to smash the glass in the roof above our heads.

Cars pile in on us from all sides. Police cars, unmanned, set to do the same as the birds. They veer towards us and Valona has to steer out of their way, and these new cars crash, piling into one another, slamming nose to nose, bursting into flames. More cars, one on either side of Valona's car, hemming us in. They get closer, until the sides of their bodies are grinding up against our vehicle.

'Keep them off!' Valona shouts and Rex leans out of the window and aims at the back of the one closest to her, as it pulls away and then steers back. We're jolted but she holds steady, aims, fires. She hits something important and the car sparks.

There's a moment where it's like all the sound has been sucked out of the air and then the car bursts into flames, stopping suddenly, exploding off the road, flipping over in front of us.

We all gape.

Jonah leans out of his window and tries the same, but the car is too fast. It collides with us and the car shudders and he slips, falling forwards, half-hanging out of the window. He drops his gun and I watch it crunch under the car as it ploughs for him. He's loose, face calm as anything, trying to pull himself back inside.

The police vehicle comes for him, to crush him against Valona's car.

I scream his name, trying to pull him back, failing. He's heavy. Too heavy.

Then Rex leans over and she takes hold of him, hauls him inside with her augmented arm.

'Wait,' she says.

She stands up, pushes herself through the broken window in the roof. One heave and she's up, and then she's gone, leaping from the roof of our car to the police car next to us, and she kicks in the window, aims down with the gun, shoots the computer that's driving it. She makes it look so easy.

And then, as the car starts to brake, as it spins wildly, she's leaping back, grappling with the side of our car, hand digging into the roof; her feet dragging on the road, she manages to get herself back, pulls herself onto the roof, slides in through the window-hole, back to her seat. She's shooting birds again within seconds.

The birds fall, one by one. Only, there are too many of them. They keep coming. And Hoyle is relentless, gaining ground; behind him, the sirens and lights of more police cars. I can see figures leaning from the car windows, guns trained on us. They'll shoot us. When they reach us, we're done for. We've got too far to go, and too much to do, still.

I can see Hoyle's face. It's still his face, even missing the jaw; and the rest of his skin is pulled away entirely, revealing the smoothness of the frame underneath, glinting in the sunlight, shining so brightly it's like a mirror. He looks at me, and he picks up speed again. Watching his legs is confusing, unnatural. Like I can't quite understand how fast he's moving.

It's good, I think, to see it; to see what he's capable of.

Jonah takes my hand, pulling my attention away from Hoyle. 'You don't belong here,' he says.

'What do you mean?'

'You know what I mean. You can't stay here,' he says.

'We'll find somewhere,' I tell him.

'No. You'll find somewhere. I'm meant to be here.'

'We started in the same place. None of us are meant to—'

But he interrupts me: 'I wasn't. Once, maybe. But I am now. I've done things. Before, I didn't know who I was, but I do now. And I have to be punished for what I've done.' I shake my head.

'None of this has been your fault,' I say.

He kisses me. He holds me and he kisses me. 'I've finally got the freedom to make a choice,' he whispers, 'so I'm going to.'

Hoyle has pulled up alongside our car. His remaining arm reaches out and he grabs us, getting hold of the window frame, and he pulls himself along, then plants his feet, trying to stop us. It's incredible to see the strength in his legs, even as damaged and beaten up as he is. What he's doing shouldn't work, but it does, his feet digging pits in the already wrecked tarmac, smoke coming from the road; and even as he does that he looks at me and he looks at Jonah and I know he's about to end everything. He could flip the car. Kill us all.

There are seconds left. Seconds until—

Jonah grabs Hoyle's arm. He grabs it, leans out of the window, starts to yank his fingers open.

'Take me,' Jonah says, and his voice is soft but I hear it anyway. Hoyle hears it as well. His eyes widen; his brow softens. 'Do it. I'm enough.' There's a weird serenity to how he says it. Hoyle stares at me, not Jonah. Around us, birds rain down in flashes of fire and metal. Hoyle nods.

Jonah looks at me. He loves me. I know it now.

I won't see him again, I know; and if I ever do, he won't know me. At least, I tell myself, he'll have made this choice for himself. At least he'll be free.

Hoyle grabs him, pulls him through the window. And then Hoyle lets go of the car. There's a thumping as we smash back to the road, as Valona gains control again, as she accelerates away from Hoyle. For the second time, Jonah is swallowed by a cloud of birds. And then the swarm of birds lightens as they stop following us, as they change direction, move away. The chase has been called off. They've got their man.

They've got somebody to punish.

I stare as Hoyle holds Jonah aloft, their figures already growing smaller in the distance. I watch as he lets him go, as Jonah drops to his knees. I can just about make out Jonah's arms, his hands reaching for his own neck; for his scars.

He doesn't look back at us.

In the sky, the cloud of birds disperses and all that's left is the heat of sun. So hot, so sudden and sharp, it's like I've never felt it before; like I'd completely forgotten how powerful it could be.

12

Valona drives and I shut my eyes. None of us speaks and I sleep.

I don't know what I dream of. It doesn't matter.

We stop, to charge the cells that power the car. Valona's worried because the roof is gone and that's where most of them were. 'You don't want to get stuck in the desert,' she says.

I go up to Ziegler as he sits at the side of the road. He's tired. He looks so old, but when I sit down next to him his eyes light up a little.

'Thank you,' he says.

'What for?'

'Doing the right thing.' I don't ask him what he means. I know. He knows. That's enough. I wonder if he always knew that this would happen, right from the start. 'I have to tell you something. I don't know if it's useful, but I have to tell you.'

'What?'

His voice is so serious, like he's worried about what he's about to tell me, about what it'll do to me. 'The New World.

The capsule ship that you took me to.' Sighs, so much air it makes him cough a little. We need water, I know. It is dangerous, being out here. 'It's not just that. The rest of it exists as well.'

'What do you mean?'

He looks up at the sky. Squints, puts his hand over his eyes, to shield against the sun. 'Somewhere in orbit is the rest of the ship. It's up there.'

'Are there prisoners on it?'

'No. God no. It was a contingency plan, nothing more. It's always good to have a contingency plan.'

'So why is it still there?'

'In case, probably. I don't know. Look, I read the files. They're on the system. It's basically a bomb shelter. The plan was, governmental people would go to it. They would stay there until everything had calmed down.'

My next question is inevitable. 'Can we get up to it?'

'I think so,' he says. He doesn't seem surprised that I'd ask. 'It'll be a miracle if it all still works up there, but . . . I don't know. The ship down here is powered up. It's got fuel. It's ready to go. The one up there, it's orbiting. The computer said it was operational. *Fully operational.*' He stands up and wipes his hands on his trousers, dust coming off onto his thighs. Dirtying them.

'Why are you telling me this?' I ask him.

'Because, like I said, it's always good to have a contingency plan.' He offers me his hand, to get to my feet again. Valona shouts that the car is ready, charged up. She starts the engine. 'Seems as good a way to end the story as any,' he says.

* * *

The cloth sea of the nomads is in the distance, away from the road, snaking its way across the landscape. It's dusk and they must have just started moving. Can't get far when there's that many of you. At least, not on foot.

I tell Valona to stop the car, that we're getting out here.

'Here?'

'Wait for us. Just for a short while.' She nods. Ziegler and I step out of the car. 'Shall we?' he asks, looking towards the nomads.

'Yes,' I say. The three of us cross the desert, waving our hands at them, letting them know that we're not dangerous. Fiona steps out as we get closer, hearing our shouts, and they rush to bring us water. We drink until we feel sick and then she holds me, briefly.

'I didn't know if you'd be back,' she says. 'You ready to join us, settle down?'

'Join you, yes,' I reply. 'But maybe we won't settle quite yet.'

I tell them where to meet me. What we're going to do. I tell them I have a plan, and that if it works, it's going to change everything. Give us another chance; a chance to be ourselves, to live our lives. To take something that we haven't ever been given: a chance.

'I don't know how it's going to end,' I say, 'how it's going to go. It's a risk, but it might be worth it.'

'We're not scared of a risk,' Fiona tells me.

'This has to be your choice,' I say. 'If you want to come with me, I want you. I want to try.'

'You're giving us a chance; how are we not going to take it?'

I nod. I tell them where to meet me. 'There's one last thing I have to do,' I say.

I tell Rex and Ziegler the plan and ask Valona to drive us. She agrees. I can tell that she's excited to be one last part of a story that will go down in history.

The drive back to Washington is arduous. I worry the whole way: that my plan won't work, that the police could end everything for us, that what's waiting for us at the other side might not be what I hope for, that it could already be ruined.

I have to believe it's not, though. And if it is? We can rebuild. We know how.

Worst case, we return here with our tails between our legs, begging to be let back into a place that never wanted us. God knows what will happen then. I'll try not to think about it. No sense worrying about what might be, what could be. Worry about what is.

Worry about making the most of the chance that you've been given.

We hide in the back of Valona's car as she gets to the front gates. She's got credentials that are going to get her through security. They don't ask questions, and they call her by her name – 'Miss Valona,' they say, like it's her second name and first name, one name, that's it – and they raise the gates. She's above questioning. I have a sense now that she's more important to the way this city works than even Ziegler suspected.

I get the feeling that, in another time and place, she and I might have been enemies. That she does things I don't agree with; that Hoyle might have one day sent me after her, Rex at my side, and we might have taken her down. But for now, she's an ally.

I tell her where we want to be dropped off. She asks me if she should wait for us, as she pulls the car up to the sidewalk outside the building.

'I think we're fine,' I tell her.

'If you're not,' she says, and she doesn't finish the sentence. She waves her hand instead, like that's going to say it all for her.

'It was good to meet you,' I say. She knows we won't meet again.

'The pleasure was all mine,' she replies. She walks over to Ziegler and hugs him tightly. 'You send me the book about this when it's published,' she says. 'That's all the payment I require.'

'I don't know that I'll be able to,' he says. 'Where we're going—'

'You'll find a way,' she tells him. Then she hugs me and she tells me that everything will be alright. Those words and nothing else. A reassurance from somebody I barely know, but I believe her. I have to.

We watch her torn-up car weave down the jagged road towards Washington. 'Won't they want to ask her about being involved with us?' I ask Ziegler.

'They'll want to ask her a lot of things. She'll be fine. She's always fine.' He smiles, a little wistfully, and I wonder for a quick moment about the two of them. Was she someone he could have loved?

Then she's gone, down the street, out of sight amongst the other cars.

The three of us look up at the building, at the doors.

'Shall we?' Ziegler asks. The glass doors shift open as we walk towards them. The person I'm looking for is in the lobby. People stare as we walk through, recognising me, recognising Rex.

Cameras whir to track our progress. We're going to be on the news tonight, I think. Nancy, the new presenter, stares as we approach.

'You're back,' she says.

'We are,' I tell her. 'And we need you to broadcast something on the network for us.'

They don't bother with hair and makeup this time. They want to, but I swat their hands away, so they let me be. Rex simply glares at them until they back off. Then we're standing in the same space as before, the camera drones swirling around us, focusing on our faces.

'Chan,' the female presenter starts, '*The Girl Who Fell to Earth*. Last time we spoke with you, you were—'

'Be quiet,' I say. I don't have time for their questions. This isn't about them. 'I'd like to speak to everybody who feels like this place isn't their home. Everybody who feels like they don't belong here. Everybody who feels scared, lost, alone. To those people, if you can see this, there is a better way. We can make a better life. You don't know me. I don't expect you to trust me. What you know of me is from a book by this man.' I indicate Ziegler. He sheepishly raises his hand. 'But that wasn't the truth, not really. I can tell you what is true: life doesn't have to be like this. You don't have to be forgotten about.'

The presenter seems flustered. She glances at one of the drones, at the holo of her lines that are being beamed beneath it for her to read. 'Chan, there are rumours that—'

'Meet us at the north-east entrance to the city. We're heading there now. There isn't much time. We're leaving this place, and never coming back.'

And then I turn and I walk out of the studio. Rex follows, the presenter nipping at her heels, desperately trying to get some sort of quote, something else off us. We've given them enough.

'What happens now?' Ziegler asks as we get back to the street, as we start to walk. Not caring about the cameras, the birds, the police. That part is done. We're leaving, and nothing's going to stop us.

I don't answer him. In front of us, I see somebody step out of an alleyway. A woman with an old network tablet in her hands, held together with tape, showing my face, my words coming from the speakers. Not a holo, even older tech than that. She stares at me. Her hair is a mess, knotted and twisted together. Clothes that barely fit her. I've never seen her before. Not in the docks, when I lived there; not with the nomads outside the city; not anywhere. She's lived in this city and I've never noticed her. I doubt that anybody has.

'I'm Chan,' I say. 'Do you want to come with us?'

She does.

We are marching. Way back, people marched in the streets to protest about what was happening to their world: the change in the climate, poverty, the hard times that normal people were enduring. They marched, beat their drums, chanted.

We're different, now. We don't have any demands; we're leaving. We're silent. As we walk, more people come to us. From the docks and the other slums, dragging their bedding, carrying their possessions in their hands, muted children hanging on to their hands; from the alleyways, health gone, eyes hollow; and from the poorer parts of the cities, abandoning a world that simply doesn't have room for them. People – haircuts and augments and fancy clothes and money – stand and watch as we go. Drones float above us, but no police. Hoyle's keeping them back, I bet. It's easier to stay out of our way; we're not doing anything wrong.

As we reach the gate in the city wall, the guards that Rex and I fought before stare at us, slack-jawed. Rex smiles at them. She wants to unnerve them; it works. The gate opens and from behind the guards, from the outside world, come the nomads, walking in their own procession. They abandon their tent-blanket shade as they march through the city gates. Fiona is leading them and she comes to me, pulls me close.

'Looks like I have got one more move in me,' she says. She looks sickly and I know she's telling the truth: she won't last much longer. At least she'll get to see a future she's never had before, before she goes. The nomads fall into line with the rest of us, and we move on as one. You can't tell a difference between the people from the docks and the nomads, and us. It doesn't matter where we're from, where we started, or who we've been. All that matters is what's to come. Trusting that something better can be made.

No one tries to stop us, which is good, because they

wouldn't be able to. Maybe they're tempted. Somewhere, in some room, somebody's tempted to try.

But there are too many of us.

Rex and Ziegler and Fiona and myself at the front. Judith, with her kids, right behind us. The soft sound of her murmuring to her children, promising them a future, finally. I look behind her, beyond, and see pregnant bellies, children who wouldn't otherwise have had much of a chance.

I take Rex's hand. She and I, walking together, and it feels like this was how it was always meant to be.

'Are you sure you want this?' I ask her.

'Yes,' she says.

'It can be different this time,' I say. She doesn't reply. 'You're not who you were, not when we left—'

'I am,' she says. 'But everything else has changed.'

The sound of our feet as we march echoes through the streets. We're marching down the middle of the road, swelling onto the sidewalks. I don't know how we'll all fit, but we'll make it work. We will.

I see the fence. Beyond it, the warehouse. There's no one to open the fence for us, and I wonder if we'll need to climb it. But then we get closer, and push, and the fence buckles and falls under the strength of us. I lead the people over it, across the grass, and into the warehouse.

We force the doors open, and yes, the alarms ring, but we don't care. We snake through the corridors, into the hangar. The hatch on top of the lander is already open. I don't know if somebody opened it earlier, or if Ziegler and I left it open the last time we were here, but it's open. Ready. Waiting.

I climb to the top of the ship, turn around, take a breath and look out at all the faces, watching me.

'We're all getting into this,' I say. I turn around and they look scared. They don't know what happens next and neither, really, do I.

So I tell them that. 'Whatever happens after here, after now? It has to be better than this. It might be hard. It could be scary, at points. But it could also be absolutely amazing. We'll make it amazing. It's a fresh start, and we're all going to make something of this. All of us, together.'

With my broken hand, I start ushering them up. It's ceaseless, the line of them. Myself and Rex and Ziegler and Fiona help them all, hiking them up onto the roof of the lander, telling them not to slip – it's so smooth, not designed to be walked on, a glaring flaw in what seems like an otherwise clever design – and then they're helping each other down the hatch, holding hands as they get onto the ladder. I don't know how many people there are here. I've lost count. Too many to be comfortable inside this thing. There are too many of us; more people than I brought down from Australia before.

Enough, I think, to populate the ship. To fill it.

I recognise some of them as they pass me and descend into the hatch, and some I don't. Maybe not everybody getting on board now is a good person. Maybe some of them harbor bad thoughts or have done bad things. It doesn't mean they shouldn't be able to come with us. That's the past. Now they have the chance to see themselves right, to make a future. We're all starting over. They will bring all of their experiences, all that's happened to them, all that's good and right and broken and fixed and still breaking and still waiting to be fixed, and together we'll build something. It'll be a place where we're useful, and where we make families or we don't, where we fight or we don't, where we tell stories or we don't. but it'll be ours to decide. It'll be a place where we're ourselves. Every day. Where we're free.

Ziegler, Rex and Fiona are standing by the hatch with me, helping people down it.

Fiona leans in close to us.

'I'm going to get on board,' she says, 'get people settled.' I hold her hand as she starts to climb down; and when I turn around, Ziegler's gone.

I find him climbing down the edge of the lander, to the warehouse floor. He looks up at me as he steps off the final rung.

'I can't come with you,' he says.

'I know,' I say. I climb down to stand next to him, to face him.

'I've got a place here. Or, I had one. I can't abandon it. I can't run away. And that's what I think this would feel like.' I tense my jaw as he speaks. 'Besides, I've got to tell your story. Your real story.'

'You could tell it up there, with us,' I say.

'I could. But I have a feeling that you'll all tell it fine without me. Down here, though? They're going to need someone who knows the truth. And I will tell the truth this time. The whole truth.' He rubs his neck. The scars there, just like Jonah's. 'Chan, I'm sorry . . .' he finally says, but I don't let him finish his sentence. I wrap my arms around him and I hold him. Around us, people are still climbing onto the ship. Almost everyone has boarded now. I can hear their voices coming from the ship below, the last few climbing down, getting themselves settled, ready for what I'm going to show them.

'I'll miss you,' I say. Both of us wet eyed. We hug again.

We don't say goodbye. Rex helps me up onto the hull and then climbs down the ladder. She leaves me there alone, lets me wait to be the last one in. I spend a last moment watching Ziegler walk away from the ship; he stops at the edge of the warehouse, watching us. I don't wave as I climb down the ladder and he doesn't wave back at me; and even when I can't see him any more, when I'm inside the lander and have pulled the hatch shut after me, I know that he's still there; still waiting, still watching.

It's crowded. People in the corridors, crammed in. There's not enough room. Kids on the beds in the bedrooms, parents sitting on the floor near them, holding their hands. I have to tread carefully. Everybody is scared, not knowing what we're going to see. I push through, apologising. Rex stands in the doorway to the kitchen and she clears a path for me through to the computer, a seat that's been left vacant for me.

On the screen, there's a button that reads The New World.

In the distance, I hear the sirens ringing. Or alarms. Maybe they're for us, but maybe they're not. Maybe there's something else going on that doesn't involve me; something much more important.

Doesn't matter, not now.

Rex shouts for everybody to hold on, then she kneels next to me, puts her arms around me. She holds me, tight as she can manage, tight as I can manage.

One of us presses the button. I don't know which of us.

I think maybe we did it together.

We jolt and lurch. It's calamity. It's fast and there's screaming from all the people in the ship who don't know what to expect, who've never experienced anything like what's happening. And there are flashing lights and the hiss of air, and it's hard to breathe and I feel like I'm being pressed into the floor, flattened, like I won't survive, and then, suddenly, it settles, and we're, I don't know, in the sky somewhere. Above the city. Up high. I shut my eyes as my ears pop, and everyone is still screaming, the ship juddering and shuddering, and I don't know if we're going to make it, maybe it's too old, maybe there are too many of us and we weigh too much—

And I hear my mother's voice for what I suspect will be the final time.

Don't die.

I won't, I tell her. I'm going to live.

Everything goes black, as it always does; as it was always going to do.

EPILOGUE

There's a loud thud, and then a hissing. I open my eyes to the sight of everybody else screaming, panicking. The little ship shudders and then there's a grinding; and then there's silence, as we hold our breath to see what happens next.

We exhale as one, it seems. Relief in everybody's faces. We're not moving any more. I stand up, and I take Rex's hand and we walk down the corridor together. Stepping over the bodies – no, the people, the people who sat here, clinging on, who trusted me. They're not dead, just waiting. We find Fiona and Judith. We ask them to come with us. This is important for them. One of them is seeking an ending, and one of them a beginning.

We're going to give them both.

On the floor, then, I see a doll, just like the one that I took for Mae. I pick it up, and I feel the hair between my fingertips, reminding me of her; as it always will. And that's okay.

I pass it to Judith, for June, her daughter. The little girl takes it, smiles, holds it out in front of her baby. She's not old enough for it yet, but she will be.

I realise how alike their names are. Mae, then June.

Everything moving forwards.

'Are you ready?' I ask Rex.

'I am,' she says.

I climb the ladder, and I push open the hatch. I shut my eyes, shut my mouth; I can't help expecting the rush of mulch from the pit. But there's nothing. No wetness, no gore. Through the crack I can hear nothing. It's totally silent.

I push it further, and the light nearly blinds me. I can't see, and then my eyes focus, and I can. I try to take it all in. The ship is complete. It's the same as Australia, in essence: the same shape, the same thick metal walls, the same floors, the same pit down here at the bottom. And then, in the middle, suspended far above me, the same arboretum. Only here the arboretum is the heart of it all; the heart of this ship. It's nothing like Australia's. This one lives and shines, so bright and beautiful and warm it's like I always dreamed it would be. And it's done its job. Plants, trees and vines and vegetation spill out of the arboretum and over the edge, running along the gang-ways, up to the top of the ship and down to the bottom, where I stand. Decades – centuries – of being allowed to grow, to run wild and free on this place, and it's a jungle; a farm; a garden. It's paradise and it's ours.

Rex wraps her arm around me, holding me steady as I shake, as we take in the extraordinary abundance of life that fills our new world; as the rest of our people climb up the hatch after us, fill the ship with joy and excitement and life and hope; as they play and climb and pick up fruit that's fallen from the trees, and run to berths to claim them as their own.

I look at Rex, and I don't say anything, and neither does she.

For now, we're home.

ACKNOWLEDGEMENTS

I'd like to thank my editor Anne Perry, for being there this whole journey, and for getting – sometimes better than I did – what it was Chan and Rex were doing, and why they were doing it. *This* is hers as much as it is mine. To her and everybody else at Hodder: you're ace.

I'd also like to thank Sam Copeland, my agent; and I'd like to thank Cath, Will, Matt and Amy for letting me bleat on at them over and over about plot points in this thing, or for reading it and telling me I'm not an idiot.

But most of all, I'd like to thank you, the reader. If you're reading the acknowledgements of book 3 of a series, you're likely a fan of it. (Or you hate it so much you want to know who to blame.) So, to you: thanks. Your support means everything. It means I get to keep doing this. You're as important to this process as anybody.

WANT MORE?

If you enjoyed this and would like to find out about similar books we publish, we'd love you to join our online SF, Fantasy and Horror community, Hodderscape.

Visit our blog site
www.hodderscape.co.uk

Follow us on Twitter
🐦 **@hodderscape**

Like our Facebook page
f Hodderscape

You'll find exclusive content from our authors, news, competitions and general musings, so feel free to comment, contribute or just keep an eye on what we are up to. See you there!

Enjoyed this book?
Want more?

Head over to

CHAPTeR 5

for extra author content,
exclusives, competitions – and lots
and lots of book talk!

Our motto is
Proud to be bookish,

because, well, we are ☺

See you there . . .

f Chapter5Books 🐦 @Chapter5Books

About Island Press

Island Press is the only nonprofit organization in the United States whose principal purpose is the publication of books on environmental issues and natural resource management. We provide solutions-oriented information to professionals, public officials, business and community leaders, and concerned citizens who are shaping responses to environmental problems.

In 2003, Island Press celebrates its nineteenth anniversary as the leading provider of timely and practical books that take a multidisciplinary approach to critical environmental concerns. Our growing list of titles reflects our commitment to bringing the best of an expanding body of literature to the environmental community throughout North America and the world.

Support for Island Press is provided by The Nathan Cummings Foundation, Geraldine R. Dodge Foundation, Doris Duke Charitable Foundation, Educational Foundation of America, The Charles Engelhard Foundation, The Ford Foundation, The George Gund Foundation, The Vira I. Heinz Endowment, The William and Flora Hewlett Foundation, Henry Luce Foundation, The John D. and Catherine T. MacArthur Foundation, The Andrew W. Mellon Foundation, The Moriah Fund, The Curtis and Edith Munson Foundation, National Fish and Wildlife Foundation, The New-Land Foundation, Oak Foundation, The Overbrook Foundation, The David and Lucile Packard Foundation, The Pew Charitable Trusts, The Rockefeller Foundation, The Winslow Foundation, and other generous donors.

The opinions expressed in this book are those of the author(s) and do not necessarily reflect the views of these foundations.

About SCOPE

The Scientific Committee on Problems of the Environment (SCOPE) was established by the International Council for Science (ICSU) in 1969. It brings together natural and social scientists to identify emerging or potential environmental issues and to address jointly the nature and solution of environmental problems on a global basis. Operating at an interface between the science and decision-making sectors, SCOPE's interdisciplinary and critical focus on available knowledge provides analytical and practical tools to promote further research and more sustainable management of the Earth's resources. SCOPE's members, forty national science academies and research councils and twenty-two international scientific unions, committees, and societies, guide and develop its scientific program.